WHAT THEY
DON'T KNOW

Also *by Susan Furlong*

Shattered Justice
Fractured Truth
Splintered Silence
War and Peach
Rest in Peach
Peaches and Scream

Written as Lucy Arlington

Off the Books
Played by the Book

WHAT THEY DON'T KNOW

SUSAN FURLONG

SEVENTH
STREET
BOOKS®

Published 2022 by Seventh Street Books®

Cover images © Shutterstock
Cover design by Jennifer Do
Cover design © Start Science Fiction

Inquiries should be addressed to
Start Science Fiction
221 River Street, 9th Floor
Hoboken, NJ 07030

Phone: 212-431-5455
www.seventhstreetbooks.com

10 9 8 7 6 5 4 3 2 1

ISBN: 978-1-64506-040-6 (paperback)
ISBN: 978-1-64506-041-3 (ebook)

Patrick:
Writing this book would have been a lot more fun if you were here to read it.

Our own evil inclinations are far more dangerous than any external enemies.

—St. Ambrose

ONE

Saturday, October 31

The predawn light casts a dismal gray through the barn as Detective Lucas Reyes steps inside and squints to gain focus, his gaze landing first on a rusted steel harrow in the corner, its tines like wet dragon teeth, then on the crime scene techs placing numbered markers, snapping photos, documenting and bagging evidence. They work silently as a biting wind slips through the dilapidated siding, spawning a ripple of creaks and pops.

Reyes shivers as the ripe odor of fresh blood coats the back of his throat. Until recently, death had been just a component of his job until it stole into his own family. Now every death is personal. He shakes off the memories, swallows hard, and moves toward the portable lights illuminating the victim's body: facedown, neck cranked hard to the left, and limbs splayed. The back of the skull is a pulpy mass of brain matter, and a pool of blood fringes the head like a hellish halo. He crouches just outside the protective perimeter surrounding the body and studies the victim's vacant eyes, bulged with shock, blue irises dimmed in death. "What did you see?" he asks.

He passes a hand above the battered skull. Violent and vicious the perpetrator delivered an initial killing blow, enough to bring the victim down. Then, strike after strike, continued in a violent rampage, until the victim's skull was pulverized. Overkill. Intense rage. It sickens Reyes.

He turns away and blows out his breath as he surveys the rest of the barn. An old tractor fender, a stack of tires, a pile of rotting timbers, several old, rusted gas cans, and a coiled towing chain. Everything layered in dust, oxidized and brittle with age. Nothing looks like it has been disturbed or used recently. No sign of the weapon.

Reyes looks upward to the hayloft and to the shadowed beams and rafters that crisscross overhead. An uneasiness shudders through him. *Why in this barn? This remnant of farmlands swallowed by suburbs?* Then he lowers his gaze, and through the gaps in the barn's siding, he studies the lights of the nearby neighborhood, homes of doctors and lawyers and CEOs, hardworking, wealthy people, with 1.9 children, a Lexus or a Mercedes, golf carts, exotic vacations, and black-tie functions. But Reyes knows that under a carefully purchased veneer often skulks an uncontrolled and lethal passion.

He steps back farther, watching as two of the coroner's assistants roll out plastic sheeting next to the victim. They work efficiently, placing bags over the hands and securing the fragmented skull to move with the rest of the body. As they roll the victim and start to place the sheet underneath, one of the assistants stops.

"We've got something here," he says, pointing to a cell phone wedged under the victim's body. It's as pulverized as the victim's skull. A tech photographs and documents the phone before it's secured. Then the victim is placed in an open body bag.

"Give me just a minute," Reyes says.

The coroner's assistants exchange a look, and then step back, allowing him some room just as the first rays of sunlight leak through a slit in the siding of the barn and graze over the body. Reyes takes a final look at the victim and makes the same promise he'd made just a few weeks ago to another victim of a brutal death, the body found in a nearby lake. No signs point to similarities in the cases—not yet—but the gut of this fifteen-year veteran cop clenches. Somehow, they are connected. "I'll bring you justice. I promise."

He looks up and nods, and darkness swallows the victim's silenced answers as they zip the bag closed.

PART I

THE UNRAVELING

TWO

Tuesday, October 27
Four Days Earlier

Outside the wind howled, moaning through the trusses of our old home like a woman in ecstasy. Inside, the fire burned hot, crackling and popping and warding off the fall chill. It was the last Tuesday of the month, our normal book club night, and we were gathered at my house—Selma, Alice, Tara, and me—settled in the living room, Moroccan rug plush beneath us, immersed in the decor's eclectic mix of whimsy and Old-World aesthetic. This would be our last book club meeting, but it was more than that, really. It was a pulled thread in the carefully woven tapestry of our friendships that had begun in college and endured careers, weddings, our first-borns, and remained constant through affairs, divorces, and much worse.

Somehow, we'd held together through it all, and now I was the first to break away. I'd made the announcement a few weeks prior, telling everyone that Ben wanted to relocate to an inner-city condo to be near his new clinic, and that while we hated to go, it wasn't like we were moving across the country. Since then, we'd traversed the emotional stages of our pending separation with trite phrases like "You're actually leaving us?" to "What will we do without you?" and finally settling on our new mantra, "There is nothing that can pull us apart."

And we wanted to believe it. So much so that we kept the evening's conversation in tone with the wine we were drinking, fruity with just a hint of somber undertones. We drank, we talked, we laughed . . . we toasted Selma's new love, Alice's finalized divorce from her cheating hubby, my husband's new clinic and the recent sale of our late nineteenth-century Victorian (thanks to Selma, realtor extraordinaire), and then there was a rare pause, culminating in a toast from Tara: "Here's to Ben and Mona and . . ." She faltered and cleared her throat. "To friendships that last the test of time and distance."

Distance? We were relocating from the suburb to the city, a little over an hour by car, almost two by train. Still, it wouldn't be the same as being next door, so I nodded and raised my glass. "I can drink to that."

And I did. We all did. Two bottles down and one more ready to uncork.

The fire burned bright, the conversation rose and fell, eyes sparkled, and glasses clinked. All in all, it was a perfect evening until Alice, always a bit of a Debbie Downer, took a shaky sip of wine and killed the mood with, "Did you catch last week's article in the *Tribune*? Remember that dead girl the cops found in Simon Lake? They think they have a lead on her identity."

The corner clock ticked off several awkward moments as we switched mental gears from compulsory but pleasant chitchat to a young woman killed, her body sunk in a nearby murky lake. Then all at once, everyone jumped in with the platitudes reserved for just such occasions: *such a terrible thing . . . that poor girl, whoever she is . . . and her family, yes, her poor family, can you imagine? And when are the cops going to find the guy?*

Selma tried to pull us out of the mire by saying how the girl's death was likely gang-related, or drug-related, and of course it wasn't someone we knew, but Alice, her voice as sharp as her perfectly manicured nails, said, "Actually, I shouldn't be telling you this, but the gal who does my hair, her husband is a cop, and she was saying that the girl *is* from Belington. Her name was Mia Jones. Any of you know her?"

Tara raised her brows.

Selma blinked. "Never heard of her."

I tipped back my glass and swallowed the dregs.

"She was troubled," Alice went on. "In and out of foster homes until she aged out of the system. People lost track of her after that and, well"—she looked at each of us, emphasizing her insider's knowledge with a dramatic pause—"the body was so badly decomposed, it took the cops a while to make an identification. Now they're calling it murder."

"That's horrible." Tara fiddled with her dark hair, something she did when feeling unsettled.

Selma tried again to get us off the subject. "Why are we talking about this? I thought we were keeping things light." She looked toward me. "Especially tonight. It's Mona's last book club."

Alice sighed. "We should be aware, that's all. Truth is, it's hard protecting kids these days, even when they have someone watching out for them."

Tara jumped in: "True. They're so easily influenced by their friends and social media. Facebook, Twitter, and Instagram, now that's the worst of them." Tara didn't have a spouse or kids, but she never hesitated to insert bits of her professional opinion as a counselor.

"That's right," Alice agreed. "Caught Bess in a lie last week. Said she couldn't come home for the weekend, because she had too much homework. Northwestern's what? A two-hour drive?"

Alice had already told me about this last week and I'd thought at the time to check Instagram to see if Gus had an account, but Alice was upset and needed a friend and I never got around to it. Now she seemed completely under control as she paused for drama and nibbled the end of a cracker, talking again only after Selma prompted her. "And?"

"And, well . . . one of her friends posted a picture on Instagram. Bess was in the background. Hashtag: *road trip.* She wasn't doing homework; she was partying in Milwaukee, and I would have never known if I didn't look on her social media."

Tara looked taken aback. "Can't believe you cyber-spy on your kid."

"Of course, I do," Alice said. "She's in college. God only knows what she's doing there."

I should look, too. Maybe Gus . . . I reached for my cell phone in the back pocket of my jeans.

"I've never skimmed Victoria's social media," Selma said. "No need."

Alice rolled her eyes. "Oh, that's right. Victoria's perfect."

Selma shrugged. "No. I just prefer to remain in denial. Life's easier that way. Bury it and forget it."

I retracted my hand. A hush settled over the room, denied memories swirling in the current of merlot. We all had things we'd buried lately, things we'd rather remain in denial about. Selma didn't let herself spy on Victoria; Alice pretended she'd moved on from her husband's infidelity; Tara acted as if she'd actually chosen to be single at fifty, and I'd denied Gus's behavior problems, making excuses and bailing him out of trouble, over and over. But now . . . "Let's get back to the book," I said, trying for a wobbly smile. "We should at least try to discuss it, don't you think?"

Tara nodded and uncorked the last bottle of wine. Glasses were refilled. Soon the conversation switched back to a happier tone and, once again, heads bobbed and tipped with laughter.

Except mine. I remained on the fringe of the conversation,

my phone heavy in my pocket as I drenched my own denials in bloodred merlot, of all things. Because, unlike the others, I recognized the name of the girl in the news—Mia Jones.

I'd heard it from our son, Gus.

THREE

We got through the rest of the evening without any more mention of the dead girl. Or Gus, for that matter. Or any hint that anyone knew what was really going through my mind. There were a few quizzical stares, concern maybe, and Tara had asked me if I was doing okay. But in the end, everyone chalked up my shift in mood to the stress of my pending move.

Selma insisted on helping clean up and carried the empty wine glasses to the kitchen while I walked Alice and Tara to the door and watched them waver off, leaning on one another as they veered toward their houses across the street. We lived within a stone's throw of each other. If Alice left her blinds open, and I squinted, I could see the televangelist that preached from her TV screen nearly every night.

Shutting the door, I retreated through the living room, snatching up the rest of the snack plates and crumpled napkins, hoping to get things done quickly so I could get Selma on her way. I bustled into the kitchen just as she slurped remnants from one of the wine glasses.

She saw me and quickly swiped the glass with a soapy rag. "Great party tonight."

"Thanks for helping me clean up," I said. "But I can finish from here. You're probably tired from work."

"I am tired. Long day. Three showings. Can you believe it?

I haven't seen the market this hot for years." She turned off the water and dried her hands. "Saw Ben today. He—"

"You saw Ben? Where?"

She tossed the towel on the counter. "Drugstore. He was picking up your prescriptions. He told me all about the clinic. Went on and on about it. It's good to see him so passionate about something. He seemed genuinely happy."

My cheeks burned hot. *So passionate about something?* I pictured her standing next to him in the drugstore line, in her pencil skirt and black pumps—slim, sexy Selma—making clever conversation with my husband as he picked up not one but two prescriptions for his stressed-out wife.

Ben said both were necessary. With everything going on with Gus's behavior and the move and everything, I hadn't been sleeping well, been a bit jumpy, weepy. He'd always said, "What's the point of being a psychiatrist if I can't prescribe something to help my wife?"

I forced a smile, ushering Selma down the hall to the door, where she opened my front hall closet and reached for her light blue trench, which was cozily spooned with Ben's parka. She turned my way with a concerned cock to her head, her sculpted shiny bob swinging gently, a dark 'do fresh from the best salon in town. "Ben mentioned that he was heading out of town for a couple days."

"A conference in Seattle. It's not going to be a problem, though. He'll be back for the closing." I reached for the front doorknob.

"I was more worried about you. So much packing and all." She pressed her lips tight, and her gaze swept over the foyer, to the front parlor with artwork on the walls, photos still displayed, and a curio case of collectable dolls in frilly dresses. Her gaze locked there, on my Madame Alexander dolls, and I swore I felt them tremble under her critical eye, even heard what

13

sounded like a little gasp. Another gust of wind maybe. Or not. I fidgeted. A small crease flirted at her brow as well. Had she heard, too?

"It's windy tonight," I said to her or maybe more to myself.

She nodded, squinting at the dolls.

I continued: "Don't worry. It just looks like I haven't done any packing, but I've actually made good progress on the second floor."

"What about your . . . your sewing room. All those—"

"Tara is going to help me, starting tomorrow. Ben's suggestion. It'll be wrapped up before the movers get here." I opened the door wide and hung onto my smile. A chilling wind whipped through the house, rattling a set of framed photos displayed on my foyer table.

She finally tore her focus from my dolls and stepped outside into the swirling darkness. I shut the door, maybe a bit too quickly, and turned my gaze to the row of plastic curls and painted porcelain faces, my heart racing with panic. The move, the stress of packing, and now a dead girl who Gus knew. My perfect life was teetering on the edge. And so was my mind.

14

FOUR

I needed answers about Gus and Mia Jones.

I checked my watch: forty-five minutes before Ben would get home. Not much time to find out what Gus knew about that girl's death. I rushed upstairs and down the hall, greeting, as always, my pretty Madame Alexanders perched on the shelf that lined the hallway. "Hello Marne, and Lizzie, and Peggy Pigtails, and you too, Cissy dear." Another step and I turned to a little blondie with wide blue eyes and molded lashes. I could feel time ticking away, but I couldn't help myself. I fingered her calico dress and bonnet, white stockings, and double-checked her black slip-on shoes. "Don't fret, Bo Beep, I haven't forgotten you. Tomorrow I'll make you something special. No time now, though." And off I went, calling out to the rest of the Madame Alexanders as I passed by.

At Gus's door, I turned and glared at Amy, an exquisite angel in a full gold brocade gown and real feather wings. I'd given her a coveted spot, right next to my son's room so she could watch over him. That's what an angel was supposed to do, right? "You've done a crap job, Amy." Her shoulders seemed to droop, and in my mind, I heard her say, *I tried, I tried*. I shook my head, instantly sorry for my words. It wasn't her fault that he'd left home. I stroked her feathered wings, apologized, and then braced myself.

Inside my son's room, I faced empty coke cans, crumpled chip bags, overflowing trash . . . Gus's usual mess. Ben had been after me to do something about it, but this room was so like Gus and because of that I loved it, just as I loved Gus, and I dreaded changing it, let alone packing it.

But wait . . . drawers sat opened with clothes falling over the edges, notebooks with pages torn out, boxes tipped over with their contents strewed about. I frowned. Gus left trash about, always had, but he hadn't left it tossed like this. And it wasn't like this yesterday when I'd come in here to pack. I looked back by the door; the packing boxes I'd brought in yesterday sat empty. I recalled bringing them in here, a bottle of wine and a cup as well, just to help me get through this and then . . . I remember I had slid his laptop out from under the bed, opened it and . . . I couldn't remember after that. Admittedly, I had a few times like that this last week when I couldn't quite recall the hours passing. Too much to do, I guessed—too little time.

His laptop still lay open on the bed. I moved to it and pressed it on, flinching at the naked woman that popped onto the screen. I'd asked that kid a thousand times to change his screen saver to something more appropriate. Maybe it didn't really matter, though—he never used this computer anymore. Hadn't since graduation when his phone became his new "go-to," which he always kept with him.

Still . . .

I typed several different passwords: *bubbles*, his old gold-fish; *trubisky*, because we saw him play at Soldier Field once; *nirvana*, his favorite "classic" band. I'd done this yesterday as well and, getting nowhere, in frustration had opened the Char-donnay. That much I recalled. Wished I had the bottle now.

I slapped the screen shut and sighed. Like I was really going to ever guess his password when he'd hardly said three words to me in months, or really since he became a teenager.

Selma was right. Denial was dangerously alluring. Can't face something? Just ignore or forget it. Denial made me look the other way more than once, rather than face the facts about Gus. He'd left us over a month ago now, but that wasn't even the longest he'd been gone. His delinquent behavior had started in high school, breaking curfew, partying, and coming home drunk or, worse, stoned.

That night that I'd heard him talking about Mia, he'd stumbled into the house around two in the morning and relief had washed over me—*he's home safe!*—and then anger, because he was over two hours late. I had gone down the hall to check on him and found him in his bedroom, crying and saying the name Mia over and over. I'd asked him if he'd been drinking again. He'd ignored me, kicked me out, and locked the door. For a couple days afterward, he was anxious, on edge, angry. Ben tried to talk to him, but as usual with the two of them, it quickly evolved into yelling, and Gus stormed out.

And Ben had let him go, just walked back into his den, and left me to watch as my son flung himself into his beat-up Camry and drove away. Ever since, I'd resented Ben for not going after him.

But now . . . the name Mia . . . Gus's behavior after that night. I didn't want to think it, but . . .

I pulled out my phone and texted him with trembling fingers: *Come back home. We're moving soon. Come back.*

I waited. No reply. What did I really expect?

Across the room, I opened his closet and inhaled the stale tobacco odor that clung to his jacket. Whether it was from him or his friends, I couldn't be sure. Not that it mattered. Cigarettes were the least of my problems. I clicked through his clothing, my fingers pausing on one of his shirts—a dress shirt I forced him to wear to a wedding for one of Ben's colleagues—an expensive shirt, end-on-end broadcloth with a distinct woven contrast, light blue thread on the warp and white thread in the weft, and I thought of that pretty little doll up in my sewing room, the one waiting for a light blue summer dress, maybe with lace around the trim . . .

"Mona?"

"Ben!" I stumbled from the closet and patted down my hair, pretending sobriety and decorum. "You're home early." I picked up a pair of jeans, folded them neatly, and put them in the dresser drawer.

"Should I apologize?"

"No, of course not." Ben had escaped from the office for the day, but where another man might have loosened his tie by now, he preserved his status in a perfect Windsor.

His brown eyes seemed sad as they studied me, and not for the first time I noted how much Gus took after him. Same eyes, same long face, same hair that would curl at the end if you let it get too long. Sometimes I wondered if that was why Gus chose to dress sloppily—big sweatshirts with angry slogans, stained tank tops, ripped pants—to hide the fact that he could pass for his father with not even much of a squint.

"I didn't expect to see you up and packing still," Ben said. "Especially not Gus's room."

"I'm not packing, really. Just looking through things. I thought I might find some answers to why he left us."

Ben's expression changed to impatience. "You're not going to find any answers in here, Mona."

"It's just that after that argument—"

He cursed, then took a deep breath, and spoke calmly. "Please don't start in on that again. We've been over this before. It was an argument, that's all. Why can't you let that drop?"

"Because you haven't told me everything. All I heard was you screaming at him. What were you so angry about?"

He raked his fingers through his hair—more gray than

brown since our troubles with Gus—then patted it back into place and sighed. He'd quit talking about Gus a couple weeks ago, maybe because their argument was too painful? Maybe to protect me? Or had the eminent child psychiatrist given up on his own son?

Tears welled in my eyes, but I refused to look away. "He was so upset when he left, Ben. All because of that argument. And now we're moving . . . without him."

"Please try to understand, Mona." He reached out, pulled me against his shirt, blue, my favorite color on him, but my muscles tensed. Instead of feeling comforted by his touch, I felt . . .? My brain finally registered the emotion: repulsed.

His grip tightened as if sensing my reaction. "I was frustrated, that's all. You get that, right? Everything that we'd worked for over the years . . . the private schools, the tutors— all that wasted potential. No ambition, just partying and video games all the time. What type of life is that?"

"Maybe you shouldn't have pushed him so hard. It was right after that argument that he ran away—"

He winced and pulled back. "You think it's my fault that he's gone."

"No. That's not what I meant."

"Then why bring it up in the first place? Did someone say something to you about Gus?"

"No . . . well . . . yes. There was an article in the paper today. We were talking about it. And Tara said—"

"Tara was here?"

"Yes. Alice and Selma, too. It was our monthly book club."

His face darkened. "I thought you said you were going to cancel the book club. Given . . . well, given everything we have going on."

"I said I wanted to cancel it, but you said that it's best to carry on like things were normal." I thought that's what he'd said. That was what he always said. I couldn't really remember now . . . "Anyway, it was our last chance to get together before we move. I figured you'd be out late anyway. Again."

He sighed, the burden shifting to him now with that single word. "You're right. I should be here more. It's just that there is always so much to do at the clinic, my clients, paperwork, and we're training a new person for—"

"A new person? What's her name?" I couldn't stop myself. The wine, probably.

He shifted uncomfortably. "How do you know it's a woman?"

"Because you said 'person.' If it was a man, you would have said, 'We're training a new guy,' or a new man, or something like that. 'Person' means it's a woman and you're afraid I'll be suspicious."

"You're always suspicious."

"You're avoiding the question."

He rolled his eyes to the ceiling. "Let's see . . . Ashley. I think."

"You don't know?"

"Ashley."

"Young?"

"Youngish."

"Pretty?"

"I haven't noticed."

"Sure, you haven't."

He frowned and looked at the tangle of clothes at his feet. "Where are you going next with this downward spiral? Seriously, I'm worried about you."

I looked around again. I must have torn through Gus's room like a madwoman yesterday. Maybe I was one. All this stress was messing with my mind, making me dredge up past worries to pile on new ones. Now the wine had coaxed me into a snit of suspicion. Enough already.

I tried for a smile, but it felt like the crazed grin of an imbecile. Still, I held onto it, offered it up to him like an olive branch. "Then give me a break. Take me out for dinner. Just the two of us. We can talk about this, work things out."

"That's all we ever do, talk . . . I've got a better idea." He wrapped his palm in mine and tugged me toward the door. "And my idea is much better for relieving stress."

I pulled my hand from his. Did he really think that sex was going to make this better? Or was this just a ploy to distract me, so I didn't ask more about the argument? "I don't think so, Ben. Not tonight."

He turned toward me, that look on his face from our college days when he'd beg me to sneak into his fraternity house after hours, back when we didn't have to pretend that we wanted each other. My brain flooded with memories and hope that maybe it *could* be like that between us again, so I offered him my hand and let him lead me down the hall. A dozen pairs of eyes followed our every step and whispers echoed around us, *lies, lies, lies* . . . I ignored them, holding onto the hope that this was more than a distraction, that tonight would be different, that we'd be okay again. Like old times. But the murmurings followed me to our bed, where my hope died as Ben and I stroked and rubbed and breathed the same perfunctory sex I'd endured lately, because it was easier to pretend that we were okay than face the truth: nothing short of Gus coming back home again would fix our family.

FIVE

Wednesday, October 28th

The next morning, I peered through the bedroom window. The rolling field beyond our house was bare and empty like a brown bath towel had been rolled over the landscape. In the not-far-enough distance, a slanted barn loomed against the morning's predawn bronze, a nostalgic reminder that our sprawling suburb was once a small farming community. I used to think the barn was quaint, but now . . . I shook my head and turned to face my affirmation wall, Ben's idea. The sage psychiatrist. It pleased him when I followed his advice. I scanned the yellow Post-it notes dotting the wall like it'd caught chickenpox. What would it be today?

One jumped out at me: *Every challenge is an opportunity to grow.*

Challenges. As if my life hadn't had enough of those lately. I shook my head again and turned to my bedside table where I picked up a long, rectangular plastic box with a little compartment for each day of the week. "Don't forget your medicine," Ben had said earlier that morning as he'd rushed to get ready to leave. My happy pills. A couple of new types. Ben said they would work better than my old antidepressant.

I'd promised him that I would take them and then asked, "How long are you going to be gone?"

"Back on Sunday."

"That long? I'm going to miss you."

"I told you things would be hectic with the clinic for a while."

"I know, but—"

"You told me you were going to use the time to pack. Didn't you say that Tara is coming to help today? To start on your sewing room?"

"Yes, but I decided to wait a little while on the sewing room . . . just in case I have a project to do. We'll work on another area today."

"Projects? We're moving soon and you won't have time—"

"Just a few small things. Don't worry. It'll all get done in time. Did you need me to get you breakfast?"

"No, no need." He tapped his stomach. "I've already eaten."

I'd wanted to say more, to talk to him about the girl they'd found in Simon Lake, about what I'd heard Gus saying that night, and ask him if he'd thought that Gus knew what happened to her, but he was in too big of a hurry and part of me didn't want to know the truth. And why ruin his mood? He looked happy about getting away for a few days. I got that. Every day he tolerated his patients' miseries, depressions, and psychoses, and then came home to face even more of it. He needed a break.

So I'd kept quiet and followed him to the door. The good wife sending her husband off happy, even though inside my gut twisted with misery at the thought of his absence. As if he read my mind, he turned back right before walking out the door, and brushed his lips over my forehead, whispering, "Don't worry, Mona. I'll be back before you know it."

I shut the door and leaned my back against the cold wood, taking a few minutes to think about the week ahead of me without Ben, and suddenly the doorknob twisted and jiggled. I stepped back and threw open the door. "Did you forget some—"

The porch was empty.

"Ben?"

The wind tossed my hair as I leaned forward and turned my head left and then right. No one.

I shrunk back, slammed the door, and cranked the deadbolt.

One step back, two . . . my gaze riveted on the knob . . . another step and another and a flutter of movement caught my eye. Golden curlicues lifted from a doll's face as a cold draft wafted through the house, swirled around my ankles, and carried with it a wave of soft giggles.

SIX

Thirty minutes later, I sat at the kitchen table finishing my second cup of coffee. The sounds in the house, the whispers, the giggles, the jiggling of the doorknob, they were products of my imagination. Weren't they? They seemed so real. But Ben had told me over and over that intense stress causes auditory hallucinations. His solution: medication and affirmations. Neither was working. I pulled my phone from my robe pocket, my finger sliding to the App Store. It was time to look for something that might offer real help.

I'd checked Facebook and Twitter weeks ago, and nothing, but I hadn't ventured onto Instagram. Alice had mentioned it last week, and I'd planned to start an account right after that, hadn't I? Yet the "Get" still showed in the App Store. Guess I hadn't finished downloading it. I sighed. I was getting forgetful, and this could be where I found my answers. I tapped the screen and watched as the data circle filled, hoping something in here might fill my needs as well.

The doorbell rang.

Tara. She was early. I hurried down the hall and spied a little body heaped on the floor. One of my dolls. "What are you doing down here?" *Did I do this?* I scooped him up and gently cupped him in my hands and sighed. Little Boy Blue. Always the mischievous one.

The bell rang again. I startled and rushed to the front of the house, my doll in hand, and yanked open the door. "Hey, Ta—" But it wasn't Tara. It was two men in suits. The tall one spoke first. "Mrs. Ellison?"

"Yes."

He held out an ID. "Detectives Reyes and Meyers. Belington Police." He was bald, with pasty skin and black, watery eyes. Fifty maybe, but with the worn look of a man much older, as if he'd delivered too much bad news in his day.

"What's happened? Has there been an accident?" My heart jackhammered. Ben? Or was this about Gus?

"No. No accident. Can we come inside, Mrs. Ellison? Won't take long." He peered past me into the house. Was it my imagination or had he zeroed in on the picture of Gus on the foyer table?

I stepped aside and let them enter but made no motion to invite them further into the house. I'd encapsulated this intrusion in the foyer, keeping them at a safe distance from my personal life until I puzzled this out.

"Saw the 'sold' sign." The younger detective Meyers said, thumbing toward the front yard. "This is a great old house. They don't make them like this anymore. Bet it sold fast. When do you move?"

His neighborly smile, accompanied by a slight rocking motion, implied "I'm just like you," but his cold gray-blue eyes reminded me of the Chucky doll in that horror movie that toyed with victims before killing them. I moved Little Boy Blue behind my back. "A couple weeks. But why—"

"Where to?"

"We're just downsizing. A condo downtown. Closer to my husband's work."

"Is your husband here now? We'd like to speak to him."

"What do you need to speak to Ben about?" I tightened my grip on the doll—the soft familiar feel of the denim fabric was comforting. I needed to stay focused.

"Just a few things regarding his work."

I exhaled, relieved. I'd overreacted, assuming the worst, as usual. Ben was often summoned to testify in court as an expert witness for the defense, even though he hated it. Ben liked to be in charge, to solve issues with logic, to resolve conflicts with measured mediation, and in the fast-moving courtroom he would often lose the sharp edge of correctness he'd so carefully honed.

Even without the pressure of our move, I knew Ben would turn them down, regardless of the case. "No, he's on his way to Seattle for an important conference at Seattle Children's Hospital. But now is not a good time for Ben to help you. Not with—"

There was a noise outside on the walk. Detective Reyes moved to the narrow window that ran alongside the door and peered through the beveled glass. "You expecting someone?"

"My friend. She's coming over this morning to help me pack." I saw her through the side window and opened the door before she rang the bell. "Hi, Tara."

She lingered for a second on the stoop, casting a wary glance at the men before coming inside. Wisps of black hair stuck out from under a colorful beanie, cherry red lips smacking on gum, hints of peppermint and her floral perfume swirled inside with the smell of brewing ozone from the low-hanging thunderclouds. We were the same age, but she looked young and fresh.

I felt old and stale. "I just need to give these gentlemen a phone number. Coffee's made in the kitchen. I'll be there in a minute."

Meyers watched her with interest as she squeezed by and hurried down the hall. That neighborly smile still plastered on his face.

Irritation pricked at me now. Why didn't they just call Ben's office? Or maybe they had, and Ashley, the "hadn't noticed"

27

pretty girl, had stood her ground, not giving out the doctor's home number. Well, good for her.

"I'll give you Ben's private cell, but again, it's not a good time." I took a pad from the entryway table drawer and started to write. Reyes fixated on the framed photos on display.

"Nice family pictures." He pointed to one of Gus. "Your son?"

"Mm." My shoulders tensed.

Meyers took out a notebook. As his pen moved over the paper, my throat tightened; it occurred to me that they'd never made house calls before when they wanted Ben to consult. "What exactly do you want to talk to my husband about?"

Meyers spoke up. "A tip came in regarding a white Range Rover that might be involved in a case. The witness was able to provide a partial plate number. A vehicle license registered in your husband's name came up in the database."

"We had a Range Rover, but it was in an accident and totaled some time ago," I said, and then wish I hadn't.

"We're aware of that." Reyes nodded. "Who usually drove the Range Rover?"

"My husband, mostly."

"Mostly?"

"Our son, here and there. Not very often, though." My gaze darted to the picture of Gus and then back to Meyers, whose scribbling clawed into my brain. I ripped the page from my own pad and gave him Ben's cell number. "Thank you for coming." I added a smile and opened the door for them to leave.

Meyers stared at the number for a moment. "We'll give your husband a call." He lifted his chin, and his voice dropped a notch. "We're investigating a murder that occurred in this area a while back."

Reyes added, "Do you know anyone named Mia Jones?"

"No. I don't know anyone by that name," I answered

quickly, too quickly, and a tilt to Meyers's head told me he realized it.

"Could we sit down and talk a minute? We have a few questions—"

"This really isn't a good time." Again, too quick, but my pulse was racing. I opened the door wider. "Gus isn't around to ask, and I never drove the car, so it'd be best to talk to Ben. I'm sure he can answer all your questions."

Meyers and Reyes glanced at each other, some covert message passing between them. Then Meyers closed his notebook. "We'll talk again soon, Mrs. Ellison." He paused as if to let his words soak in, more threat than promise, and then turned and walked through the door.

Reyes stayed put, pointing at the doll in my hand. "Can I see that?"

I glanced at Meyers, already out on the steps, glad *he* hadn't asked. I still felt hesitant but handed the doll over to Reyes and watched as he studied him carefully as if trying to figure something out.

He finally said, "Little Boy Blue, right? My mother read that rhyme to me. Let's see . . . Little Boy Blue come blow your horn, the sheep's in the meadow, the cow's in the corn . . ." He shook his head and chuckled. "Afraid I can't remember the rest."

I smiled and finished it: "But where's that boy who looks after the sheep? He's under a haystack, fast asleep. Will you wake him? No, not I—for if I do, he's sure to cry."

"That's right." He looked down at the doll again. "Sure brings back memories." He passed it back, his expression softer. "Good memories."

He left. I watched through the window as he made his way down the walk, my brain flooding with images: the car, Ben, Gus, and . . . memories.

SEVEN

Tara stepped into the foyer. "What was *that* about?"

"Nothing, just someone looking for Ben." I headed for the kitchen.

She was right behind me. "Someone? You mean the police, don't you? They looked like cops."

I gently propped Little Boy Blue on the counter, out of the way of spatters and splashes but close enough that he didn't feel left out of the conversation. I straightened his straw hat just a little and sighed. I had no intention of discussing this with anyone. Certainly not Counselor Tara. "Routine questions. That's all."

"Don't do this, Mona. This is me you're talking to, not Selma or Alice. Me. Your best friend. Don't shut me out. If there's a problem, I can help."

I filled two mugs and passed her one, coffee sloshing onto the counter. I swiped it with a dishtowel. True, Tara might seem too nosy at times, but it was her job to get patients to open up, so who could blame her? Selma would just dismiss my problem and suggest a shopping trip—denial and all that—and Alice would offer a prayer, her solution lately for everything, but Tara was a friend and a professional counselor. Not a psychiatrist like Ben, and there was value in that. At least to me. Ben would analyze my issues and give me a quick solution, usually in the form of medication, while Tara would actually listen to my problems and help me find solutions.

"Mona?"

"What?"

"The cops. What did they want?"

I sighed. "They just needed Ben's opinion on a case. His professional opinion. You know, he consults all the time on court cases and things. I gave them his number, that's it."

Complete silence for a moment while Tara sipped her coffee with a pensive expression. "It's that girl, isn't it? The one they found in the lake."

My head snapped her way. "What? Why would you even . . ." I bit back the rest, my skin prickling. She overheard it, right? That was all. But my fingers held tight to the cup as I looked at Tara, her head tipped now, assessing me. I hated that. Why did she do that? It was the kind of thing Ben did, as if at that angle they can slip under my lies. *All the better to see you with, my dear.*

"The clinic," she said.

"What?" I'd lost track of the conversation again.

Tara spoke softly now, in that "it's okay" tone that counselors use. "Ben's new clinic for the homeless. The girl might have been a patient there."

I closed my eyes briefly. I should have realized this was likely one of the reasons the detectives had come by the house.

Tara toyed with her cup. She reached for the doll and picked it up, studying him closely. "Did I hear that cop say something about a Range Rover?"

Blood whooshed in my ears. She'd overheard more than I thought. And she knew that the police didn't come just because of the clinic. It was because of the witness who'd seen the Range Rover that night. They had questions. For Ben. Or . . . they'd also asked about Gus.

31

My stomach clenched and I shifted my cup in my left hand as the fingers of my right slid softly over my belly where a pink scar still rested under my jeans. Ben had kissed it last night, murmuring that it was my badge of courage, that's what he always called it, as if I had a choice back then.

"You okay?" Tara's cocked head lowered to my line of sight, her gaze intense.

"Fine." There was nothing courageous about me then or now.

Then she looked back to the doll, her brow furrowed as she turned Little Boy Blue over a couple of times. "Who is this supposed to be anyway?"

I brightened, glad for a shift in the conversation and was halfway through reciting the nursery rhyme when her phone rang.

"Alice. Hi." Tara sounded chipper when she answered, but didn't look it, as if disgruntled at the interruption. "I'm in her kitchen now. Yeah, she's right here."

She put me on speaker and Alice said, "Oh hi, Mona. I saw some men at your house this morning. Never seen that vehicle at your place before. Everything okay?"

I bristled. "Just some business thing for Ben, nothing important . . ." My voice trailed off as a flash of color through the kitchen window caught my eye. A cab turned the corner and was heading down our street. I left Alice hanging and scurried to the front of the house for a better look. I parted the front drapes. Tara shimmied next to me with the phone, Alice still on speaker.

"Looks like Selma's going somewhere," I said.

The cab idled in Selma's drive, white smoke spewing from its exhaust. On the speaker we could hear shuffling as Alice went to her window as well. We all watched as Selma popped out of the front door, dragging her carry-on and wearing a pencil-thin skirt skimming perfectly sculpted calves, a fitted turquoise cashmere sweater, and nude-colored stilettos to lengthen her already statuesque frame. She climbed ever so demurely into the back seat.

"How does she do that?" Alice asked over the phone. "Wear that tight skirt and still function?"

Tara chuckled.

I frowned. "Wonder where she's going?"

"A quick trip with her new boyfriend," Tara said. "She told us last night."

"She did? Must not have heard her."

"Yeah," Alice said. "Seems serious with this new guy."

Tara snorted. "Seems serious with every guy she dates. Remember the guy she brought to the neighborhood picnic last summer? She thought he was the one. Good looking, charming and all, until you got a few drinks in him. He hit on every woman at the party."

Not me.

"Liquor brings out the worst in people," Alice said. "It's the devil's brew, the bane of—"

"We get it," Tara said.

But Alice was right, I thought. Liquor brought out the worst in some people. It did in Ben. Back in college, he got wasted at his frat's New Year's Eve Party. We all did. I'd passed out, woke up, couldn't find Selma, my ride, and finally stumbled upstairs to one of the frat house bedrooms and . . .

"It meant nothing." Ben had told me time and again. "We were both drunk. It won't happen again."

I took a steadying breath and returned to the kitchen, grabbing my phone off the counter and pretending to read my to-do list. Another tactic recommended by Ben: focus on positive actions when the brain spirals. It usually worked. Right now, not so much.

Tara followed me, and I could feel her gaze, but I ignored her as she continued with Alice, changing the subject. "It's early for you, isn't it? Especially after our night last night."

"Yeah, well, I want more than anything to climb back under the covers and sleep it off, but Milo has other ideas. He started whining at seven this morning. You know how puppies are. Pee, eat, poop, play, repeat. They're like babies, I swear."

"Exactly why I don't have one," Tara said, and the conversation turned to all the great reasons Alice figured Tara really should get a dog. And Tara's excuses about why she had no place in her single life for one.

I tuned out, scrolled through my screen, found the Instagram app. It'd finished downloading. I quickly tapped open the app, moved through the prompts, entered my email and a password, and picked a username, something simple that no one would recognize, and then typed Gus's name into the search bar, my heart pounding as a dozen Gus Ellisons filled my screen. I scanned the faces and then there he was—shaggy dark hair; a barely grown beard, not much more than stubble, really; brown eyes too big for his thin face . . .

"Are you still there, Mona?" Alice asked over the phone.

Tara looked my way for a second, and squinted at my phone. I pulled it close, screen facing away from her prying eyes.

"Mona?" Alice asked again.

Tara's features tightened with concern. "We'll call you back, Alice." She quickly wrapped up the call.

"What did the cops really say, Mona?"

"What do you mean? I told you already, they—"

"I know what you told me. But it didn't sound like just a business thing. And you're upset. I can tell."

"I told you everything, okay?" I snapped.

She took a step back and held up her hands.

I felt bad. "I'm sorry. It's this move. I don't think I can do this. It'd be different if Gus were here, planning to go with us but . . ." I slipped my phone into my pocket, shrugged, and dumped my coffee into the sink. My hand shook. "I think I need some rest. Can we postpone this? I'm sorry, you took the time and . . . It's just that I'm not feeling all that great and—"

"I completely understand. You don't have to explain anything to me. I'll come back later this afternoon." She placed her hand on my arm and lowered her chin, her expression firm. "No need to be overwhelmed. I'll be here to help you."

"Right." I sighed. But my fatigue wasn't from the stress of packing but caused by fears over Gus and his involvement with Mia Jones, and I could never release it, not even to a friend.

EIGHT

As soon as the door shut, I cradled Little Boy Blue against the soft fabric of my sweatshirt and scurried upstairs, down the hallway to the back of the house—offered a nod and quick hello to Sissy, and Robyn, and Bo Peep—and continued up another flight of stairs, narrow and rickety, past the attic entrance, and then up one more set of stairs, this one spiraled, with one . . . two . . . three turns that led to a thin door. I opened it and stepped into the tower room; my little bird's nest perched high above the neighborhood.

Once inside, I began to relax, my muscles loosening and the dull ache behind my eyes melting away. I turned up the dimmer switch just so and exhaled my stress. This was my happy place.

I'd left the dark paneled wood walls unpainted, with age stains and fastenings adding to the sense of timelessness. On the windows, heavy maroon drapes kept the prying sunlight from damaging my precious world. My sewing table rested in the middle of the room, with fabrics stacked neatly around a scarlet settee and matching Queen Anne chair. Spools of thread stood ready in trays, and doll hair of every hue filled plastic bags like brown and auburn and dirty blonde cotton candy. A small cabinet held little arms, some at rest, others with fingers grasping for life. And on one wall, a shelf of glass eyes of every shade: cerulean blue, green envy, deep brown, and purple sparkle. They stared at me, waiting for a body and watching my every move as I pieced together each perfect doll.

The round space of my tower room felt like the full circle of life, where dismembered limbs and glossy eyeballs and straggles of hair awakened in my hands. This is where I found my peace. Right here in this room.

I gently tucked Little Boy Blue on a shelf between two regal boudoir dolls with plunging necklines and painted lips. "Behave now," I told him and moved to the front windows that overlooked my cul-de-sac, careful to remain partially concealed behind the brocade drapes as I caressed the gold tasseled tiebacks and stared over the neighborhood.

Alice was just turning the corner with Milo tethered on a red leash and wearing an argyle doggie sweater. A gust of wind whipped at her hair and rattled my window and I thought of Ben's flight. He would have left his office already, maybe even be at O'Hare. I opened my weather app and scanned the report. Severe weather was predicted throughout the Midwest, but it looked like he'd be flying just north of the worst of it. What a relief. But I feared something worse than weather in our lives. I dialed his number, hoping to catch him before he boarded, got his voicemail, and sent a text: *Call me when you land. Important.*

A flash of movement drew my gaze to Tara's front window and told me she was already inside, going on with her day. Good. I planned to do the same. I settled in my chair like a queen on her throne and regarded my subjects: shelves and shelves of dolls, each and every one orderly, and well behaved, as children should be. Such good company, they were. And loyal, too.

"I can trust all of you, right?" I whispered. Their steady expressions and earnest eyes told me I had nothing to fear. "Okay, then. Let's see what Gus is up to." Excitement fluttered through me as I opened Instagram again and clicked over to Gus's timeline, and then my stomach lurched as an image of the wrecked Range Rover filled the screen—hood crumpled, doors popped, airbags puffed out like giant marshmallows. I read Gus's comment:

ellison_gus18 My dad did this.
#totaled #roll #wrecked #rangerover

The post was over three months old and I hated that he'd kept it online or even posted it at all. The night Ben wrecked the Range Rover still haunted me. How had he even survived this?

Anxiety gurgled in my throat as I skimmed the comments:

View all 21 comments
melbax WTH man
14w 1 like Reply
mockingbir everyone ok?
14w 1 like Reply
   gus_ellison18 @mockinbir yup
maggy.vi ☹
14w 1 like Reply
Jlgimme sorry dude
14w 1 like Reply
   ellison_gus18 @Jlgimme yeah gone forever
ICU2 I know why.
1d Reply ♡

I stopped. *I know why.* Strange. What did that mean?

I scrolled down to the next post, a photo of Gus sitting on the edge of a stained mattress, wearing that black T-shirt I hated, and behind him, a window framed in tattered curtains and partially covered with plywood.

4 likes
ellison_gus18 somewhere in the crib. f*cked up.
#lifesucks #staystrong #partyhard
View all 2 comments
July 19

yungceo ya man.
15w 1 like Reply
ellison_gus18 @yungceo yessir
15w Reply

F*cked up? Party hard? My face burned hot. Had any of the other mothers seen this? And who was that next to him? A girl? Mia? She was cut off in the picture; I could only see her arm, part of her shoulder, a lock of jet-black hair, and her palm resting on Gus's thigh, a cigarette between her fingers. My skin pricked. I tried to enlarge the picture, only to see a white heart flash on the screen. The likes increased to five. What? Oh, no! I tapped the red heart under the post, and it went blank again. *4 likes.* My own heart was pounding.

Gus had never shared about girlfriends but had let slip a few times a "her" and "we," so I'd figured he'd entered that dangerous territory of relationships. It was about that time when he changed, started acting up. At a certain age, friends become more influential than parents. I wished I could go back to that time when I was the most important person in his life. But wishing didn't make it so. Still nostalgia overcame me as I went back and read what he'd put for his profile.

ellison_gus18
bhs2019 . bears football . Fear Nothing . YOLO!!

My mind flitted to when Gus was ten, the perfect age, before puberty set in, before his big rebellion, before girls, and we were at a Packers/Bears game, the sunlit gridiron, the chanting crowd, and smells of buttery popcorn, yeasty beer, the tang of boiled hotdogs, and Gus wedged between Ben and me. Such a perfect day.

I typed Mia Jones into the search bar. A dozen Mia Joneses

popped up, many with flower pictures or goofy pet icons instead of images. I clicked on each one, but none of them seemed to be the right age for the dead girl. Of course, kids use cryptic handles for themselves half the time so maybe using her name wouldn't even help.

Gus had said her name over and over that night he was distraught. If he knew the truth about Mia's death, why didn't he just talk to me about it?

I looked closer at the photo with the mattress. The location under the picture said Belington. Gus was somewhere close by with this girl, in a boarded-up house, on a mattress, doing God knows what. It could have been Mia. Or not. I scrolled back to the picture of the totaled Range Rover and to ICU2's comment and clicked on the name:

ICU2
The profile picture was blank. Nothing, just a silhouette.
Posts 9 Followers 0 Following 1

I clicked on "Following." ICU2 followed one person: *ellison_gus18*
My breath caught.

The nine photos on ICU2's profile were generic, no descriptions, no hashtags, no people, just pictures of places and things, and each posted two days ago: the high school, the library, the mall, the skate park, and Pizza Man. It dawned on me: these posts were snapshots of Gus's life, his normal hang-out places, even the pizza place where he used to work. My heart rate kicked up, and so did a little voice in my head: *Gus, Gus, Gus* . . . Was he reaching out to me through social media, trying to tell me something? Could it be possible?

My hopes soared as my finger zipped over the screen, moving through the posts with more excitement, studying each one closer. A couple of the posts were different than the others. One was of two heart balloons tangled in what looked like tall brown grass. The other, a photo of a red metal park bench.

I had no idea where these balloons were, or why there was a photo of them, but I'd seen red park benches like this down the road at Simon Park.

The park where Mia's body was found.

NINE

It took me a while to find the bench that matched ICU2's post. It rested near a bend in the path, under a bare-branched maple. When I finally did locate it, I sat down and craned my neck until my view matched the photo angle in the post.

ICU2 created this account just a couple of days ago, and only yesterday posted, "I know why" on Gus's three-month-old, wrecked Range Rover image. Why? Some sort of cryptic message? For me?

I searched my phone and found the newspaper article Alice had mentioned:

The Belington Reporter, October 24. The remains of a body discovered in Simon Park last month have been identified as Mia Jones, a seventeen-year-old local woman. The victim was first discovered on September 19, when Belington Police responded to a 911 call reporting human remains on the bank of a lake in Simon Park. Police believe that the victim's body could have been submerged in the water for several weeks. The authorities refuse to make any additional comments on the case at this time, but ask that if you have any information or leads regarding Ms. Jones's death, please call the Belington Police Department at . . .

The article went on to paint a picture of Mia Jones: young teen, raised by a single mother, an impoverished childhood, high school dropout. How long before the cops found a connection between her and Gus? Or had they already? I remembered how the detectives looked at Gus's picture in the foyer.

I swayed a little as I worked myself onto my feet and started down the path toward the lake. A young mom scurried past me with a bundled baby in a stroller, and I thought about Gus at that age: warm, soft, with doughy baby cheeks and coffee-colored eyes. I'd treasured those days. Squishy-pea days, I called them. Baby Gus loved peas, eating them until green mush oozed out the side of his sweet little mouth. Such tender times, those baby days. They gave way to the playful toddler days, when I'd pretend to be a horse and he'd crawl onto my back, thrashing my braid like a rein: "Giddy up, horsey. Giddy up." Then the wonderful, inquisitive years between six and eleven, before the angsty tween years started, when he grew like a pole bean, learned to read, and obsessed over matchbox cars. Teenage Gus—taller than me, wiry thin with traces of facial hair, and eyes hard and set against the world—was no longer sweet and innocent . . . Where had time gone?

I paused on the path and shot out a text: *I can't make this move without you.* Another dozen steps and I stopped again and added another text: *Your dad misses you too. I need you home. We need you home.*

A few more steps and I stopped again; this time I shook my head and pocketed my phone. I was acting like an obsessed mother, wasting time following random social media posts when I had so much to do at home, sorting and packing and clothes to make for . . . I looked up. Ahead, a young man stood at the edge of the pond, staring out over the water. His back was to me, but his dark hair, his posture, the way his shoulders slightly stooped under his sweatshirt . . . *It can't be . . . Gus?*

Gus was here? "Gus!" I screamed, but the wind swallowed my voice.

I cut over the grass—*I knew it, I knew it, he was reaching out to me!*—and yelled out his name as I ran . . . "Gus!" But he didn't move. Why couldn't he hear me? Was he ignoring me . . . no, that couldn't be it. He'd led me here with his posts. I needed so much to see him again. "Gus!"

He finally turned around.

I stopped. "You're not Gus."

His startled blue eyes studied me, taking in my sweatpants, baggy and stained under my old worn wool coat I'd snatched when I rushed from the house, messy hair, no makeup. Then his eyes softened. "Are you okay, lady?"

I lowered my gaze, my breath still ragged from my short sprint. "I'm sorry. I thought you were someone else." This man was much taller than Gus and older, his hair two shades too dark. He didn't look like Gus at all. *What is wrong with me?*

"Do you need help?" he asked. "Can I call someone for you?" His hoodie had a North Central College logo on it. Gus had talked about going there. Ben had higher aspirations, but I thought a small college made sense—keep him close to home and out of trouble.

"No. Really, I'm fine." I turned away, sweat trickling down my cheeks—or was it tears?—and started back to the path, stumbled, bit my tongue, cursed, righted myself, and kept going, my head down. Blood swirled inside my mouth, pain swelling on the edge of my tongue when thunder cracked behind me. I startled and turned back. The kid had disappeared, maybe making his way around the lake's path now, but something shiny and distorted swirled in the reeds near where he'd stood: the twisted skins of a pair of Mylar balloons, silver and red, the same color of the balloons in ICU2's post.

Raindrops fell on my face and tapped the surface of

the lake like invisible hands on a keyboard. The clouds were churlish and cruel, and my mouth went dry.

In retrospect, I should have left the park at that moment, shut down Instagram, and never looked at another one of ICU2's posts again. But I didn't. Instead, I moved toward the lake, my nerves twitching as I neared the balloons, once round and silver with red hearts, but now deflated to nothing but shriveled Mylar that hung shredded from dry reeds.

I waded shin-deep into the ice-cold water, sludge pouring into my shoes. The water churned up blackish green strands of slime and reeked like gamy socks and pungent urine. The odor coated the back of my throat as I squatted down and reached, and reached, until my fingertips latched around the balloon strings.

I tugged and jerked, but the strings were snagged on something under the water. Determined now, I leaned in for a better grip, but my feet slipped on the scum below, and I plummeted forward, my left hand sinking into the muck. Putrid blobs of muddy goo splattered my cheeks.

I gagged, coughed, lifted my chin, and gulped fresh air before plunging my hand deeper under the water, my fingers probing along the base of the reeds until they nudged something solid. The balloon weight. Probably a little bag of sand, wrapped in a colorful foil and attached to keep the once helium-filled balloons rooted.

I gave it a yank and the mud released the weight, nearly toppling me backward. But it wasn't a balloon weight. It was a mud-caked doll, the balloon strings wound around its neck and knotted tightly like . . . like a noose.

My brain stuttered, my thoughts racing so fast that it couldn't keep up, then my body kicked in, and I scrambled back to the bank, splashing and hyperventilating. More thunder, and lightening now, and I shouldn't have been near water, but I squatted down and dipped the doll over and over, stroking the grime and mud away.

The poor thing was naked and covered in mud. Is that how Mia was found? Facedown? Naked? Not naked, I hoped. And shuddered, my head filling with Gus's voice from that night, *Mia, Mia, Mia*, over and over like a manic mantra, as I stared at the doll, discarded and thrown into the murky water, mud and silt now oozing through her every orifice.

I dunked her again and ran my fingernail along the crevices of her joints, flicking away sand and sludge and tiny pebbles. Then I went to work on her face, rubbing the dirt lodged in her eyes, and the dip above her chin and her hairline, and I thought that there were so many other things, not just Gus's words that night, but other things that I needed to know and to understand in order to figure this out before the cops did.

"Blythe," I whispered, as I brushed muddied curls away from her face, recognizing the sweet features of her oversized head and wide round eyes. I knew her. And she was much more than an iconic fashion doll, now without a stitch of clothing. Blythe was my very first doll, given to me by my mother all those years ago, and now discarded for dead.

"You poor thing." I pulled her close, terror striking at my heart as I realized that this also proved that there was nothing random about ICU2's posts. They were meant for one person. For me.

TEN

I pulled into our driveway, parked, but kept the engine running. Rain pelted the windshield. I cranked up the heat and turned to Blythe. "You're home now, right where you belong." I kept my voice cheery, for her benefit, but as I stared at our home, the detective's earlier words echoed in my mind: *a great old house.* And that it was: situated on a rise at the edge of our suburb, it was the original estate, built to withstand time with a solid foundation and a third-floor attic dormers, a tower with a turret, and a shady porch. Historic, stately, impressive, or so I used to think. Now it seemed tired and sad, in disrepair. Much like me. And now Blythe.

I had dialed Ben's number twice since leaving the park, with no answer. His plane was scheduled to land over an hour ago, and he should have seen my text by now. Why hadn't he called? Worries mounting, I dialed his office. Maybe they'd heard from him.

"Child Psychiatric Associates." The woman's voice chirped pleasant, yet concise, efficient. Efficiency was important, Ben always said.

I took a deep breath, steadied my voice. "Dr. Ben Ellison's office, please."

"One moment."

Music came over the line and I began pulling at my eyebrow hair. A nervous habit. Ben hated it. I found it soothing.

"Hello. This is Dr. Ellison's office."

I knew this voice. Tammy. A big woman, brown hair, thin lips, lots of makeup. She handled prescription refills. Handled my prescriptions. "This is Mona Ellison. I'm—"

"Hi, Mona. Tammy."

"Yeah, hi, Tammy. I'm trying to reach Ben, but he's not answering his phone."

"Uh, Dr. Ellison's out of the office today."

"I know." Did she think I wouldn't know that? "It's just that I need to get ahold of him. He's not answering his phone. I'm wondering if you've heard from him. Has he called to check in?"

"Well, no, and I wouldn't expect him to normally." I heard the shuffling of papers and a muffled voice in the background— no doubt she was busy, probably swamped with her regular work and helping Ben with the new clinic. "He might be in flight still. Maybe if you wait—"

"No," I said. "His plane was scheduled to land an hour and ten minutes ago."

"Oh. Well, you might try his hotel later."

"I forgot to ask him which hotel he's at. Do you have that information?"

A long, impatient sigh sounded over the line. What had Ben said to her about my prescriptions? That his wife was having trouble with her mind? Forgetting things? Obsessing?

"We've been disorganized with the move and all," I explained. "I'm sure he wrote down the name of his hotel—I just can't find it."

"I understand." Although her tone said she really didn't. Or that she understood only too well about her boss's forgetful, fretful, troubled wife. "I don't know where he is staying. Someone else handles his travel arrangements now."

"Ashley?"

"Yes, actually, it is Ashley."

"I haven't met her yet."

"She's new. Just started a couple weeks ago."

"Well, can you put me through to her? Maybe she can help me out."

"Uh . . . I would, except she's not here today."

A pause. Or more of a purposeful hesitation? What wasn't she saying?

"Where is she?" *Seattle? With my husband? Is that why I can't reach him?*

"I'm sorry, Mrs. Ellison. I . . . I can't really say."

"You can't, or you won't?"

"Excuse me?"

"I need to get ahold of my husband, Tammy. It's urgent."

"I understand, but—"

"No, you don't."

She was still talking, but I hung up. *Liar. You know where he is.* I imagined them having a good laugh about right now. Poor Mona Ellison, so paranoid, delusional even, Ben should up her meds.

Damnit, Ben. I shot him another text—*Call me. It's important!!* My eyebrow hurt, my skin was raw, tears welled in my eyes, but I wouldn't give in to crying. I swiped them away, turned off the engine, tucked Blythe protectively under my jacket, and went into our empty house.

Alice showed up a half hour later with a bag of takeout from the neighborhood deli—veggie wraps, baked chips, and drinks; a soda for me; a bottled water for her. Alice didn't do meat, or sugar either. She believed in clean eating. Since her divorce, she'd become a believer in a lot of things: the many benefits of apple cider vinegar, Jesus and angels, yoga and bitcoin investments, regular colon cleanses, and even though she's not a Catholic, she's now a true believer in Marian apparitions and demonic possession. She was obsessed with the demonic for a while, even suggested that inanimate objects like my dolls could be cursed and have spirits attached to them. I took offense to that. She didn't even know my dolls.

Now she set the food on the kitchen table along with the day's newspaper and explained that Tara was running late to help with the packing and had asked her to fill in with lunch. As if they didn't trust that I'd fix myself something to eat.

"Have you seen today's paper . . . Oh . . . your eyebrows, have you been picking them again?"

"No. Yes. A little bit, I guess."

"You shouldn't do that to yourself."

I shrugged and pointed to the paper. "Thanks for bringing this. We're not getting the paper now. Canceled our subscription already."

"It's got an article in it about that girl, Mia." She unfolded it to the front page, where the lead story was an article on the murder. A photo of Mia Jones took up an entire column.

"This"—she tapped the page—"this picture is getting to me. Before she seemed so distant, not real to me, but now I can't stop thinking about . . . just look at her. It's disturbing. Someone so young and pretty, and she ended up murdered right down the street."

The face of a young girl stared back at me. Obviously not the current Mia, but an old school picture. She was maybe fifteen in this photo, with a dark braid, full cheeks, a hesitant smile, and round, wide eyes. My mouth dried out. I looked away and snatched my soda, my mind drawing comparisons. Mia's deteriorated body on a morgue table, Blythe plucked from those murky pond waters and now upstairs in my tower room, her body dirty and naked and stretched out on my mending table waiting for me to tend to her. I shivered. Thankfully, I'd found Blythe before she'd suffered more damage.

Alice chomped down on her veggie wrap, shreds of lettuce falling onto the table. She chewed and talked at the same time: "Can't imagine what her last moments were like. How scared she must have been. Makes me sick to my stomach." She took another bite, chewed while looking sideways at my unwrapped sandwich. "Fuel up," she said. "You're going to need energy to take on that attic when Tara gets here."

I plucked a slice of cheese from the folded wrap and nibbled the corner, while she went on about the article. "What really bothers me is that she was found just five minutes from here. I mean, I go running at Simon Park all the time, or I used to. Can't stand the idea of it now. Don't think I can ever go there again. Can you?"

She'd finished her sandwich and was picking at the label on her water bottle as she spoke. Little flakes of paper piled up on the table like snow in a snowstorm.

My eyes zeroed in on the pile and I thought of my father. It's always the little things that trigger the ugliest of memories. The smell of his cigarettes, mixed with the rotten cabbage smell of sulfa from the refinery where he worked, the way he picked the label off his beer bottles until they piled up like shed reptile skin, fitting since he was like a viper, coiled and ready to strike, not just with his fist, but with names like *retard, loser,* words that stuck and hurt more than any physical blow and plagued me even into adulthood. I often wondered if that's part of what attracted Ben to me. Out of all the women he could have picked, he saw the brokenness in me. Something that he could fix. A project.

Now, like most projects, I'd become tedious. "I haven't heard from Ben yet," I mumbled, more to myself than Alice, but I followed it up with, "I'm worried. He said he'd call as soon as he landed. I don't even know his flight number. I hope something didn't happen to him."

She got up and went to the sink to refill her water bottle. I scooped the paper pieces into my cupped hand and shoved them deep into my pocket.

"It's probably just a weather delay," she said. "Weather can cause all kinds of accidents. I don't blame you for worrying, but you need to try to stay positive. Same advice I gave to a couple women at choir practice this morning. They were all worked up about this article, worried that the killer is still out there, prowling neighborhoods, looking for another victim, like a serial killer. So, I reminded them that the Jones girl was living on the street, so it was probably either a prostitution thing or a drug deal that caused her demise. Don't you agree?"

Nothing like putting a positive spin on things. Airline accidents, serial killer, prostitution . . . *Drug deal gone bad.*

#f*cked up. #partyhard. My fingers itched. I wanted to get back on my phone and look at Gus's posts. Especially the one with his eyes hooded and bloodshot. Was he high?

I set my wrap aside and rubbed my temples. "I went there today." My voice cracked and I hated it that I wasn't strong enough to handle this. "To Simon Park, to the lake, and I thought I saw Gus there. I swear, Alice, it was so real. Like it was him, only when I got up close, I saw that it wasn't Gus but some other guy, we even talked and then . . . I don't know. He was gone. Like maybe I imagined the whole thing. What's wrong with me?"

Alice sighed as she came close, dipping her head to catch my gaze. "There is nothing wrong with you, are you serious? You've got major stress. This would be a lot for anyone. I know you don't like to hear this, but you can pray about this. It helps, really it does."

Alice gripped my hands in hers and closed her eyes, her lips moving in a silent prayer, when my phone rang. It was Ben.

I yanked my hands from her grip and started for the back stairs. "Sorry. I've got to take this."

ELEVEN

"Mona. I'm sorry," Ben said right away. "My flight was late, then I was running behind for my first meeting and I didn't turn my phone back on until just now."

"I was worried about you. The weather, and when I didn't hear from you—"

"Have you practiced your mindfulness today?"

"No, I will . . . it's just that . . ." I shut our bedroom door, scooped up his pillow and hugged it close. I lowered my voice even though Alice had already excused herself, and I now heard the front door close. "The police were here," I whispered. "They asked about our old Range Rover. A tip was called in or something, but they think it's connected to the girl they found in the park. They know who she is now. Mia Jones."

Background noise wormed over the line: the low murmur of voices and faint music, someone laughing, clinking silverware.

"Ben?"

"I'm here."

"They asked about you and your work and then they kept looking at Gus's picture, you know the one in the foyer by the front door, and what if they think Gus had something to do with her death? And now he's gone. It looks bad. And do you remember how Gus was acting back then? I think . . . maybe he—"

"What did you tell the police?"

"Nothing. Just that we had a Range Rover, but it was totaled."

"Did they ask about Gus directly?"

"Not really . . . but Ben, they asked if he drove the Range Rover. I didn't know what to say . . . I couldn't lie . . . I told them that he did sometimes." My voice sounded screechy. My throat felt tight. "That wreck . . . do we have some sort of record on it? A police report?" We would, wouldn't we? For insurance.

"Calm down, Mona. They have to check with everyone who owns a car of that make and model. Routine questions, that's all. Don't get all upset and do something stupid."

Do something stupid? What did he mean by that? I picked at the pillow's seam, memories filling my mind: a broken glass, red juice oozing over the floor and sinking into the cracks in the linoleum, Daddy standing over me, anger, fear . . . *"You stupid little girl. What were you thinking? Answer me! Answer me!"* My body shaking, tears streaming, as spit pooled on the edges of his cruel mouth. And I had no answer to give. *"I'm so sick of your crying."* And my fingers, small and soft, wrapped around my doll, the only comfort I knew, and his hands, rough and calloused, wrapped around the back of my neck, hair tearing from my scalp and pricks of pain as he yanked my head back and forced me to look up at him, then the putrid smell of beer and cigarettes on his breath as the final ultimatum was delivered: *"Stop it! Or I'll give you something to really cry about."*

"I found Blythe today," I blurted.

"Blythe?" Ben paused. "Do I know her?"

"My doll." How did he not remember Blythe?

Another long pause, then, "Maybe it would be best if I sent someone over to be with you."

"I don't need a babysitter, Ben."

"Of course not. I was simply suggesting that—"

"Tara's coming here anyway. She's going to help me clean out the attic."

"That's wonderful. I'm so proud of you."

My heart soared. "I'm trying, Ben. I really am."

"I know you are, dear . . . oh, hold on."

I heard the muffled sound of a female voice in the background. He came back on the line with a long sigh. "Honey, I'm sorry, but I need to go."

"Who's that talking to you?"

"Mona, I have to—"

"Is it Ashley?"

"Who? Oh no. Come on, Mona. Don't be this way. I've got to go, okay? I'll try to call back later, but my schedule is tight. Please try to understand."

"Wait!" But he disconnected. I didn't have a chance to tell him about the man I saw at the park and how I thought it was Gus, and . . . and that he seemed to vanish into thin air. What would he say about that? *Relax, Mona. You're overreacting. Don't let it . . .* what? Get to you? Upset you? Unravel you more than you already are?

I blinked back tears—*maybe I am unraveled*. Going to the lake. Thinking a stranger was Gus. I snatched a tissue and blew my nose. On my nightstand was the medicine case that Ben had carefully filled for me before he left. I reached over and popped open the compartment for PM. Two little pills stared up at me like beady little eyes. I swallowed them dry.

Alice had left and Tara wasn't due to arrive for another half hour, so I ran a brush through the snarls in my hair, tied it back, and headed downstairs to Ben's study. Might as well keep busy packing.

I surveyed the room. Among other things, my husband was a tidy man. His papers were stacked with edges aligned, pens parallel to the edge of the desk, books in a perfect pyramid, paperclips all in a row, as straight and evenly spaced as obedient soldiers, no dust, no disorder . . . not a single thing was out of place in this miserably neat room. For a psychiatrist, Ben had his own set of issues. Maybe that was what made him so brilliant. *Crazy knows crazy.*

I avoided the desk and started by pulling framed photos off the wall, wrapping each and carefully stacking them in a box. Next, a couple pieces of artwork, and then I moved to the bookshelves, stacking the books on the desk so I could sort them by weight: *An Unquiet Mind, The Handbook of Narcissistic Disorders, A Journey Through Madness*—I chuckled. Haven't we all been on that trip? I kept going: *Handbook of Differential Diagnosis, Psychopharmacology* . . . A sliver of white peeked out from the top of this book. I opened it to the marked page: a section on antipsychotic medications and saw that Ben had made notes in the side margins. His handwriting was narrow and slanted, but even so, the word "Mona" popped off the page. Also, the words "recurrent acute psychosis."

I slid the book back onto the desk, acid rising in my throat. *Psychosis?* Of course, Ben would have set his analytical mind to piecing together my issues. That was what a psychiatrist did, fitted symptoms to diagnosis. Round peg in round hole. But psychotic? Is that what Ben had thought? Depressed, anxious, maybe, but I've never been psychotic. I glanced again at the page; my name bordered a long list of drugs. And it hit me: off-label use. Ben frequently mentioned how some drugs had benefits for an issue unrelated to the drug's originally intended purpose. Was that what he was looking for here? Something that worked better for my depression. Don't second-guess the expert, I told myself. My head throbbed. I took a deep breath, my fingertips massaging a circle over my left temple as a voice hissed in my mind, *"Don't trust him."*

* * *

The attic ran along the front side of the home, long, narrow, dark, with only a couple small dormer windows, old and cloudy like cataracted eyes. They were stuck shut, hadn't been opened in years, and the whole room felt like a suffocating lung. My skin itched.

"Over here," Tara called out.

I followed her voice to the far corner, where she stood next to a stack of boxes. We'd been working for most of the afternoon and had made good progress. Now, she had an empty mason jar in her hands. "Why do you have so many of these?" she asked.

"I forgot about those. Wow. It's been years. I got them for a steal at a garage sale back when Ben and I went through our organic gardening phase." We'd just bought the place, a unique find with a large yard, on the edge of an open country field. A pocket of paradise in Chicago suburbia, isn't that what Ben called it? I'd gotten bit by the gardening bug. We both had. Organic, homegrown veggies. I was going to grow and preserve them. A poignant yet pleasant memory, and I found myself relaxing at the thought that I could let some memories—and these jars—go. I could move on.

Tara replaced the jar and weaved the top of the box closed. "I don't remember that phase."

"It was cut short by the breastfeeding and diaper-changing phase."

"Aw, yeah, well, that would do it."

I pointed to an open area by the door. "Let's put it in the 'donate' pile over there. Looks like most of this stuff will be going to new homes."

The attic rafters sloped down to studded walls, lined with musty cardboard boxes, stacked two or three deep with over a decade of castoffs. None of it would fit in the condo. I sighed and flipped open a box: old books, a pocketknife, polished rocks, a baseball glove . . . Gus's things.

And there was the problem: the attic was a graveyard of treasures, unused things, but too sentimental to discard. I closed the box, taped it shut, and moved it to what was going to be a 'keep' pile along with one of his old baseball bats, all of it destined to end up in a storage unit somewhere.

We worked like this for a while, until Tara traipsed over and flopped down on an old recliner near me. Dust particles poofed off the cushion and rode along a stream of dim light from the overhead bulb. She coughed, sucked in more dust-filled air, coughed again, and pointed at my open box. "Oh wow, what's that?"

"This?" I pulled out an old tweed jacket, brown Irish herringbone with elbow patches and a breast pocket. It still smelled like the tobacco Ben used to smoke, back when he was into pipes. Nasty habit. Glad it was short-lived.

Tara popped out of the chair. "It's so retro. Can I?"

I handed it to her. "Ben's. From our college days. He thought it made him look sophisticated."

"I sort of remember him wearing this." She wrapped it around her front side, sniffed, and screwed up her face. "You could dry clean it. Tweed is in again."

"No, donate. He's never wearing it again."

She took it off and put it in the donate pile. "So much family history up here, huh?"

"Some, sure. But a lot of junk, too." Maybe the pills had softened my edge, maybe telling Ben about the cops had released that burden, or maybe it was just the sight of those stacked and sorted boxes, but I felt better. Maybe I didn't need mindfulness exercises as much as forward progress.

I came to a small box that'd been shoved beneath an old desk. I opened it. And gasped.

58

SUSAN FURLONG

"What is it?" Tara asked, craning her neck.

"Nothing. Just . . . something I'd forgotten about." An old inside-out sweatshirt that I'd shoved up here a while back. I pushed it away, about to relegate it to the discard pile, but my fingers paused on the worn-soft, time-faded fleece. Images and memories and possibilities all blurred together, and an idea came to me; I knew a way to put this to good use.

Tara stepped closer.

"It's nothing," I repeated and closed the box, crisscrossing tape across the top, back and forth, three layers deep, and then moved it aside. What would Ben say if I told him about this sweatshirt? He'd tell me to dispose of it and never mention it again. *Leave the past behind and move forward, Mona.*

A creak on the attic stairs startled me.

Tara heard it, too. "What was that?"

I forced myself to relax. "The wind, old wood, thin walls . . . who knows? This house has a soul of its own."

She hugged herself and rubbed the top of her arms.

"Ben and I used to think this was our dream, saving an old gem like this, restoring it to its original grandeur, filling the rooms with babies."

She laughed, her voice tight and high-pitched.

"We never did finish our projects—"

Suddenly a loud *Bang, bang, bang!* echoed through the house.

Tara's eyes popped wide.

My muscles jittered with adrenaline. "I'm sure it's just the boiler kicking in. The temp must've fallen." But it'd never sounded like that before, had it? Maybe just because we were in the attic? Yet a chill crept over me and light seemed to drain from the attic's dusty air. Part of me ached with hope that it was Gus, but I knew better and had already made a fool of myself once today. I wanted to reach for the soothing comfort of one of my dolls, but instead I reached for the baseball bat I'd found earlier. "It's after seven," I said, struggling to keep my voice even. "I think we should call it a night."

She nodded and fell in step behind me as I moved toward the door, pulling strings on the overhead bulbs, my grip tight on the bat.

TWELVE

The wood on the landing moaned under our weight and we hesitated, Tara's breath on my neck, a seesaw of heat against my cold skin, as we listened to the whirl of the wind and the *ticktock* of the old grandfather clock. Time felt suddenly soupy, like fear had slowed its passing.

I nodded toward the stairs, squeezed the bat tighter in my sweat-slicked palm, and we proceeded down the steps and into the hall, where we stopped short. The hallway floor was littered with tiny bodies, facedown, face up, piled on top of one another, like a mass grave. I spun dizzy in the silence, and then sunk to my knees, tiny sobs spurting from my mouth. "My, my, my . . . my dolls."

Tara got down on the floor with me. "Mona, Mona, it's okay."

I crawled on my hands and knees to Sissy first, and turned her over, breathing a sigh of relief. She was okay. No breaks. Then Zelda and Clara and Scarlett, all my beautiful Madames were fine, and then something sharp sliced through my jeans . . . "Oh no. No, no, no . . ." Porcelain shards. I shifted and found the broken, jagged face of Bo Peep staring up at me. "No!"

Tara touched my shoulder. "She can be fixed, it wouldn't take—"

"No!" I batted Tara's hand away. "Who did this? Who did this to my babies?"

"No one *did* this, Mona." She pointed to a long piece of wood plank half hanging from the wall. "The shelf came loose, just gave way, that's all."

"No, someone did this. Someone is after me."

"Mona, honey. You know that's not true. Here, let me help you pick up and we can go downstairs, maybe open a bottle of wine . . ." She reached out again.

I shrank back. "No. You don't understand, you never did."

"Mona!" Now she sat back, her feelings hurt, but I didn't care.

I groped the floor, gathering the tiny shards. "I can fix you, I can." I carefully plucked part of Bo Peep's lip from the crack between wood planks. "I can fix you."

Looking back at that moment later, I realize how fiercely I longed to talk to Ben, tell him about the desperate hollow feeling in my stomach, the sudden pain creeping over my skull, the bothersome and now constant twitching in my left eye. *I can fix you*, he'd whisper, followed by a pill or two and kisses in all the right spots. Why was he gone, yet again?

"This is Ben's fault. He's never here anymore. Neglecting things around the house."

"I'm sure he means to take care of things, Mona. He's been a little distracted lately."

Distracted with his lover, I wanted to say, but didn't. I kept the words buried. "Thank you for all your help this evening, Tara," I bit out. "But I think I want to be alone right now."

"Oh, Mona, I can't leave you like this. Let's have—"

"Go!" I clutched the injured Bo Peep and sprung to my feet, blood surging hot through my veins. "Just leave me alone."

Her eyes narrowed and I thought she was going to argue with me, but then her pupils sunk into dark exhausted circles. She shook her head as if resigned to her thankless task of helping me, and although part of me wanted to take back my harsh words, I just wanted her gone.

"Okay, Mona," she relented. "Try to get some rest this evening. I'll be back tomorrow."

An hour later, I answered the door in my pajamas and robe.

It was Detective Reyes. And it was the second time he'd rung my doorbell today. "Mrs. Ellison. I know it's late, but a few questions have come up in the investigation and . . ." He looked down at the bandage on my hand. "Something happen?"

"Just a little accident."

"I hope you're okay."

I opened the door wider and craned my neck, looking over his shoulder. His nondescript sedan sat empty in my drive. Detective Reyes had come alone. A ploy. Two men on my doorstep would be intimidating. One stood a better chance of charming information out of me.

"May I come in, Mrs. Ellison?" His eyes, deep brown and sincere, were framed with expressive brows, thick and precisely arched. My finger flew to my own brows, plucked thin and scraggly from worry and anxiety, and I thought about how damn attractive Detective Reyes's brows were, reminding me of someone I couldn't quite place. My gaze fell to my bare feet, stumpy toes, red chipped nail polish. *Tell him to leave*, my mind screamed, but when I looked up again, he pinned me with a stare, and I remembered how he'd held my doll earlier, gently and with compassion.

I nodded for him to come inside, and we stepped into the living room, where Bo Peep was splayed on the coffee table like an accident victim in the OR.

"Oh, my," he said, pulling a peppermint candy from his pocket. He unwrapped it and popped it into his mouth. It clanked against his teeth as he sucked. "What happened to her? Can she be fixed?"

"She can be put back together, but she'll never be the same.

No one . . . I mean, they . . . never are the same once they're broken."

He picked up a tiny splinter of her fractured face, rose blushed. "Her cheek," he said. His voice almost seemed sad. "Is this porcelain?"

"This particular one is an unglazed porcelain. Bisque, actually."

I watched as he examined the piece, rolling it between his thumb and forefinger, and a strange mixture of warmth and irritation crept over me. "You said you had some questions?"

He gently placed the piece back on the table. "Yes, a quick follow-up on a few things we discussed earlier."

We moved to the chairs. I cinched my robe a little tighter and crossed my legs. I noticed that he had bags under his eyes, and stiff black whiskers dotted his square jawline.

He continued: "You said your husband is a psychiatrist. Can you tell me a bit about his job?"

"He helps people, kids mostly. Troubled kids."

"Does he ever talk to you about his work?"

"Of course."

"How about The Caring Place?"

"Yes. His clinic. He's proud of his work there. Do you know of it? It's a brand-new facility off Dearborn. They help teen runaways."

"I do. You're part owner."

"A silent investor. I came into some money, unexpectedly, and helped get the place started. Ben brought on a few other local doctors and therapists, but it was his project. His passion."

"His passion?"

I shifted and recrossed my legs. "He wants to help as many kids as he can."

"That's admirable." He nodded and smiled, and then I saw it: just the slightest hint of dimples in his wide cheeks, and with those distinctive brows, now I knew. Mason. He looked like a grown version of Mason, the Boy Story doll that lived only a couple years on the market. A boy doll that came with a storybook.

"Ma'am?" He'd asked something and I'd missed it.

"Oh, The Caring Place. Yes, it's something he's always wanted to do. For as long as I can remember, anyway. He had a rough childhood. His parents divorced; it was hard on him. He understands where these kids come from." Where I come from. We all come with a storybook of sorts, some more horrific than others. I wondered about Detective Reyes's story.

He scribbled something on his notepad. "Does he talk to you about his clients? These kids he's so passionate about?"

I sensed a shift in the conversation and saw no hint of dimples now. My answer came slowly. "Sometimes. Nothing specific, though. Client privilege."

"When was the last time you spoke to your husband?"

"Earlier this afternoon. Just briefly."

"Did you mention that we'd been here, asking questions?"

"Uh-huh. Why?"

"Did your husband mention that Mia Jones came to visit him at the clinic?"

"No," I said, and from the way he paused in sucking on his peppermint, I knew he didn't believe me. "It was a short call. Just to tell me he'd landed."

"You sure he never mentioned that earlier, Mrs. Ellison? There's a record of Mia Jones visiting The Caring Place on several occasions. And since her name has been all over the news, he might have mentioned knowing her."

I swallowed. Blood pounded in my temples. "It's a clinic. There are several doctors there. A lot of kids come in for counseling and treatment, each therapist probably sees a dozen kids a day. There's no way he'd know all of them."

"Yes, but not all of them are murder victims. You'd think that would stand out. Be something worth mentioning."

I inhaled, held my breath for a few beats, and then slowly and quietly exhaled, maintaining a straight face even though inside me a brew of fear and anxiety threatened to bubble to the surface.

He paged back in his notebook. "You said earlier that your husband flew out late this morning to Seattle for a conference."

"Yes." My skin prickled now. I'd told him this already. Told him all about the conference. "He's supposed to return on Sunday."

He cleared his throat and scribbled something in his notebook.

"If you don't believe me, check with his office, they'll tell you the same thing."

"We did that. We couldn't reach the woman who made his travel arrangements, but we'll check back." He paused and then asked, "Does your husband suffer from depression? Mental disorders?"

"No!" *That would be me.*

He cocked his head, regarding me closely. "Mrs. Ellison, are you having trouble in your marriage?"

A dull pain appeared at the back of my head and spread over my skull. "Why do you . . . We haven't been communicating well, that's all . . . we're both stressed with selling the house, Ben's new clinic . . ." I was cold all over, but my cheeks burned hot. Did Detective Reyes know something I didn't?

Under the buzz in my ears, I heard him asking more about Ben's clinic and our plans for moving and I mumbled off nonspecific answers while dread swelled inside me. "You mentioned that his conference was sponsored by Seattle Children's Hospital," he said.

"Yes, he was excited about it. He told me that their psychi-

66

atry and behavioral medicine team has introduced some cutting-edge treatments in the field."

He nodded and came back with, "We were unable to reach your husband by phone, so we contacted the hospital. They said that he's not there. There is no conference, Mrs. Ellison. No one at the hospital knew anything about it."

~ PART II ~

NO MORE PERFECT WIFE

THIRTEEN

The power drill felt solid in my hands. I secured a heavy bit, rammed it into the hole, and leaned into it. The drill spun. Metal sparks flew. The lock popped. I stepped back, eyed the mess, and pictured Ben's rage when he found out I'd drilled the lock on his file cabinet. It had always been off-limits, Ben claiming that it contained sensitive client information. Which I'd believed and accepted. Seemed that was part of the problem. I'd accepted everything that Ben told me. *Well, not anymore.*

Now desperation fueled my actions as I searched through the top-drawer files, each with different colored labels, all lined up neatly and each neatly labeled, some regarding ongoing research that he was doing for various journal articles, but the majority pertaining to the start-up of the clinic. The second drawer held more of the same. No secret files jammed with love notes, no receipts for expensive hotel rooms, no indication of where he'd gone instead of Seattle, or even anything out of the mundane. Why even keep this locked? Then I came to the last file and my fingertips brushed against something hard: a plastic box duct-taped to the back of the file drawer.

Here are the love letters, I thought as I ripped it out and opened it.

But no letters, no receipts.

Cash. And a lot of it. Bundles of hundred-dollar bills. A quick estimate: ten thousand dollars. Maybe more. Anxiety zipped through me. *What is this?* I gathered up the bundled bills and found a torn piece of notebook paper mixed between them. An address was scribbled on it. A place on Farnsworth. I'd never even heard of the street. What was there? A hotel? Was it where Ben hooked up with his lover? The woman he was away with now? Did he use cash to avoid a trail of hotel credit charges or . . .? I'd sometimes suspected his lover might be Selma, or maybe that "didn't notice" pretty Ashley at work, but now I wondered . . . was Ben *paying* for sex? I shivered, as if a cold, grimy dirt coated my skin every place Ben had ever touched.

I shoved the bills back into the box and the box into a drawer and buried the address in the terrycloth folds of my robe, my fingers touching on something else, a crumpled yellow Post-it: *every challenge is an opportunity to grow.* Ben's wisdom for me. Post-its that kept his troubled little wife optimistic, to help her face reality, or so he said. Were they Ben's personal mantras, too? Had Ben taken on the challenge to keep his affair from his wife? Seen an opportunity to exploit his sexual appetites in other ways? And how wise was it to hide his little secrets, thinking I was too stupid, too faithful to his mantras, to figure it out?

My heartbeat throbbed in my temples; I knew what was coming next: a meltdown, what Ben called a Black Hole. I'd fallen into that Black Hole in the past and lost track of time and logic. I couldn't afford that now. Not with everything on the line. When Ben saw me spiraling, he'd hold my hands, look into my eyes, and give me a pill, cooing, "Take a deep breath and clear your mind, think rationally, slow down and look at things from a calmer perspective, don't jump to conclusions . . ."

So I did that now. I closed my eyes, took a deep breath, and then another, and I thought through all the different explanations for this secreted cache of money. It could be for anything, right? Not just an affair, but maybe . . . a special trip. Or a gift for me. Or a fund for Gus's education. I would have liked that explanation . . . but wait. It was stuffed in a box, not secured in a bank or savings account waiting for some special surprise purchase. I opened my eyes and looked at Ben's once tidy office and saw drawers skewed, metal shavings and displaced file folders littering the floor. I'd taken the challenge of Ben's lies and tried to learn the truth, but now I faced even more questions. Why was the money hidden? Where had it come from? And the even bigger question: *What will I do now?*

I left the office mess, retrieved Bo Peep from the living room, and retreated upstairs to my happy place. Inside the round, womb-like tower room, my muscles instantly relaxed. Gently, I placed Bo Peep and all her parts on my worktable and flipped on the overhead light. A series of gasps filled the air. The others were upset. I could understand their concern. Poor Little Bo Peep, a cracked skull, their worst fear, except for the Plastics, who worried more about becoming brittle in their old age, especially if they were left to bake in the direct sunlight.

"It'll be okay," I assured them. "Mama will fix her."

I prepared my tools: latex gloves, epoxy, tweezers, hog ringer, and scalpel . . . and another round of gasps filled the air. Not my dolls this time. Just the wind seeping through the poorly fitted window casings.

I knew the difference.

"Easy now." I kept my voice low and soothing as I cut along the edges of Bo Peep's hairline, removing a small bowl-shaped portion of bisque, jagged along the broken edge, half an eyebrow still clinging.

I blinked back tears. It was so difficult to see a child hurt and broken, much like my Gus was now. *Oh, Gus. If you were here, I could fix you too. I know I could.* I turned my head and peered across my worktable to yet another broken child, Blythe, swaddled in a clean cloth, still resting after a bath I'd given her earlier, her sleepy blues frozen in a permanent wink.

Mud and gunk from the river had lodged behind her left eye, which was unable to close, and now stared ahead wild and blue, like a zombie. "I'll fix you too, sweetie, don't worry."

But who would fix me, I wondered? Not Ben. Never again.

A tear fell and made a round spot on Bo Peep's blouse. Then another and another and I pushed away and moved to the window, parting the heavy drapes, and looking out over the dark street. Tree branches swayed and the asphalt glistened as rain dashed through the glowing halos of the streetlights. Every house was dark, except Alice's. Still awake, she was propped up in her chair, watching television with Milo on her lap. I squinted at her screen. That televangelist again. Her fixer?

I sighed. Tomorrow, I'd go to the address I'd found with the money and confront Ben's lies. From here on out, I was going to be my own fixer.

FOURTEEN

Thursday, October 29

Ben would never have met a woman in a place like this. No matter how much he'd wanted to have sex with her. The house was a mess. Boarded windows, paint shedding, weeds choking the front yard, mildew creeping up from the foundation.

I put the car in "park," pulled out the slip of paper, and rechecked the address. Had he written it down wrong? No, not Ben. He didn't make those types of clerical mistakes. There was a reason he had this address written down and hidden inside the box of cash.

I stared at the house, wishing I could see past those boarded windows, and then a memory nudged me. I'd just reached for my phone when a girl squeezed through a crack in the side door and came my way, head low, long hair hanging around her face, hands shoved in her pockets. My hand moved to the gear shift but then I paused, because the girl was so young, so blow-over-in-the-wind thin and not threatening in the least. I attempted to make eye contact, but she dipped her shoulder and walked past me, brushing hair from her face with ringed fingers.

Back to my cell and Gus's Instagram: *somewhere in the crib. f*cked up.* The girl's hand with rings on every finger, and boards covering the windows, the same as the windows in Gus's post. This could be the same house. Is this where Gus had gone? And Ben knew about this place?

I turned off the engine, left my purse on the floorboard, pocketed my phone, and locked my car door. If it was still gray and cloudy, this neighborhood with its tired homes and trash-blown street would look beyond desperate, but this morning's sunshine brightened things a little. Except my mood.

And this house. Nothing could brighten this house. It looked abandoned and completely closed up except for the propped-open side door. I knocked, no one answered, but footsteps sounded behind me.

I wheeled.

It was another girl, maybe fourteen, head bowed, a black skull cap over stringy hair, hands clenched. There was something about her that looked vulnerable, sweet almost. A glimpse of freckles sprayed across the bridge of her nose, and I was reminded of a much younger child. No, that wasn't it. She reminded me of Maggie, my freckled-faced Madame with the lime-colored dress and the sweet hazel eyes. But my warm thoughts vanished when this real girl's gaze met mine, her own hazel eyes cool and indifferent, and I knew that whatever innocence this girl once had was long ago stripped away.

"I'm looking for someone," I said.

"Your kid." A statement.

"Maybe."

She shrugged and pushed past me. I followed. We entered the kitchen, dank and moldy, with graffitied walls and cracked linoleum. Black bugs scurried across the countertops and under the fridge. The girl didn't seem to notice and headed to another room, me still behind her. Then I saw the sofa from Gus's post and my stomach lurched.

There were a couple more kids there, a girl on a dirty

mattress, cross-legged like a yogi, completely stoned, upturned arms tracked with red pricks. On the sofa, the same sofa where Gus sat not too long ago, was a guy looking weird, with light streaming in from the cracks in a nearby boarded window and dissecting his face like stripes on a flag. He seemed sober, but cagy, brown eyes intense and greedy and fixed on me.

The freckled-faced girl walked over and sat next to him, her hand on his knee. "She followed me in. Says she's looking for her kid."

"It's just us. Your kid ain't here. Leave."

"His name is Gus." I showed him the post and pointed out the sofa. "He was right here."

"He's not here now."

"I've been looking for him and—"

"Get the hell out of here, lady."

"He might have been friends with a girl named Mia Jones?" I tried.

The girl tensed. "Mia?"

The guy stood, snatched her wrist, and yanked her to her feet. A small yelp escaped her lips, and then she laughed as he playfully dragged her across the room and pushed her against the wall. She wrapped her arms around his neck.

"Wait. I need to find out about my son."

They ignored me, his hand running alongside her body and under her shirt. She arched her back and raised her chin, mouth gaped open like a hungry bird. He slid a pill out of his pocket, placed it on his tongue, and leaned over her, practically swallowing her lips, his tongue pushing deep into her throat. I watched as her eyes darkened and her face turned hard, and I imagined Gus here, in this room with a girl, doing . . . these types of things. This could've been him and Mia. My skin crawled. My heart ached. This was no place for my son.

FIFTEEN

Inside my car, I blasted the heat and squirted hand sanitizer into my palm. The alcohol-tinged liquid seared into the cuts left behind from the sharp-edged pieces of my poor baby's broken face, but I welcomed the pain, even squeezed out more liquid and rubbed it directly into the slices on my fingertips. The sting reached my nerves, making my eyes water. Good. Physical pain always eclipsed emotional pain. It also sharpened me, made me more alert, and ready. I needed to be alert because I felt so, so close to Gus right now. The answer was within reach. That girl knew Mia, and she might know Gus, too.

I sunk back into my car seat, the house in my peripheral vision, and went back to my phone, to Instagram, and scrolled Gus's posts again, skimming over the one of him here on that crappy sofa with some girl's hands on his thigh. The girl I'd just seen? Or Mia? The weeks-old post could mean any number of girls had filtered through that slime den during that time.

It disgusted me. I moved on, stopping on a selfie of Gus standing in front of a mirror, holding his phone—dark jeans, sleeveless T-shirt, biceps flexed.

I'd read this already, skimmed it really. It'd bothered me before. It bothered me still.

ellison_gus18 so over high school. glad to be free from that hell hole. there was a time that i wanted to belong and be cool and be a part of everything but now i know that it doesn't matter what anyone thinks about me. advice to you younger bros do whatever the hell you want because #lifeisshort #free #high-schoolsucks #imsad #nomore #overit

View all 5 comments

King4Night h. s. sucks. never going back there, man

    22 w 1 like Reply

              ellison_gus18 lmao

Jwatts Yaeess Sir

    22w 1 like Reply

AustinL20 haha that's what i'm saying dude. no more crap

    22w 1 like Reply

This photo was dated in May, right when school had finished, but trouble had emerged much earlier than that, sometime between freshman and sophomore year. Bad music, bad language, violent outbursts. The darkness in Gus frightened me. And both Ben and I were shocked by it. *Our boy doesn't act like this! We've raised him to know better!*

I'd turned to my husband, the brilliant child psychiatrist, the man who dealt with troubled kids every day and asked, *What's wrong with him, Ben? Could he be sick, something to do with*—but he'd cut me off with his own worries: *What will our friends think if they find out that he has problems?* And for the moment I, too, would worry about what they knew or didn't know and what they would think of my perfect family, the one with the boy who turned bright red with anger over the smallest things, who slipped off to school only to return to lock himself in his room, who avoided meals with us. What would my friends say, or Ben's colleagues think? So, we covered it up, avoided questions, denied this was real, pretended this phase would be over soon. Because how would it look if Ben, a noted child psychiatrist, couldn't control his own kid?

When we couldn't cover it up anymore, we excused it. Laughed it off. Boys will be boys, male hormones and all that. But Gus withdrew and started not coming home at night, "staying with friends," he'd say. *Normal young adult behavior,* Ben had said. *Let him grow up, be his own man.* Be his own man? What did that even mean?

I glanced at the house. Ben obviously knew about this place. Did he condone this type of behavior? He should have told me about this. I would have put a stop to it, and then maybe Gus wouldn't have severed communications with us and left me feeling guilty and sad and lost.

And now angry. Anger surged through me. This was just one more of the many secrets Ben had kept from me.

I took a deep breath, rubbed at a kink in my neck, and turned back to Gus's posts. I found one from his junior year in high school, before things had gotten so out of hand: Gus at Windy City Pizza, the place where he'd worked for several years.

He was in his uniform, black pants, a red T-shirt with the Windy City Pizza logo. Flour and shredded cheese and bits of pizza topping covered the stainless-steel counter behind him. He held up a loaded pizza.

ellison_gus18 #lovemyjob #pizzaman
View 2 comments
AustinL20 coming for mine in a while
76w 1 like Reply
King4Night friend discount
76w 1 like Reply

Gus was smiling and happy, just as he should have always been. I tapped on the picture—ten likes—and as a heart grew over the photo, my own heart grew with happiness. Finally, something positive. I scrolled and found the other happy pictures, ones I'd only skimmed over before, but now . . . *Tap, tap, tap. Heart, heart, heart. Like, like, like* . . . Wait! My finger hovered over the screen. I'd liked over a dozen posts.

Now what? Leave them? Unlike them?

I sighed. @momofone could be anyone. No one would ever know it was me. Truth was, I should have done this a long time ago, showed Gus how much I appreciated that happy time in his life.

There is no end to the things a mother can feel guilty about.

Not a father, though. Ben seemed to be able to easily move forward. To a whole new woman, even. Last night, I painstakingly pieced Bo Peep's face back together, along with the shattered pieces of my own life, and made some decisions: I wasn't going to move to the condo with Ben. I wasn't leaving Belington; I needed to stay near our son.

Now, anxiety wormed through my mind at the thought of telling Ben, and my brain got stuck in a dark loop of rumination: Ben angry, Ben hurt, Ben pitying me . . . on and on until I caught a glimpse of the girl slipping back through the door, her head down, all her attention focused on the phone in her hand.

I scrambled out of my car and called out to her. "Excuse me!" I rushed around the car to catch up to her. Her pupils were still pin-pricked. "Hey . . . I noticed earlier that you seemed to know Mia."

Her grip tightened on her phone. "Seen her around, that's all." She took a couple steps forward.

"Wait. I'm Mona."

She gave me a look that said she couldn't care less about my name. I followed up with, "Do you live here with . . . uh?"

"Ronnie. No. I don't live nowhere. I'm free that way."

"What about your family?"

She tensed and looked angry. "I don't have family."

"I'm sorry." Then, "How'd you meet Mia?"

"I knew her from the shelter where I stay sometimes."

"Did she hang out here with you? At this place?"

"Yeah. We partied together sometimes. Me and Ronnie and her."

"Did Mia ever bring a guy around. Dark hair? Gus?"

"Yeah, sometimes . . ." Her gaze fixed behind me and she grew agitated.

I turned and saw a group of guys down the street, coming our way. One was on his phone but put it away when he spotted us. He jabbed his finger in our direction.

The hair on my arms stood up.

"Jax." Her voice was tiny, like a little girl's.

"Jax?"

"My boyfriend," she said. "He's gonna kill me. He doesn't like me to be around Ronnie."

The guy who just had his tongue down your throat. Wonder why? I grabbed my car's door handle and pulled it open. "Get in my car."

"What? I can't."

I reached out and gave her arm a little tug. "I can get you out of here. I know a place where you can go."

She shook me off. "I'm fine."

I looked back at Jax and shrugged. "You sure?"

She hesitated, her eyes darting between me and the group of guys coming our way. The one who had been on the phone, Jax, was shouting something at us. "Maybe just a quick ride."

We scrambled into my vehicle, and I jammed the keys into the ignition, one eye on Jax. He'd started running our way and was almost on us. My fear-riddled mind registered small details about him, dark pants, stocking cap, a tattoo covering his entire neck and inching up the right side of his face.

His red, angry face.

"This is crazy," she said. "Jax's not gonna like this." But she didn't try to leave.

I cranked the wheel and lurched to a stop.

He'd reached my bumper now and was slamming his fist on my hood. "What the hell, Ru, get out here!"

His friends joined in, banging and screaming. Across the street a big woman was on her porch, pointing a cell phone our way.

Jax grew more intense, jumped onto my hood, crawling toward our windshield, his tattoo throbbing blue anger. "Get out here!"

She balled up in the passenger seat, hands over her head, trembling, and hysterically muttering over and over, "Go, go, go . . ." I jammed the gear and slammed the accelerator. Tires spun and squealed, and then caught pavement, and we shot forward, throwing Jax from the hood.

People were yelling and pounding on my car's side and following us, but I kept going, not looking back. *Don't look back, Mona,* but the girl swiveled in her seat, wide-eyed at the guy on the pavement behind us. "Jax!"

"He's fine. Put on your seatbelt." I turned off Farnsworth and toward a strip of fast-food places I'd passed on the way into this godforsaken neighborhood. I was sweat-soaked; under my jacket I could feel my shirt sticking to slimy skin. No wonder. I had some strange girl in my car, close enough that I could smell her body odor, an odd mixture of weed and the musky smell of old sex. I'm stupid about kids at this age, obviously, since even my own quit talking to me, and I had no idea what to say to this one, so I asked, "Ru, is it? Is that short for Ruby? I love that name. Are you hungry?"

"You tried to kill my boyfriend."

A chill swept over me. Her voice was no longer scared

or worried, but venomous and laced with hate. "I didn't. He tried to kill *us*. I was just getting out of there. Trying to protect you."

She reached for the door handle. "Let me out. I'm going back. I've gotta see if Jax is okay."

"Are you crazy?" I cringed. Wrong word choice. I always said the wrong things. Crazy? People thought that about me and I hated it. "I'm sorry . . . I didn't mean . . . You're not . . ."

She pounded her fist against the car door. I startled, tightened my grip on the steering wheel, and tried to control my breathing. Maybe she was crazy. *Think through your next words, Mona.* "Let's be reasonable, Ru. Jax was threatening us, we had to get out of there. It was a matter of safety."

"He's pissed, that's all. He didn't want me hangin' with Ronnie."

"Being angry isn't an excuse for threatening someone."

"It's my fault. I shouldn't have gone there."

"Then why did you?"

"Because I can't just stop. It's not that easy." She sunk back into the seat, scratching the skin on her arm, back and forth, until it sprouted blood. Her fingers were long and skinny, like bony tentacles digging into her flesh. She was coming down off her high.

And she was scared, I decided, not angry. She sounded angry, but it was fear driving her actions. *Masking.* A term I'd heard Ben use more than once, it meant showing one emotion, a safe emotion, when you're actually feeling something different, an emotion that you're ashamed to show. In Ru's case, anger masking fear. Fear of Jax's retribution, fear of abandonment, fear of not getting her next fix, whatever . . . we all did it, I did it, and why did I even care about this right now? I needed to know about Gus. This might be my only chance, and I was letting it run like water through my fingers.

She had her phone out now and was pushing numbers. "Ya know what, I am not crazy," she said. "You're the crazy one here. This is kidnapping. I'm callin' the cops."

My skin crawled. I couldn't explain this to the police without linking Gus to the murdered girl. "I'll let you out, I promise. I'll let you go. I'm pulling over. You can put your phone away."

I whipped into a vacant lot sandwiched between a minimart and a lube shop, and something crunched under my tires. Glass? A flat tire wouldn't be good. Not in this neighborhood. *I'm obsessing. Did I take my meds this morning? I can't remember.* "I just need to know if you've seen my son at Ronnie's house. Dark hair, brown eyes, Gus is—"

"I know who he is, okay? I already told you I did."

Hope washed over me, and then faded when Ru reached for the door handle again.

I slid my finger over the safety lock. How low I'd sunk, keeping this girl in my car when she wanted out—it *was* kidnapping, but she'd understand one day when she was older, when she had a child of her own, and really, if she got there with this lifestyle, but what did I care if she wanted to be stupid and go back to the abusive boyfriend? She was so far in denial that she couldn't see that he mistreated her. Too young to realize—

An image of myself at her age flashed in my brain. *Was that me too?* I was her age when I'd met Ben.

And suddenly, the weight of time smothered me. All these years, if I'd only made a few different decisions, like back in college, when through my own drunken haze, I'd seen him with Selma, kissing her and running his hands over her body, and what did I do? Gave him a pass, continued the engagement, married him. A broken doll I was back then, my pieces scattered by my own father. My emotion: unworthiness. And I masked it with confidence and the façade of a perfect engagement to a perfect man.

"What's wrong with you, lady?"

I blinked.

"Did you hear me? Let me out of this car."

"You don't understand. This is about my son and I need to know—"

"Then ask your husband. Yeah, that's right. Ask Dr. Ellison."

"You know . . . you know my husband?"

She had her phone out again. "You really are nuts." She started pushing numbers. "That's it. I am so done with this crap."

I slid my finger along the door panel and clicked open the locks. "Go," I said. She bolted like a freed animal.

SIXTEEN

An hour later I rang Tara's doorbell and waited. I heard noise behind the door and shifted from foot to foot, hugging myself, still shaky from my encounter with Ru.

The door opened. Tara looked down at me. "You look like hell. Where have you been? I came over but you weren't home."

I shuffled again, my gaze drawn to the jack-o'-lantern at my feet. Its orange flesh carved prematurely, it was now shriveling around the eye sockets, with wrinkly lines radiating from its clown-like mouth. An old man without his dentures who wouldn't even make it to Halloween.

"You told me to come by after lunch," she said. "We were going to finish the attic, remember? Where were you?"

I looked up. "I'm sorry. I forgot . . . I—"

"What's going on, Mona?" She stepped back to let me inside and offered to take my coat, but I kept it on. "You got my message, I take it," she said.

"No, what message?"

"Come on back to the family room, I'll explain."

There was something about Tara's house, the pastel colors, the plush textures, the way light seemed to stream through her windows even on cloudy days. A cotton candy feel. I felt better already, just being here.

"Perfect timing," she added. "We just opened a bottle of wine."

"Oh, I didn't know that anyone else—"

"It's just Alice. And she's part of the reason I tried to call you. We need to talk. It's important."

Alice sat curled up on the sofa, her legs close to her body and a glass of wine in hand, mascara smudges under her eyes. *We need to talk. It's important.* I coughed, the saliva in my mouth sucked dry by sudden uneasiness.

"Hey, Mona," she said.

"Here, sit down." Tara handed me a full glass of wine.

I swallowed a mouthful. It slid into my empty stomach like a hot sword. I settled into the club chair and noticed Alice's eyes, glossy wet with red vessels popped along the edges of blue irises. They hovered in front of me like a raw wound. "What's going on?" I asked.

Her mouth turned downward slightly. She shot a look at Tara, who reciprocated with a slight nod.

"The police stopped by earlier," Alice started. "Probably because I live directly across from you, maybe they went by the Reynolds' house next door, too, I don't know. But they were investigating Mia Jones's death and they asked a lot of questions about Gus."

"Gus?"

"He drove your old Range Rover back then," Alice said, waiting for me to elaborate. When I didn't, she continued: "I didn't tell them anything, Mona. I promise."

"I don't know what you mean—there's nothing to tell."

"I mean, I swear I didn't say anything about your marriage, or about—"

"My marriage? I don't have marital problems. Not like you and—"

She jerked back.

"My marriage is fine really"—but not really at all—"and our issues with Gus are nobody's business but ours, so I'm not sure what you would have said to the police anyway."

She blinked a few times. "That's not what . . . I wasn't saying that there's something wrong with your marriage. But the officer was asking about you and Ben, that's all that I meant."

Heat flushed my face. I'd taken the defensive, which only proved I had something to defend. *Stupid*. Too late now. I took another drink and my stomach gurgled loud enough for everyone to hear, but we pretended we didn't. I set my glass on the coffee table, squirmed a little. My coat felt bunched under my armpits, and I couldn't get comfortable in the chair. Tara's brightly lit family room in lemon yellow felt like the glare of a bare bulb in an interrogation room. They were staring at me.

Tara spoke up. "But this summer, with the . . . situation . . . with Gus."

"All kids have issues from time to time."

They both nodded. Almost in unison. Silently.

Of course, they knew he'd started staying out at night, and then quit coming home altogether. How could they help but know; we practically lived on top of each other on this block.

Alice folded her hands tightly on her lap, and studied them intently, before speaking again. "Remember at the fourth of July picnic and we were in my kitchen and you were upset over something with Gus?"

"No. Not really." I'd blocked out most of the summer. Natural, Ben had once told me. Our brains are smart that way. They know how to keep the unpleasant memories locked in a safe place.

"Well, I do," Alice said. "You were so upset at the time, and well, I didn't know what to tell you, but I did promise to pray for you."

A sharp pain emerged behind my eyes. Memories nudging to get out.

She continued: "You were angry over a girl Gus had started seeing. Today, when the police asked me about Mia Jones, I

89

suddenly remembered where I'd heard the name. You'd said it that day. Just once, but you—"

"No." I swallowed hard. "You must have misheard me. There was another girl . . . Maria . . . she was older than him, not from around here." I rubbed circles around my temples. "I'm not feeling so great." I stood, the room spun, wine on an empty stomach, but I somehow made it to the door with Tara behind me, walking me out.

"We didn't want to upset you."

"No. You didn't. I'm fine."

She opened her mouth as if to say more, but I quickly stepped down the steps, avoiding her eyes. We made plans for more packing in the morning, and I assured her a couple more times that I was okay before I turned toward my house.

And stopped.

Reyes's nondescript car was parked on the curb in front of my house.

SEVENTEEN

I heard their voices before I saw them.

Meyers first. He stood on the backside of the boxwood hedge that separated our yard from a small strip of community green space and the field beyond. He had his phone out and was taking pictures of the back of our house. I swallowed the urgency to scream or wave my arms at them. Control, I needed to show control.

I cut across the yard and found Reyes crouched down among the tangles of branches, examining a natural path, trampled by young feet years ago, when neighborhood kids used our yard as a shortcut to the field.

"What are you doing here?" I asked.

Reyes stood and brushed down the front of his khaki trousers. He tugged at the brightly colored scarf tucked into his parka as he spoke. Hand-knitted from multicolored yarn: yellow, brown, burnt orange, stiches missed, rows uneven, the thing was a mess. A gift? From his wife? Girlfriend? Whoever she was, she was a horrible knitter.

"Mrs. Ellison," he said. "Nice to see a bit of sun, don't you think? More rain in the fore—"

"Why is he taking pictures of the back of my house?" Cool but direct.

"Because we talked to some of your neighbors today and

we're trying to piece together some of the information they gave us." He pulled at the scarf again. "Have you heard from your husband yet?"

"Neighbors? Which neighbors? I don't understand. What did they say about me?" Reyes and Meyers exchanged a look, and my hand flew to my forehead, fingers swiping at my brow a few times before I gave one of the hairs a good pluck. "They lie all the time. Last year that woman next to me, Ramsey's the last name, backed over my garbage cans and then tried to blame it on Gus, when I'd seen the whole thing as it happened. I called you guys. It's probably recorded somewhere."

"We know what it's like to have neighbors like that," Reyes said, gesturing to Meyers. He nodded but his eyes narrowed.

Reyes pushed on. "A charge was made to your husband's credit card."

"We don't have credit cards, unless . . ."

"Mrs. Ellison?" Reyes was waiting for me to finish.

"Ben and I used to have a problem with credit card debt—it was my problem mostly." Dolls. I could admit it. I had an insatiable appetite for dolls. Bought them by the dozens. And there was always another outfit to sew: fancy dresses, jackets, bonnets . . . but it wasn't just me. Ben had a spending problem, too. Meals out, mostly. Expensive meals. We cut up the charge cards after an evening event with a few of his colleagues at one of the city's 'gastric phenomenons,' as Ben described it, netted us over a thousand dollars on the card. "We decided to stop using credit and we cut our cards. Both of us. So—"

"The charge came through from a gas station outside Scottsdale, Arizona," Meyers said.

"Arizona? There must be a mistake. Maybe someone stole his identity. He's never mentioned Arizona . . . I . . ." My cheeks burned hot.

"Is there something more you want to tell us, Mrs. Ellison?" Reyes asked.

They both stared at me, waiting, but I had nothing to say. Finally, Meyers shook his head, and then pointed to the common area behind our house, which sloped down to a narrow road that ran along the backside of our subdivision. Beyond the road, was nothing but field and the barn, which I could see from here. My eyes riveted on the barn and my thoughts started to drift before I realized Meyers was speaking again. "Open space back here, isn't it? Gives you some privacy, and a place for neighborhood kids to toss a ball. Bet kids cut through here as a shortcut."

"Used to. All the kids around here are grown now. Most of them in college . . . or gone away."

"It still looks like it's used," Reyes said, his finger following the path into our backyard. "If not, it'd be overgrown like the rest of the yard, and the hedges would have filled back in."

My gaze followed the path. Even this time of year, after the first few frosts had beaten down the grass and shriveled most of the weeds, our backyard still looked messy; a downed branch, rotting and insect eaten, an overgrowth of wild, tangled barberry bushes, clumps of brown-headed flowers. Why had we let things get so bad back here?

"Maybe it still gets used and you just don't know it," Reyes suggested.

"Maybe. I don't know."

"Kids grow up and change," Meyers said. "They meet up with the wrong crowd, get into trouble sometimes."

Reyes added, "Someone mentioned that you were having trouble with Gus over the summer. That he was sneaking out, partying and getting home late, sometimes drunk."

I crossed my arms. "Most teens go through a stage like that."

"That's what I hear," Reyes said. "My daughter is only ten, but I'm already dreading the teen years."

My gaze darted back to his scarf. *A daughter?*

"Especially dating," he added.

Meyers chuckled. "I feel bad for anyone who tries to date your girl."

The lines around Reyes eyes deepened as he smiled. "Not many guys want to date a cop's daughter, that's for sure. I wouldn't have at that age. Would have been too scared to even try." He shifted and looked directly at me. "I can imagine it's no easier for the parents of a boy."

Emotion bubbled up in me. This was my worst nightmare, the cops suspecting that Gus killed that girl. This couldn't happen. Wouldn't happen. *Calm down, Mona. No one knows that Gus was even dating last summer.* Well, Alice did. But she swore that she hadn't told the police.

"Did Gus have girlfriends?"

"I don't know. I don't think so, no one serious, or he would have told me. Why would it matter anyway?" I sounded too defensive, noticed my folded arms, and uncrossed them. Too late; Meyers's eyes followed my movement.

"We're just trying to make sense out of something," Meyers said.

"Make sense out of what?" How much did they know? What if they'd already made some other connection between Gus and Mia Jones?

"Neighbors have seen different cars parked on the back road, late at night."

I gave an angry shrug. "So what? I see cars out there all the time."

"I bet you do," Meyers said. "It's secluded, no street-lamps, no traffic, it's like a bit of country in the city. Not many places like this still around for kids to park, drink, hook up, or whatever." He looked over the field, his gaze settling on the barn.

I shoved my hands into my coat pocket and shifted, avoided looking back there. "I'd like to head inside. I've got things to do."

"Sure," Reyes said. "Just one more thing: Is it possible that Gus had a girlfriend he'd take back there, you know, for privacy? A white Range Rover was seen parked along the edge of the field a few times early last summer, with a girl in the passenger seat who matches the description of Mia Jones. Would she have been there with Gus or—?"

My stomach seized. "I can't answer that. You'd have to ask him."

They cast a glance between them, with quirks of questions in their eyes, so before they could ask more, I ended with a dismissive nod and walked past them. I wished I'd given a better answer, something to make them go away. I didn't want to discuss my son with them at all. What I really wanted was for my son to come home again, so we could deal with the miserable truth of it all together.

EIGHTEEN

Friday, October 30

Womp, womp . . . 3:00 a.m. and the damn cellar door was blowing in the wind. Rain pounded the window and voices haunted my dreams. Only I wasn't asleep, just wished I was.

I rolled over and nestled deep into the covers, and squeezed my eyes shut, but the sound of the banging door kept me awake, along with the voices that now hovered on the edge of my mind. They were usually held at bay by one of Ben's magic pills, but now were back with a vengeance. They had always been strongest in the morning, like they'd been smothered under a heavy blanket all night and couldn't wait to escape. This morning they'd become loud and distinctive . . . *Gus, Mia, water, gone, cheater, cheater, cheater . . . Womp, womp.*

Yesterday afternoon seeing Reyes and Meyers prowl over our property had taken a toll on me. Invasive, demanding, condemning. *Answer me!* The haunting voice from my childhood hammered at my brain, and I'd had no excuses to offer for my failures, no justification for anything I'd done. After I'd stomped off from Reyes and Meyers, my determination to take charge quickly collapsed in an onslaught of voices, opening the swirling torrents of another Black Hole. Breathe, I'd told myself, but the current was too strong, and I'd filled my wine glass and let the alcohol wash out the voices. Then, I'd fallen asleep, or passed out, and now the remnants of a nightmare still churned in my mind. I'd been driving, rain pelting my windshield, streetlights and buildings whizzing by my window, whiskey and cigarettes, calloused hands, my father's angry face and . . . I shivered, pulled the covers tighter, but here was too much noise outside and inside for me to fall back to sleep.

I needed a distraction.

I reached for my phone and checked messages. Almost two days now and nothing more from Ben. He'd lied about where he was going, what he was doing, and now I wondered if he'd even be coming home. Did I even want a cheater, a liar to return? What could he say to fix things now? Yet Ben always had answers for me, reasons why my mind had tilted on overload, why I'd assumed the wrong things when in reality . . . but this time Ben had lied *in reality*. He was not in Seattle at all.

Womp, womp.

I searched the phone again. Nothing. I'd quit counting the days long ago when I'd ever hear from Gus. I tapped the Instagram icon and scrolled through his profile again, savoring each picture, each memory, good and bad, and then got stuck on the Range Rover post and ICU2's comment, *I know why*. What did Ru, or Ruby, or whatever her name was, know about Gus that she wouldn't tell me? She'd said to ask Ben, but I couldn't even reach him now.

Whispered words rolled through my mind: *cheater, cheater, gone, gone . . . Womp, womp.*

I gritted my teeth against the pounding of the door and the echoes in my head and swiped my finger across my screen to cut over to ICU2's profile, anything to distract my spiraling—anxiety shot through me.

I sat up and threw off the covers. A new post on ICU2's

Instagram: our backyard, the swing set, the rotting tree, the overgrown vegetable bed, and . . . an open cellar door. #riding-outthestorm

I snatched my robe, threw it on as I clutched the phone, and rushed downstairs, voices following and buzzing my brain like angry bees. ICU2 was in my yard, now, waiting? With answers for me about Gus or . . . could it be Gus? Calling out to me somehow? Halfway down the stairs, the narrow window by the front door flooded briefly with light. I hurried to the door and flung it open. The red glow of taillights turned the corner and faded into the night.

Womp, womp, womp . . .

I dashed down the porch steps, ready to call out to the now empty street, but call what? Ru? ICU2? Gus? Rain pelted my face and my slippers sunk into the saturated ground, my robe drenched, my hair, too, but I didn't care, I kept moving. I headed for the cellar door to find the answers that clawed to be released. I was #ridingoutthestorm.

Black rain clouds engulfed the moon, and the only light came from the backdoor bulb, which cast a strange finger-like shadow across the backyard. I glanced to the hedge line by the back of the property, near the path that Meyers and Reyes had pointed out. That's where the photo in ICU2's post must have been taken. It was the only spot that would have provided the right angle to get both the swing set and the cellar door. It was also the same spot where Meyers stood yesterday afternoon. But why would Meyers—?

The slosh and thump of footsteps. I pivoted, scanning my surroundings, and then wheeled toward the sidewalk at the *slap, slap, slap* sound of running on pavement. I searched the walk, the road, saw nothing in the dark, but knew I hadn't mistaken the sound.

"Hello!" I called, my voice half-swallowed by the wind.

Womp, womp, womp . . .

I stood, rooted in fear-infused confusion: twenty more yards, and I could reach the cellar door, see if some answer awaited me there. Or was it a trap? Should I run back inside the house, lock myself inside, call 911? And say what? A car had driven on our street and my cellar door was open?

Now other sounds welled up from inside me, as I heard soft whispering, a man, a woman, no, two women, laughter, an angry voice.

They're watching you . . . watching you . . .

And my gaze fell on the sycamore tree, split in two last year by lightning, and in the shadow of it . . . "Gus," I whispered, and then yelled. "Gus! Guuuusss!" I plunged forward, my slippers stuck in the mud, and I fell forward as my voice echoed in the air, dogs barked, lights flipped on, the whole neighborhood lit up. I raised my head from the wet grass, reached out my arms, grasping for . . . but he had disappeared. "Guuuusssss . . ."

My arms fell to the ground, mud squishing between my fingers and I sunk deeper and deeper into the blackness.

I woke later that morning to the smell of coffee wafting in the air along with faint memories of Tara and Alice removing layers of my wet and muddy clothing and helping me into bed. I rolled over and grabbed my cell off my nightstand. After nine. My nails were dirty and my skin smelled wormy, and as my morning brain haze lifted, memories of #ridingoutthestorm emerged. I shook them off and began my morning bathroom routine. Ben always said that routine helped anchor me, and now I focused on every inch of my shower, the hot water pouring over me, relaxing me, washing away last night's misery. After my shower, I drifted to the vanity and wiped a circle in the fogged mirror. Despite steaming hot water, I still shivered. Then, I heard voices, not inside my mind this time but rising from the floor vent. Soft murmurings, punctuated by Tara's hyena-like laugh. I cinched my towel tighter, got down on all fours and leaned my ear toward the cast iron grate. Mostly garbled mumblings, but a few distinct words came through: stress, worried, move, blah, blah, blah . . . nothing new. Everyone thought I was cracking under pressure. But then Tara's voice came through loud and clear: "She thinks she saw Gus." And more words from Alice: "Breakdown . . . Ben . . . meds . . . home soon."

I lurched back, blinked, and sucked in a sharp breath as last night's events came racing back again: the cellar door, ICU2's post of my backyard, the taillights, and someone by the syca-more . . . Only now, in the flood of the bathroom lights, cleaned and dried of last night's half dream state, everything felt surreal.

And now my friends were talking about me like I was some sort of crazed lunatic? I wasn't. I had heard the cellar door, had seen . . . someone.

I went back to my nightstand and typed a text to Gus: *Was that you last night? I think I saw you. Did you see me, too?*

I waited, hoping for just one response: *Yes, I saw you, too. ICU2. ICU2.* And I slapped my hands to the sides of my head, the voices crowding in again. I needed them to stop.

I reached for my pillbox. Yesterday's PM compartment was still full, as was the AM compartment. Ben always reminded me of my pills, but he hadn't been here and, besides, I'd been angry with Ben. He'd betrayed me. Lied over and over. Could I trust him with anything? Could I trust him with my meds?

My fingers hovered over the box, but I left my pills untouched—maybe later, not now. I didn't want my thoughts dulled, not quite yet, not while I felt so close to knowing the truth.

I dressed and headed downstairs, slipped my still wet boots from the hall closet, avoiding Tara and Alice, who were in the kitchen talking about me, and snuck outside to the backyard, inhaling and holding cool air in my lungs for a second or two and then exhaling, long and slow, expelling the anger that zipped through me. Tara's words churned in my mind: *she thinks she saw Gus.*

I did see someone. It had to be Gus. He'd made the post, and left the cellar door open, flapping so I'd go there. Only Gus, Ben, and I knew it did that when left open. I stared at it now, a green metal bulkhead door, wedged against the side of the house like a giant slice of puke-green cake. When we first bought the house, we had plans to convert the cellar into a wine room. Ben was into wine. We'd drive up the Michigan coast every year and visit vineyards, sipping and tasting along the way, lodging in one of the lake coast villages with their cute boutiques and restaurants, lighthouses and ice cream shops. But once Gus was born, we forgot about our wine room, and now we rarely came down here. Over the years, the hinges had rusted, leaving the doors wobbly and loose. We kept them secured with a wood dowel rod threaded through the handle, where it was now. I realized either Tara or Alice must have slid it back into place last night.

I removed it and opened the door. Musty air rolled up from the depths: earth and damp rock mixed with the faint smell of bleach. Just before we listed the house, Ben had me thoroughly clean this space. Everything neat and tidy and in good order just the way Ben liked things. It all seemed so silly now; Ben wasn't even around to care if . . . I shook my head. *Forget Ben.* I needed to focus on the cellar and the message meant for me.

I stepped carefully down the moss-covered concrete, grasping the stone walls on either side to stay steady. A web grazed my face. Something scurried over my fingertips. I flinched. Spiders. Light from the door behind me barely lit the dank room. I continued forward with my flashlight app, searching for something, anything Gus might have left behind for me. A shadow shifted in the corner, and I heard claws on stone and a series of squeaks that sounded like a squeegee raking wet glass. A rat, I thought. A dull ache spread over my skull and faint whispers circled inside my head like the distant rising and falling chirping sound of cicadas on a summer evening. And then my light caught on something, and I froze in place, staring harder, my pulse banging in my ears.

"Mona, are you down here?"

I looked up to see Alice outlined against the sunlit door. "Yeah. I'll be right up." I bent, and ran my hand along a pile of rope, curled like a snake ready to strike. I ran its coarse length through my hand and brought it to my neck, sliding it along my skin under my neck, feeling the slight burn of rope on flesh.

"Mona! What are you doing?" Alice stood at the base of the steps.

I scrambled to my feet, and let the rope drop from my fingertips. "Sorry. I'm coming."

"What are you doing with that rope? Mona! Is that what you . . .? Dear God."

"There you two are." Tara appeared on the steps. "What's going on?"

I tried to explain to Alice about the rope, but she was already halfway up the stairs, giving her version of things to Tara. "Mona was in the cellar, wrapping a rope around her neck."

I followed and secured the door behind us. Tara whimpered, "Oh, Mona. Why?"

"No. I know what you're thinking, both of you, but that's not what I was doing. I told you last night that I saw . . ." I pulled out my phone to show them the post with our backyard, but my hand shook. They wouldn't believe me. I knew that now. No matter what I said to them or the detectives or Ben . . . My voice faltered and Alice offered a comforting hand, but I sunk to the ground, wet grass soaking into my jeans, and my head swirling with dizziness, like I might pass out.

Tara leaned down, ran her hand over my shoulders, and said, "Come on, Mona. Let's get you inside. You need to rest."

NINETEEN

They cleaned me up again, tucked me back into bed, and hung around while I pretended to be asleep. It took a while, but Tara slipped out first, Alice staying behind to check on me a few more times. She fussed about, tucking in my covers, and praying.

I'm fine, Alice. I'm fine. Just go away.

I kept my eyes closed, contemplating my situation, desperation growing inside me. A half hour later, after Alice finally left, I picked up my phone and did two things: I opened Instagram and typed out a message to ICU2: *What's next?* But I hesitated. The posts, the doll submerged in the pond, the cellar door . . . ICU2 had some sort of intimate knowledge about Gus, and about Mia Jones's murder. If they took that info to the police, it would look like Gus killed Mia. I couldn't let that happen. But it was really the unknown that caused me to hesitate. ICU2 could have been anyone, someone dangerous, a threat. Did it even matter? If I wanted to protect our family, I had to fully enter into whatever sick game this person was playing.

I hit send.

Immediately the voices in my head taunted me: *Stupid, stupid, they have you right where they want you now.* "Shut up. Not true," I said back. "This isn't about me, it's about Gus."

And then I did the next thing. I made a phone call and hurried to get dressed.

* * *

"This is highly unusual." Doctor Adler eyed the baggie of colorful pills I'd placed on his desk. He was Ben's friend, and Gus's therapist, a peculiar old man with a dry sense of humor and low alcohol tolerance. We shared a table at last year's Psychiatrists of Chicago black-tie gala, and I'd endured three minutes of Gershwin's "'S Wonderful," staring down at his molted scalp as he maneuvered on the dance floor, drunkenly steering me into other couples. But sober, he was one of the best psychiatrists in the city and a friend of the family. When I called him today, he'd quickly agreed to work me into his schedule.

He regarded me with a curious gaze. "What are these for?"

"Well, that's what I'm here to ask you."

He furrowed his already heavy brows. "Maybe you should explain. I'm not sure why you have all these, but if you're confused about which is which you could have just asked your doctor or pharmacist and—"

"Ben is out of town."

He frowned all the more. "Certainly, Ben didn't prescribe all of these medications. Who is your regular doctor?"

"Why would I go to another doctor? No one knows me better than my husband." Like I'd share my anxieties and fears with anyone else, or let Ben's community of doctors know— well, know anything. The pills were just a way to see Dr. Adler today, a way to get answers to some of my questions.

He leaned forward and emptied the baggie of today's pills onto a sheet of paper. He examined each pill, sorting them into separate groups while referencing his computer and mumbling to himself. I pointed at the two multicolored capsules. My happy pills, Ben had called them. And they really did work. At least at first.

"I know what these are for," I said. Then I separated out a yellow pill, the one Ben said would zap my anxiety. It didn't. "And maybe this one. I can't remember. The others must be over-the-counter. He just recently added them. One is a sleep aid, I think, but I don't know what the others are for—that's why I brought them to you. I'm hoping you can help me."

"You said on the phone that you've been feeling dizzy."

"Yes."

"Any other side effects?"

"Sick to my stomach. Most nights I don't sleep well even with the sleeping pill. And I . . . my friends think that I'm hallucinating, but I'm not. I'm pretty sure I'm not." *Pretty sure.* I wasn't sure about anything anymore. Except the voices. They were rearing up now, hot and angry, hissing through my skull like a million hornets. Right now they were pushing me to ask my real questions, to get on with it. I fumbled with my fingers in my lap, uncertain how to ask.

He was still messing with the pills. "Where are the original containers for these medications?"

"I don't know. Ben fills a dispenser for me. I don't know where he puts the bottles. Probably throws them away." No need to clutter things up with empty pill bottles. I folded and unfolded my hands. "Did I mention the headaches? Terrible headaches. Like I said, Ben's out of town and I can't reach him about my most recent symptoms." I nodded toward the meds. "So, what do you think?"

"Have you had side effects before?"

"Here and there."

"Have you ever discussed them with Ben?"

"Yes, but he tells me that the benefits outweigh the side effects. But I'm not sure anymore. I've gotten worse over the last couple days." *Probably because I'm not taking them, or*

*maybe because I fear my husband is on a getaway with some
cute young thing and the police are breathing down our necks
and—*

"You mentioned possible hallucinations."

"What? No, what I said was that my friends think I'm hallucinating." I shouldn't have mentioned it at all. It made me sound
crazy. If I was crazy, I wouldn't have come here, right? Come for
the answers I really needed.

The voices buzzed, *So get to your questions!*

"What prompted your friends' concern?"

"A silly misunderstanding." I smiled, or tried to, and then
adjusted in my seat. "I never thanked you for always being so
kind to my family."

"Of course. But what—?"

"Especially to Gus." Dr. Alder smiled at the mention of
Gus. Good. Now I could ask. "Has Gus ever mentioned a girlfriend to you?"

His smile faded. "Mona, I don't feel comfortable discussing
your son's sessions. Maybe we should focus on the issue at hand.
I *am* concerned about these medications."

"I was only wondering because something has come up that
might involve Gus and I think you could help me piece things
together. I have so many questions. Our current situation is . . .
well, I'm sure Ben told you about it. Anyway, I'm wondering
when the last time was that you saw him."

"I haven't seen Ben in—"

I raised my hand. "Sorry, I'm rambling. I always do that
when I'm anxious. No, I mean Gus."

He leaned forward just a bit, as if assessing how to answer.
Instead, he asked, "Would you say that you've been feeling more
anxious than usual?"

"Yes. Definitely yes." I circled my finger around the pile of
medicines and landed on the tiny white pill. "That's what this is

for. Ben just added it last week. It helps, but not enough. Obviously."

I waited while he turned back to his computer screen and spent the next couple minutes typing and scrolling and frowning. Finally, he said, "There is no indication in your prescription history that this medication has been prescribed to you. None of these medications are over-the-counter, Mona. They're only accessible through a doctor's prescription. Maybe you're not seeing another psychiatrist, but perhaps a friend or . . ."

"No. Ben gave me these. All of them." *Why is he avoiding my questions about Gus?*

"I can't imagine that Ben . . ." He shook his head and pushed the two capsules my way. "These are for depression. These are the only two I can recommend based on the medications charted in your records. Taking anything else might cause more adverse effects. And you need to remain consistent with these. Have you taken today's dose?"

I slid the antidepressant capsules into my pocket. "I have a bottled water in my car."

"Good. When did you say Ben is coming home?"

"Sunday."

He glanced at the clock. "I have another patient right now, but as soon as Ben returns, tell him to call me. I need to discuss this with him. There must be some mistake here." He cupped his hands around the rest and scooped them into an envelope, sealed and labeled it, and set it aside before forcing a tight smile my way. "I'm glad you brought this to my attention, Mona."

The voices buzzed, angry now. "Of course. Thank you for seeing me." My heart raced. I had been dismissed but I still needed to know. "Just answer one thing about Gus."

"I don't know if I can. Ethically—"

"When you saw Gus last, did he seem angry or overly upset, or . . . did he say anything about leaving?"

His expression softened. "No. None of those things."

I nodded and thanked him again.

On my way out of the building, I stopped at the trash can by the door and threw away the two capsules. Then I sat in my car, its motor running, the purr of it drowning out the voices now. Or maybe they'd quieted because I had my answer. Gus hadn't been angry or upset or planning to leave. But the effect of Dr. Adler's words was already wearing off and the pain of not knowing enough, of fears I couldn't calm or fix, remained.

Where do I go now? The motor ran and I delayed a decision. Then, maybe out of frustration, I checked my phone.

The image of our backyard grabbed my focus first, but then I saw one of ICU2's posts that I'd missed last night, one just before the backyard photo. Two brick buildings side by side with an alley running between them. If I'd had to guess, I would say it was taken in downtown Belington, somewhere around the warehouse block. There were several old buildings down there like these, many of which had been converted to apartment buildings.

The picture didn't show much, except for part of a sign, maybe a restaurant, or a market. Part of a parked car was visible, too. I widened the photo to get a better look at the vehicle, a smallish silver car of some sort. Nothing that seemed familiar. I manipulated the frame even more and saw what I was meant to see: a wheelbarrow.

A wheelbarrow in a downtown alley? But it was there. I could only see it when I enlarged the photo. Grainy, but clear enough for me to know it was a wheelbarrow. *What are you trying to tell me?*

And then I remembered: Ben and I, raking the yard with Gus, our little helper. *I can do it. I can do it.* His battle cry as he used his own rake, just like Mommy's but smaller. And then riding on top of a wheelbarrow full of leaves, crimson and gold and rust, the crisp smell of fall, laughter, and the feel of a family working together. My family. A perfect family.

Was this our wheelbarrow? When did we use it last? Cold dread rippled through me. I shivered and adjusted the heating vents so that hot air blasted directly on me. And then Dr. Adler's voice, *adverse effects*.

My husband had been feeding me a hand-mixed cocktail of drugs over the past month, uppers, downers, antidepressants. Was I delusional like my friends thought? Suffering from psychoses, like Ben wrote in the side margins of his book? Or were these things illusions created by the toxins still running through my bloodstream? One thing was no illusion: detectives had been at my door, in my house, scouring my yard, and my family's reputation was on the line.

I headed downtown.

TWENTY

The alley smelled of fried meat and urine. It ran between two brick apartment buildings and a Mexican restaurant with a large red printed sign: CARMEN'S, a match to the red "EN'S" in ICU2's post. I found our wheelbarrow on the other side of a dumpster, just sitting there, handles protruding outward, and its cart open to the sky and heaped full of stuff. A man was slumped against the side of the building, just a few feet away, surrounded by black garbage bags, and a cardboard box flattened underneath him. I moved closer, my skin tingling, on high alert.

ICU2 had set up this photo with nothing showing in the wheelbarrow, a picture that had lured me. Why?

The man stirred as I approached and smacked his lips before his head slumped again. His boots were on his lap, military-type, tattered with no laces, and on his feet, threadbare wool socks, yellow-nailed toes poking through. A crushed cigarette dangled unlit between his soiled fingertips.

I quietly walked past him and leaned over the wheelbarrow. It was crammed with empty cans and a stash of greasy wrappers around half-eaten food . . .

"Get the hell away from my stuff!"

He hoisted himself from the pavement and started toward me. Body odor permeated the air. He stopped an arm's length from me. Two, maybe three steps. A flurry of fear came over me.

"Don't touch none of that." His voice was low and thick and wet with alcohol. His left eye ticked. Blink, blink, blink . . . I got caught up in it. He noticed and scowled.

"Where'd you get the wheelbarrow?" I asked, trying not to look at the blinking eye.

He tilted his head back, laughed crazily at the sky, his teeth all small and pointy like a cartoon monster, then he dropped his chin, and his face suddenly flushed with anger. "You a cop, ain't you? Someone stealed this piece of crap and dumped it here and now you come to say I did it?"

I shook my head—"No, no, that's not it"—and reached into my coat pocket, while he looked on hopefully, eagerly, but all that I had in there were a couple wadded tissues and some loose change, which I pulled out and offered on the palm of my hand. "I just need to know about the wheelbarrow. That's it. Who left it here, do you know?"

He turned his nose up at the coins. "The supreme frickin' god of all the universe, why the hell do you care?" His expression changed again, and he jerked and looked over his shoulder. "You hear that? They're after my stuff."

I looked around. "Hear what?" Did he hear voices? This poor man. He's suffering from a mental illness and probably has no family to help, no doctor to take care of him, and . . . and without Ben, this could be me. "What's your name?"

He fully faced me and after a long gaping pause, he said, "John."

"No one is going to take your things, John. It's just the two of us here." I enticed him again with the coins. "The wheelbarrow?"

He glared at my palm.

"This is all I have, I'm sorry. If I had more, I'd give it to you. I would." I did have more but, in my purse, back in the car, and part of me feared if I went to get it, if I even glanced away from this man, that he'd be gone, and I'd be left with no answers.

He stared off for a second, digging his dirty nails through his beard, then turned, and picked the coins off my palm. "I know what you're really after."

"Information, that's it. I'm not here to take your things . . ." My voice trailed off.

He'd walked over to one of the black plastic bags stacked by his cardboard square and rifled through it, eventually pulling out a small plastic doll with long dark hair and a frilly blue tutu over a leotard. My heart ached.

"This yours?" he asked, holding her close to his chest and stroking her hair.

"No. She's not mine," I whispered, watching how tenderly he treated her. His whole demeanor had changed. Dolls are special that way.

I squeezed my eyes shut and the world spun. My own empty arms ached to hold one of my dolls at this very moment.

"Lady? You okay?"

I opened my eyes, tears blurring my vision. "This isn't my doll." But I recognized her. I'd had my eye on this sweet little girl for some time. She was part of a line of dolls that had been retired for almost a decade now, and I already had most of her friends: Jasmine, Alyssa, Kayla, Lola, but not this one.

Not Mia.

TWENTY-ONE

Her tiny hand grasped mine with urgency, the waters below the Fox River Bridge swirling dark and angry and waiting to engulf her, swallow her whole and wash her into the next tributary and the next until some river, somewhere, spat her pale, slimy remains into the sea. Or perhaps she'd be buried, I thought, under layers of mud and silt until her little body disintegrated into tiny particles and floated away, scattered forever, so no one would know. No one would blame my Gus for her death. Never.

I had to do this. For Gus.

For Ben and me.

For our family.

The voices murmured in my ears. *For Gus. For Gus.*

"I'm so sorry," I whispered. Her brown eyes pleaded with me, *no, no, no,* but I thought of those posts and knew that there was no choice. Mia in a wheelbarrow . . . Someone knew about Gus and Mia and what had happened that night. I had to let her go, but the voices, they were arguing and growing louder like the dial on the radio had been turned up inside my head. I hesitated. Listened. *Do it, do it, do, it.* Then from far back in the recesses of my mind, another voice emerged, this one small and tiny and helpless. "Help me, Mommy."

* * *

A half hour later, I pulled into our driveway with Mia on the seat next to me. It was late afternoon and both hunger and anxiety burned raw in my stomach.

I reached over and unstrapped Mia. "You'll have to stay out of sight," I told her, opening my bag and pushing her to the bottom, hidden away, anonymous. I couldn't afford for the police to find her. In my mind, I calculated the risks. Who knew besides me?

Only homeless John.

I'd known I couldn't leave Mia with him, so I'd offered him the only thing of value I had on me at the time, a gold watch that had belonged to Ben's mother. She'd had the habit of tapping it when she was annoyed with me. *Do you have any idea what time it is, Mona? Tap, tap. It's not good for Ben's digestion to eat dinner after six o'clock, tap, tap, tap. What type of mother lets a child stay up this late? Tap, tap, tap* . . . Good riddance. To the watch and Ben's mother. She'd passed a while back, on her seventy-fifth birthday, which was very timely of her. Anyway, paying off John cost me the watch and another sixty bucks for being parked in a loading zone, but I would have paid anything to protect Gus.

Gus. He'd been so angry when he left . . . I shook it off. The best thing I could do for Gus now was to keep him out of Reyes's crosshairs.

Mia in a wheelbarrow. I shivered. *Our* wheelbarrow? My eyes darted around as I leaned in and whispered into my bag, "I'll take you to your friends soon, but first we need to check something out."

Our shed had grown a deeper shade of green over the years and lost its balance. Now it leaned into our red maple tree like a friend in need of support. The door was unlocked, which surprised me, because we usually kept it padlocked. Or we used to. I hadn't been out here for a while. No need because either Ben or Gus always took care of the yard.

Inside, a bare space where the wheelbarrow usually waited, but I'd suspected that. Nothing else was missing, though. Nothing else was even out of place. Flowerpots cleaned and stored for the winter, tomato cages neatly stacked, hoes and rakes and our push lawnmower, garden hoses properly drained and tightly coiled, and one entire wall covered in pegboard hung with small hand tools: shovels, a saw, a hand trowel, clippers, a claw hammer, and a mallet. All of Ben's tools, lined up and hanging straight. I often wondered if Ben's neatness was an outward manifestation of an ordered mind, or a way to compensate for the chaos that lurked beneath the surface of our lives. In this case, the shed's interior echoed neatness while the outside sagged from neglect and time.

A noise from behind made me turn. "Oh, Alice!" My heart thudded in my chest. "You scared me." I gripped my bag tighter. *Shhh, Mia. Don't give us away.*

Alice stared at me a beat too long, and then plastered on a smile. "Looks like you're feeling better, Mona?"

"I am." I came out of the shed and shut the door.

"Thought you were going to stay in and rest this morning. What are you doing?"

"I was looking to see what all needed to be packed out here."

She seemed pleased with my answer. "Good." She held up a take-out bag from our favorite chicken place. "You should eat something first."

"Where were you at this morning?" Alice asked as we sat at the kitchen table. It was almost two-thirty, and we were just sitting down for lunch. I unwrapped my sandwich. Alice had a salad. No dressing.

"I ran a couple errands downtown." I'd put my bag on the counter and got busy eating. The bun was soggy with chicken grease and mayonnaise.

Alice ate her salad quickly and talked with her mouth full. "I'm surprised you went shopping this morning after everything last night. Have you talked to Ben?"

I shrugged and snatched a fry off the pile between us.

"He needs to know what happened last night. About your episode outside on the lawn and . . . this morning in the cellar."

"Let's talk about something else."

"Mona, I think we should discuss this . . . oh, wait a sec." Her phone screen had lit up with a notification; she tapped it and checked her texts. A smile broke over her face. "It's Bess."

Of course, it is. Her daughter kept in constant contact with her. A pang of jealousy shot through me. I reached into my bag—my knuckles brushing against Mia's soft hair—and pulled out my phone. Nothing.

"She's just checking in with me," Alice cooed. "Isn't that sweet . . . oh! She's sending a pic of last night's sorority mixer."

She texted a quick message and then showed me a photo of Bess with a few other girls, heads pressed together to fit the frame, smiles all bright and white and colorful drinks in their hands.

I pushed the rest of my sandwich away.

"Don't you love Bess's dress?" She looked off and sighed as if remembering some moment from her past. "I don't know where Bess would be without her sorority sisters. Remember how that was?"

Oh yeah, I remember how it was. Struggling to keep up, working an extra job on campus so I could afford dues and party clothing. I barely stayed afloat, even with financial aid.

Alice was still reminiscing. "We were so young and hopeful back then. We thought we could have it all. Careers, money, and a great guy, remember that? Things didn't turn out quite that way, I guess." The edges of her mouth turned downward. "I'm glad that we didn't know better."

This was about Rick. Alice was still hurting from his infidelity. I got that, but why did she keep saying "we?" Was she insinuating something about Ben and me? I searched my mind for something to say, something nice, but I wasn't feeling nice. I was pissed and the silence grew heavier. Finally, I fell back on the old cliché: "I can't imagine."

This thing with Ben and me, it was nothing like her and Rick. Was it? "I mean, it must have been so difficult to hear that your husband . . . I'm so sorry, Alice. I wish I hadn't seen . . ." My voice trailed off.

I'd been the bearer of the bad news back then. I was in my sewing room when I saw Rick and . . . well, I thought at first it was Alice in a red wig, a little cosplay in the bedroom. I'd chuckled, but then it hit me: she'd left for the week, visiting with her mother in Indiana. But Rick wouldn't cheat, I thought dumbly, but before it even registered, their clothes were off and well . . . yes, Rick did cheat.

That's how stupid he was. You'd think he would have closed the blinds.

"I wasn't shocked. Not really." She sighed, long and heavy, like someone had just let the air out of a balloon. "For months he'd been coming home late and heading straight to the shower. But no soap could wash away the stench of their sin together. I used to lay awake at night thinking about him touching her and making a thousand excuses of why it might not be true, how he would never do something like that to me. By morning, I'd have myself convinced that I was just imagining it all."

"You never said anything. I wished you would have talked to us." But maybe she did. In every group of friends there were cliques. In ours, Alice and Selma were their own special group, close like sisters, sharing secrets and private jokes. Even back in college, they were a pair, both cooler, prettier, more popular than Tara and me. "Did you tell Selma?"

"No . . . no, I couldn't. I could hardly believe it myself. Didn't want to believe it, I guess. Even with all the obvious signs."

My nerves pricked. "Like what?"

"Well, he changed all of his passwords, never left his phone unattended, took forever to respond to my calls and texts, and I found things, valet tickets, cash receipts, things that I couldn't remember doing with him. People said things to me, you know, like dropping hints. Afterward, I found out that everyone at his office knew about it. I did too, I just . . . well, it was like we talked about at book club. I was in denial."

My heart fell.

"I convinced myself that there wasn't a problem because I wanted to believe that things hadn't changed between Rick and me. And I think that's what finally drove him to do what he did."

"What do you mean?"

"He didn't have to bring her to our bed that night. He did it on purpose. To knock me out of denial. And you know what? I'm glad he did. Sometimes it takes something big to bring us back to reality."

"Something big," I repeated.

She sat back, folded her hands neatly in her lap, and stared at me.

I picked at a couple of shreds of lettuce that'd fallen on the table while my mind raced. Ben was nothing like Rick. Ben was . . .

"Denial is such a strange thing. Wouldn't you agree, Mona?"

"I wouldn't know, I . . ." A flicker of color drew my attention outside the window. Down the street a taxi turned the corner. "I think Selma's home."

* * *

We went out to see her, Alice beating me across the street, she and Selma collapsing into a hug. I stood off to the side like a bump on the sidewalk, not quite knowing how to insert myself. Selma looked relaxed, dark hair pulled back in a messy bun, sunglasses, skinny jeans, sweater, and jean jacket. "Like these?" she asked, twisting her leg out to show off knee-high leather boots.

I looked, but instead of seeing her boots, I zeroed in on the luggage next to her and the tag: PHX. Phoenix. Arizona. That was where Meyers had said that Ben's last credit card charge had been traced. Anger and envy swelled in me until I blurted out, "You were in Arizona with my husband."

Selma flinched and stepped back. She looked at Alice, wide-eyed and gape mouthed.

"With Ben? No," Selma said. "That's crazy."

"Ben's in Seattle," Alice said, slowly, as if my words had just sunk in. "Remember? He went to Seattle, not Arizona."

I ignored her and pressed Selma. "You've always been in love with him. Even in college."

Selma reached out to me. "Mona, that's not—"

I batted her hand away. "I saw you two together."

"What are you talking about?" She rubbed her wrist. "You're not well, Mona. You need help."

"Back in college," I bit out. "At the New Year's frat party, upstairs in one of the bedrooms."

"What? That wasn't me. And that was a long time ago. Haven't you moved past that yet?"

"Don't make this about me. This is about you, you and Ben."

"Ben and—?"

"I should have never let you list our house. All those times he said he had to meet with you to sign paperwork—"

"This is crazy."

"Crazy?" My voice was high, stretched thin, ready to snap. I took a step forward, my fist clenched. "Did you just call me crazy?"

"No! You're really pissing me off now, Mona. I don't know what's going on with you and Ben, but if he's sleeping with someone, it's not me."

"What's crazy is that I didn't see this a long time ago. Or I didn't let myself see it. Denial." I zeroed in on Alice. "That's what you were trying to tell me just now, isn't it? All that talk about Rick and being in denial about his affair. You were trying to warn me that I've been in denial about Selma and Ben."

Alice looked panicked. She grabbed the suitcase with one hand and Selma's arm with the other and pulled her toward Selma's house. "Let's get you inside," she told Selma.

They left me there on the sidewalk, rooted in unvented rage, hate swirling inside my gut. Dark, oily, terrifying.

A few minutes later, maybe more, I couldn't tell, I felt a hand on my shoulder. I turned my head slowly. Tara had joined me on the sidewalk. "Alice just called. She told me about what just happened. About your argument with Selma."

"She did?" I felt suddenly tired, weak, as if I'd just been spit back out of heavy waves, left flailing on the sand.

"Do you really think Selma is having an affair with Ben? Does that really sound like something Selma would do? You two are friends."

"I thought Ben was in Seattle, that's where he told me he was going to be, and then I found out he was really in Arizona. He lied to me."

"Maybe there's a reason—"

"Yeah. Selma is that reason." I was catching my breath again now, the facts coming back slowly.

Tara tilted her head and spoke to me like I was a two-year-old. "Is it possible that you're overreacting to things? Or maybe you're imagining something that's not really there."

Wrong, Tara. Ben lied. Flat out lied. What's left for the imagination?

"Not just this thing with Ben," she continued. "But other things too. Like Gus."

I flinched. "What do you mean?"

"I mean, that somewhere in your mind, you know that you're imagining more than what is there."

"I do?"

"I've experienced this with clients. A minor form of paranoia. It's more common than you know. Let me ask you this: Do you ever feel like you're waking up from a dream because suddenly you see things differently? And then you start to wonder if everything you've been experiencing has been constructed inside your mind? And maybe it's not true. Not the way you thought it was, anyway?"

Yes. I don't know. Maybe . . . I don't know.

She started in again without waiting for my answer. "You've been under an incredible amount of stress. It's understandable that you're going through something." She nudged me toward Selma's house. "Let's go inside. We need to talk. All of us."

"No, I don't want—"

"This is important, Mona. You're going to be moving soon and who knows when we'll be together again. We've all been friends for too long to let things end this way." She tugged my arm again. "Come on. We're going to sit down and talk this through."

Selma's sofa was sleek and beautiful, but not very comfortable. I shifted a few times and finally settled on the edge of the cushion, crossed and uncrossed my legs, and kept my hands clasped tightly in my lap. I felt shaky, on edge, and my teeth were so tightly clenched that a dull ache had spread from my jaws to my temples.

"I didn't even know Ben was in Arizona," Selma started. "My boyfriend, Seth, was down there for a conference and asked me to meet him for a couple days. That's who I was with. Not Ben."

She couldn't quite look me in the eye. *Proof that she's lying.* "I've never heard you talk about Seth until now."

"What the hell, Mona? You think I'm making up a fake boyfriend? That's crazy."

Did she just call me crazy? Again?

"I've been seeing Seth for over a month now. I've never even thought about Ben that way. Why won't you believe me?"

"Because you're lying."

"Okay." Tara threw up her hand. "That's enough, Mona. Isn't it possible that you're mistaken?"

I shook my head. "No, no I'm not. I saw the two of them a couple weeks ago at the café by his office."

Selma shrugged. "So? We were going through paperwork for the sale of the house."

Yeah, right. When I saw them, they were both laughing, and Ben looked so . . . so content. I hadn't seen him look that happy for months. "It looked like more than just business to me."

Selma straightened and looked around the room. "What do you mean by that?"

"I saw the way you were looking at him."

"Looking at him? We were signing paperwork, that's it. This is so bizarre."

Alice nodded. "You're not thinking right, Mona. Selma saw how infidelity destroyed my marriage, destroyed me. She wouldn't do that to someone, especially not a friend."

Everything is about you, isn't it, Alice?

"Mona," Tara said. "Remember what I said outside earlier? You could be experiencing a minor form of paranoia. Your judgement is off, and things may seem real to you, but they're really not."

Nausea bubbled up from my stomach, and the voices said, *Trick, trick, trick.* "I'm not out of touch with reality. I know exactly what's going on."

Alice shifted impatiently. "No, Mona. Tara's right. Think about it. Last night in the yard, you were having some sort of hallucination. Then this morning, when I saw you down in the cellar with the rope . . . what was going through your mind? It was like you were possessed or something."

Possessed? She's been watching too much Faith TV.

She continued: "It scared me to see you like that. I'm afraid for you. What you might do. We all are."

"I wouldn't do that. I wouldn't." I looked down. A prickle of blood had sprouted on my left hand where my nail had punctured the skin. I swiped it away.

Tara cleared her throat. "You told us that you had seen Gus last night."

"Why are you bringing up Gus? I thought we were talking about Selma and Ben."

The room had settled into an uncomfortable silence. I fidgeted with my phone and sent off a text to Gus. *No one believes me.*

Tara finally spoke again. "You're never without that phone. You constantly have it in your hands. Who are you texting?"

I set it down on the coffee table and folded my hands again. "No one."

Selma rubbed her neck and sighed.

I set my jaw. That sigh. Impatience? I imagined her postsex conversations with Ben: *How does it feel to be with a real woman? Not a crazy one?*

124

"I feel like this is my fault," Alice said. "Ever since book club, when I brought up that murdered girl, it did something to you."

My left eye twitched. *Can they see it twitching?* "I'm fine. Really."

But I wasn't. I was shaking all over. I raised my fingers to my brows and lowered them again when Alice sent me a sharp look. "I think Mona needs to rest now," she said.

Tara tensed. "No, we agreed that she needs to hear this. It's for her own good." She turned to me. "Mona. You know that Gus is gone, right? That he isn't coming back?"

The room fell silent. Except for the voices, they were relentless: *Gone. Gone . . .*

"But there's always hope in Jesus," Alice whispered. "Hope that you'll—"

"This isn't the time for that, Alice," Tara said.

"Stop. Both of you," Selma said. "This is too much for her. We should let Ben handle this."

Handle what? Admitting to their affair? They were talking about Gus just to keep me distracted from—

Tara's voice cut through my thoughts: "I talked to Ben earlier and he thinks this approach is best." Then to me. "I know this is hard, Mona. And I'm so sorry, but Gus isn't coming back. He died. Don't you remember? He passed away."

Pain cut through my skull like a live wire, my vision blurring. Images crowded like a swarm of black flies. I squeezed my eyes tight, trying to force them away.

"Suicide," Tara said, her voice mechanical and emotionless. "He'd run away and was gone for a couple days and then you found him in the barn. It's only been a few months. This is a common form of shock. Your brain can't process all the grief. What you saw was deeply troubling. That's why you're struggling now."

No one spoke. Their glaring silence rubbed raw on my nerves.

I opened my eyes and felt naked in front of these women, my life and fears and guilt all laid bare.

I glanced at my phone on the table. My fingers twitched. I wanted desperately to text Gus. I closed my eyes a brief moment and shook my head. No, what I wanted desperately was to *hear* from him. As I had each time, I'd texted him.

Instead, I looked away from the phone and faced the three of them. "You're wrong," I said. And they *were* wrong. They thought I'd lost touch with reality and believed Gus to still be alive. But I knew Gus was dead—I knew it all too well. The gut-cutting pain of it was simply too much to bear without pretending that he might still reach out somehow, that he would/could text me back, that I could see him walking at a distance or hear the echo of his voice calling for his mother. Easier to pretend. To deny.

They were wrong. I knew he was dead.

What I didn't know was what part I had played, or Ben had played, or Mia had played in his death. I had to know.

Why did you do it, Gus?

TWENTY-TWO

The text from Ben came as I left Selma's house: *Booked an early flight. Landing a little before midnight. We'll talk when I'm home.*

Typical Ben. Nothing, no explanation, not even any excuses. Of course, he'd expect to come home and simply explain away his lies and that I'd take him right back, and we'd continue as if nothing had ever happened.

I went home and dragged myself and a bottle of wine to my doll room. I kept the lights off, crossed over to the window, and pulled up the blinds. This window faced west, overlooking the field, the dusky sky, and the barn that loomed like a dark-hatted man on the horizon.

I sat motionless, watching the sun set, shadows lengthen, crawl across the landscape, and then looked at the moon, the second full moon of the month—some call it the Hunter's Moon, when men and animals alike slaughter meat to store up for the long winter ahead, and tomorrow was Halloween.

Memories flooded my mind of Halloweens past: trick-or-treating, Gus as a dinosaur, a ninja, a demented scientist (that one was fun to make). He was always the best costumed kid in the neighborhood, and loved to parade around with Tori and Bess, their plastic jack-o'-lanterns stuffed with candy, and glow sticks around their wrists. Then later, after we'd tucked our sugar-comatose kids in for the night, Alice, Tara, Selma, and I would gather for our annual Halloween drink and movie night, or Shots and Scary Shit night, as Selma called it. Last year we watched a Stephen King classic and drank Bloody Carries . . . ha, ha. We were so clever. And such close friends.

That was before Gus died.

Nothing was the same now.

I opened all the drapes and let the moonlight flood through the room, casting shadows over the faces of all my friends. My only true friends. Then I plucked from the crowd my new besties: Blythe, Mia, and Bo Peep, and they watched unblinkingly as I set the scene for a party, not a usual-type party, but a pity party, because I couldn't bear to drown my sorrows alone.

When everything was ready, we gathered in the middle of the room, a soft quilt plush beneath us, me in my grimy sweatpants and sweatshirt, they in their finest hats and gloves, and Bo Peep in the new dress I'd sewn for her from part of the sweatshirt of Ben's I'd found in the attic a couple days ago. I never could stand to let a good piece of fabric go to waste. Then, I filled our teacups (mine full-sized) to the brim with wine, bloodred merlot of all things, and made a toast. "To you, Bo, and your lovely new dress."

"Why thank you," I heard her reply. And my heart lightened a little. It felt good to have friends who appreciated the little things I did. I tipped my cup and drank, we all did. At least I think they did. And then we talked about Gus and toasted the good memories, and then the conversation turned to more recent developments, like Blythe, and her perseverance in the pond (which also called for a toast), and Mia, our newly acquired friend (another toast), and then I choked back a couple of alcohol-laced sobs and raised my teacup again, higher this time, my eyes filled with love for each of them. "Here's to friendships that last the test of time and distance."

I finished my cup, refilled it again, and offered to top off everyone else. They were fine. We carried on like that for a while: we drank, we talked, we commiserated. The conversation rose and fell, eyes sparkled with tears, and teacups clinked. Or at least mine did as I refilled it, over and over. The wine was doing the trick, my anxiety had been subdued, my sorrows adequately drowned, and I was feeling better, maybe even ready to face Ben, until Blythe, always a bit of a Debbie Downer, killed my inner drunken peace with, "Did you hear what Tara said earlier? That she'd already talked to Ben. Seemed strange considering you hadn't been able to reach him and he's *your* husband."

I did hear her say that. A slip of the tongue on her part, and I'd heard it, but it didn't even register. Why was that? Denial again?

Ben and Tara. Ben and Tara, a hundred tiny voices whispered. And they were right. It made sense now. The way he talked about her, admired her skills as a counselor, the reason she'd never married, and . . . was it possible, all this time I'd thought it was Selma and Ben at the frat party, because of Selma's dark hair, but Tara also had dark hair . . . and then I remembered the question I'd asked myself a few days ago: Where does a world-famous psychiatrist go for his own type of crazy?

All these years we'd kept our troubles private, especially our troubles with Gus, and done so for Ben's sake. To protect his reputation as a child psychiatrist, and I had done what he asked, kept it bottled up, put on a good act, covered, lied, pretended, denied, until the denial became real and I . . . I didn't even confide in my best friend.

But he did.

Ben had confided in Tara.

She knew everything, didn't she?

After all these years of keeping family secrets, he'd told them all to my best friend.

WHAT THEY DON'T KNOW

I squeezed my eyes shut and clasped my hands over my ears as the aftereffects of wine throbbed in my head, and my insides burned with humiliation and anger as if my family had been violated by Ben sharing with Tara. Secrets about my Gus, my child, things no one should know but his parents. Rage boiled inside me, hot and fierce, as my world spun out of control. *Ben and Tara, Ben and Tara . . .*

TWENTY-THREE

Saturday, October 31

Just after midnight, I woke, prostrate on the floor, surrounded by hundreds of dolls, their bodies twisted and turned in every direction like a bomb had gone off in the middle of a crowded stadium. My poor babies. *Who did . . . ?* Then I remembered the rage I'd felt earlier, over Ben and Tara. *Did I do this?*

I avoided a small puddle of congealed vomit and picked up the almost empty bottle next to me, and tipped it back, clearing my mouth with the last dribble of wine.

This was my only retreat, my happy place, and now . . . I moved to the window, leaned against the sill, and reached for my phone, to scroll through Instagram, and the pictures of Gus there. Happy pictures, and I thought maybe this could be my new happy place now, this virtual world, where time stood still and pretending was the norm. But when I opened the app, the first thing that popped into my feed was a post from ICU2.

The barn.

I looked up, through the window, and then down again at the photo. When the shot was taken, it had been a bit lighter outside, late twilight, but the angle was the same. Exactly the same. This picture was taken from . . . from this window.

And it was posted over six hours ago. When I was at Selma's? No, after that, but when? I came straight home from Selma's.

My gaze darted around the room—was someone else here, in my house?

I wheezed in a long breath, my throat constricting with fear and anxiety, my legs swaying underneath me. I must've had the time wrong. That was it. I grasped for facts, tried to put it together in my mind: it was around four o'clock when Selma got home, we'd argued, we all talked . . . it must have been around five when I got back here and started drinking. So this was taken over six, almost seven hours ago, which would have been around the time . . . no, that couldn't be. Something was off in my thinking. Too much wine, that was the problem.

Yet another look at my phone and it was unmistakable: a photo of the barn, posted at that time, showing the view from this very window. Why?

I leaned forward and pressed my face against the windowpane, allowing the coolness to force out the final bits of the alcohol haze in my brain, when a tiny orb of light flashed in my peripheral vision. I pulled back and squinted through the window, watching as the light bobbed along the ground, zigzagging toward the barn. Someone was heading for the barn. ICU2 had posted that picture just for me to see, and now ICU2 was heading for the barn and wanted me to know. Wanted me to follow. Who was ICU2?

Gus? No, no, I told myself, shaking my head, keeping out the illusion, the vain hope, that he still lived. I had to clear my head, keep reality in check. Not Gus.

Ben? I checked the time. His flight landed about forty-five minutes ago, but the drive from O'Hare would take at least an hour, so he couldn't be here yet. Could he?

Yet it was someone who knew about Gus, about Mia, about me. Someone with the answers that I needed to sort through my pain and guilt and grief.

I should wait for Ben.

The voices agreed—*Don't go to the barn. Don't go to the barn.* They followed me down the stairs and stayed with me as I threw on my boots, coat, a pair of gloves, and headed outside. *Don't go to the barn. Don't go to the barn.*

I crossed the yard and stopped by the shed, leaned against the door, and sent a text to Ben, just in case: *Is that you in the barn?*

I waited, but there was no reply.

Fear churned in my gut, the voices grew louder—*Don't go. Don't go*—but I pushed them away and started for the barn, my need for answers greater than my fear.

The smell of wormy earth and fungus swelled from the ground as I trudged through the muddy field, and as I got closer, I heard the faint creaking of the old barn walls shifting under the weight of the wind. The sound set my nerves on edge, as I remembered the sounds I'd heard that night I found Gus. There were a lot of voices now, all of them screaming through my head: *Turn back, go, leave, ICU2, Gus, Ben, Mia, Kill, Kill . . .* and I vacillated, forward a couple steps, then back again, my legs heavy as I finally squeezed through a small crack in barn door and inhaled the smell of dust and gasoline, grease from the piled-up machinery, and moldy straw. The voices were still echoing in my brain but had narrowed down to a single word: *Gus, Gus, Gus . . .* and then cutting through it all, one voice: "Hello, Mona."

~ PART III ~

NO MORE DENIAL

TWENTY-FOUR

Saturday, October 31
Present Time

It's cold in the barn. As cold as a grave. Rightly so, thinks Reyes, as he watches the body bag being zipped over his victim's legs and torso, and then looks up to see Meyers arriving on the scene. "Wait," he tells the techs. "One more minute, my partner just got here."

They back off as Meyers joins him. He takes one look at the skull fractures and markings on the victim's face, and says, "I hate cases like these. How could someone do this to another person? And she was a pretty woman, too."

Reyes gives Meyers a quick glance, noting that his face is pale and slick with sweat, despite the low temperature. This was a difficult crime scene. Ben Ellison placed the 911 call a little after one thirty this morning. Dispatch said he was so hysterical that they barely got anything intelligible from him.

"Sorry, I'm late," Meyers says when Reyes doesn't respond. "Should I step out while you do your communicating thing?"

"I don't communicate with the dead," Reyes says. "That would be strange. I simply talk out loud to them at their death scene. It helps me get a sense of things. But if you have something else to do, that'd be fine with me."

"Right. Have your chat. I'll go check to see if they've turned up anything outside."

Other officers are canvasing the surrounding fields, hoping to find the murder weapon, but the markings on her face and head are distinctive enough. Reyes squats close and whispers, "Did he use a hammer on you?"

He doesn't expect much in return. He remembers from questioning her that she was an exact person, she picked and measured her words carefully. She gave him little to no information, even though he sensed that she knew more. No doubt she'll be just as elusive in death as she was in life.

He stares at her face, or what's left of it, blue skinned, haunting eyes bulged over chiseled cheeks, her red lipstick garish on her bloodless lips. He closes his eyes and tries to imagine the first blow, her reaction—did she turn and glimpse her assailant, or was she dead before she got a chance? His mind felt like a lightning storm, striking out in a dozen different directions. Why here? The same place where Gus Ellison killed himself. Two deaths in the same barn. And another death, Mia Jones, killed and dumped not more than a few miles from here.

Meyers pops his head back in. "Hey, buddy. You better come out here. They've found something."

Reyes follows him outside, and they start to weave their way through parked vehicles toward a group of officials huddled out in the middle of the field when one of the officers peels away and runs in their direction. "It's a female," he says, out of breath. "Exposure's bad. I'm going for blankets. Transport's about five minutes out."

Reyes starts jogging, jagged cornstalks left over from harvest snagging his trousers. Meyers is right behind him.

"She's unconscious," one of the officers says as they near the group.

Reyes pushes through them and stops. It's Mona Ellison.

She's in bad shape, limp, with blue tinged lips. Reyes whips off his fleece-lined jacket, tucks it around her torso, and nestles the warm collar around her cold cheeks. "Hang in there," he tells her. He can't afford a second woman dead out here tonight.

The officer continues to fill them in: "She came to briefly but was talking crazy. Didn't make sense at all." Reyes recognizes him as Officer Cagle. Young, inexperienced, shook. First homicide scene probably.

Fifteen years as a cop, five of them as a detective, Reyes has seen his share. He was an inner-city transport, his wife threatening to leave him if he didn't move to a smaller town with less crime. They moved to Belington, and Teresa left him anyway. Cancer. She was thirty-eight. Now it's just him and Stella.

And little had they known back then that the size of the town didn't matter much. Crime was crime. Just as much evil, maybe even more, occurred in the sleepy suburbs as it did in the roughest neighborhoods of Chicago. And solving them took time. Time away from family.

Cagle continues babbling: "Ben Ellison is being talked to at his residence and the rest of us were searching the field for the weapon and . . . I almost missed her, she's wedged in the tractor tire rut behind this clump of stalks here, and well, what if I'd missed her, she might be dead now."

Reyes nods. "Easy to miss. You did good. You're right, she wouldn't have made it out here much longer." Was she going to make it now? "Where's the damn ambulance?" Then to Cagle, "What position was she in when you found her?"

"She was on her side. Left side."

A couple others arrive with standard-issue blue blankets. They hand Reyes's jacket back to him and start wrapping her. Reyes looks over his shoulder to the barn and then turns back, his gaze cutting across the field to a distant row of trees that border the forest preserve. "She was running," Reyes says. "Away from the barn, but not toward her house. It would have made more sense to run toward her house, or one of her neighbors, where she could have gotten help. Unless she wasn't looking for help. Or her fears stemmed from her house. Or a neighbor's."

"She was probably panicked," Meyers says. "She either found the body and freaked out, or she witnessed what went down in there and ran." Meyers kicks at the ground and glances back at the barn. "My guess, we've got something bat ass crazy going on here and it's coming from that neighborhood."

"That'd be my guess, too." Reyes looks past the barn, to the houses, each as distinctly stand-offish or reclusive or demanding of attention as their owners. One of them now with a very dead owner.

Crime Report

Belington Police Department   Case No. 3167 – 9824
Offense: Homicide
Victim: Tara York W/F
Location: Vacated barn, field adjacent to Harvest View
         Subdivision
Means: Bludgeoning
Weapon: Blunt Weapon/Undetermined
Reporting Officer: Lucas Reyes, Detective

Details: (Preliminary) *The 911 call came into dispatch at 0138 from Dr. Ben Ellison, who reported a possible homicide. Responding patrol officers Cagle and Schmitz arrived on the scene at 0204 hours and found the body inside the barn, face down, with obvious fatal head injuries. I arrived at the scene at 0317 hours. Crime Scene Lead Tech Michael Sievert was on the scene and supervised evidence collection. The victim was*

photographed, and the body released for transport by Deputy Coroner Charles Rand at 0702 hours. Actual time of death TBD pending autopsy report. Victim identified by Dr. Ellison as Ms. Tara York, age 52. At approximately 0728 hours, a second person, identified as Mona Ellison, age 51, was found unconscious at the scene and transported to Belington Hospital.
Time-to-date: Fingerprint analysis: pending. Footprint analysis: pending. Autopsy: pending.

Report filed by: Detective Lucas Reyes

TWENTY-FIVE

B en Ellison doesn't look like a man who'd been up half the night worrying over his wife, or distraught over the death of his neighbor. When they arrive at his house later that morning, his shirt is fully buttoned, his tie square, his trousers unwrinkled. He sits at the kitchen table across from Reyes and Meyers, his posture perfect, hands wrapped around a coffee mug. The house is quiet except for the ticking of a grandfather clock.

"I would like to go to the hospital to check on my wife," Ben says.

Reyes taps the phone fastened to his belt. "Just checked and she's still in the ER. You won't be able to see her for a while, and we just have a few questions. It won't take long."

Ben inhales sharply and swipes at his face. "Please make it quick. Mona needs me."

Right, buddy. Where were you all this time she was needing you? Dispatch had said he was nearly unintelligible when he'd called; he was Mr. All-put-together now. Was his cool now a coping mechanism? Or was the hysterical phone call a ruse? He claimed to have come to the barn looking for his wife and discovered Tara York's body with no sign of Mona. "We need to go through the particulars again, Mr. Ellison." Reyes refers to the notes from the responding officer's initial interview with Ben Ellison. "Your plane landed at O'Hare at eleven thirty-nine p.m. and you arrived home at what time again?"

Ben sighs. "After one, I believe. I wasn't keeping track of time. I came into the house, but Mona wasn't here. That's when I looked at my phone and realized she'd sent a text asking me if I was in the barn. I was concerned, so I went there looking for her and I found Tara. I checked for a pulse, but it was obvious . . . her injuries were . . ."

"You left the barn after that?"

"I . . . I was scared. It was dark, the blood, I don't know . . . I called nine one one as I ran for home."

Reyes skims the initial interview report. After he'd called 911, Ben Ellison, unable to tolerate the sight of Tara York's blood, stripped and threw his stained clothing into the washing machine, showered, and changed into clean clothing.

Reyes switches topics. "You told your wife that you were in Seattle at a work conference."

"Yes, yes and I can explain that. You see, Mona is fragile right now and if I'd told her the truth it would have . . . uh . . . let's put it this way. It would have been detrimental to her well-being."

Reyes says, "I don't understand. What were you doing in Phoenix?"

Ben clears his throat. "Uh . . . well, I participated in a three-day intensive therapy program at a private center outside Phoenix. A grief therapy program," he emphasizes and then adds, "Sometimes the therapist needs therapy. Mona was already under so much stress, and I didn't want her to know that I was . . . uh . . . well, I guess you could say that I fell prey to the common pitfalls of the masculine psyche. I wanted to put on a strong front for my wife."

"So you lied and told her that you were going to Seattle," Reyes says.

"That's right. The hospital in Seattle is known for their research in pediatric psychiatric medicine. I'd expressed an interest in their conferences before, but the timing had never worked out. I shouldn't have lied, but I did it to avoid distressing her with my own issues. It seemed like the right thing to do at the time."

"What was the name of the program out there in Phoenix?"

"You want to verify that I was there?" Ben rakes his hand through his hair. Then pats it back into place. "Look, I'm not lying. It's not easy for me to admit that I needed help, I'm usually the one doing the helping."

Meyers rips a page from his notebook and slides it across the table, and then hands him a pen. "Could you write the name of the program for me?"

Ben talks as he writes. "Gus's death has been difficult, as you can imagine, and now Tara, out there in the same barn . . . I'll never forget finding her like that." He finishes and hands back the pen. "What was she doing out there at that time of night?"

"We haven't determined that yet," Reyes says.

"Oh." Ben fidgets, clasping and unclasping his hands. "Is that all then?"

"Just a few more questions," Meyers says.

"Can't they wait? I need to talk to the doctors who are treating Mona. There are things they will need to know about her condition."

"Her condition?" Reyes asks.

Ben inhales sharply. "Mona is being treated for severe depression. Before I left it seemed like she was doing better, but then I received a call from Tara yesterday afternoon saying that—"

"Ms. York was able to reach you?"

"Yes. She called the clinic where I was staying . . . I should back up a little. Tara had been counseling me, just since Gus's death. She was the one who recommended the program in

Phoenix. She had an emergency number for me. She called out of concern for Mona."

"Let me get this straight," Reyes says. "You told your wife that you were traveling to Seattle for an orientation for your new position, but you'd really gone to Phoenix for this special therapy program, which Tara York recommended?"

Ben blinks nervously. "Yes, that's right. Mona isn't herself, you understand, Gus's death took a toll on her . . . well, the trauma, everyone processes trauma differently."

Meyers is taking notes. "You said that Tara called because she was concerned about your wife?"

"She indicated that Mona was acting irrationally, hallucinating, withdrawing, and there were times that Mona couldn't account for her whereabouts."

Meyers looks up from his notebook. "Blackouts?"

Ben nods. "Perhaps. I can't be certain. Tara also mentioned an angry outburst toward Selma. She lives across the street. She's another one of their close friends."

"An argument? Do you know what about?" Reyes asks.

Ben straightens his tie. "No. She said she'd explain more when she saw me . . ." He sighs. "Tara did mention that Mona was acting paranoid, thinking that people were out to get her."

Meyers scribbles away in his notebook.

"And she saw her with a rope," Ben adds.

Meyers looks up. "With a rope?"

Ben nods. "Tara and Alice, that's another of her friends, found Mona in our cellar with a rope around her neck. At least that's the way Tara described it to me." He sighs and gets up, heading toward the coffee pot on the counter. "Does anyone want more . . ." His voice trails off. He's stopped at the counter and is staring out the kitchen window.

"Mr. Ellison. What is it?" Reyes asks.

"There's a news van outside on the street. The press."

He wheels around, his expression panicked. "Why are they here?"

Reyes chooses his words carefully. "This is bound to be a big story. Belington doesn't see a lot of homicides."

Meyers picks up on Reyes's lead. "And now we have two within the last six months."

Ben's previously composed expression now pales as his gaze scans the street again.

"Had your wife mentioned to you that we'd been trying to contact you about Mia Jones?"

"Yes, yes, that girl found at Simon Park. Mona told me you'd come by asking questions." He still glances out the window.

"About Mia Jones," Reyes coaxes.

Ben smooths away invisible wrinkles on his shirt. "I didn't know the girl. I wish I did. Perhaps I could have helped her. Now, I really must—"

"She'd been to The Caring Place," Meyers says.

Ben lifts his chin. "I wouldn't know about that. She wasn't my patient. Maybe one of the other doctors or counselors? You should check with them." He reaches into his pocket for a set of car keys. "I am leaving now."

Reyes stands. "We'll be right behind you. We'll need to question your wife before you see her."

TWENTY-SIX

I'm embedded in a cream-colored capsule of limp curtains and beeping machines. My wrist throbs where they placed the IV, and a heavy layer of blankets pins me to the bed. I search my brain for the reason why I'm here, but all I come up with are the constant voices that continuously hover in my gray matter. I close my eyes and begin to drift and open them again when the curtain squeals on its track.

I glance over, expecting to see a nurse, but it's the detectives from before, Reyes and Meyers. I turn my head away.

"Mrs. Ellison. How are you?" It's Reyes. He sounds concerned. I know better. "Detective Meyers is with me."

I keep my head turned, but nod.

"I've got good news for you," Meyers says. "Ben is back. He's waiting outside in the hall. He's anxious to talk to you."

I look at the detectives. Ben is here? I should feel excitement, but it seems more like fear. Then the facts from last night begin falling into place.

Reyes studies me closely. "Do you want to see Mr. Ellison?" he asks.

A bolt of anxiety burns through my stomach. *Last night in the barn, Tara and . . .* "No. I don't want to see my husband yet."

Meyers drags one of the chairs to the far end of the room and sits down, notebook in hand, while Reyes sits on the chair by my bed.

Reyes tilts his head. "Why not?"

I shrug.

"Did you see Tara in the barn last night?" he asks.

Blood in the barn. Blood everywhere. "Yes. She's dead."

He nods slowly. "Yes."

I draw in a shaky breath and close my eyes again. I just want to sleep. The voices call to me and I just want . . .

"Mrs. Ellison," Reyes prods. "Please, try to tell me what you remember."

I roll my eyes his way and lick my dry lips. "I remember blood. A lot of blood."

"What else, Mrs. Ellison?" Reyes speaks softly. Gently. His eyes have that same look as they did that day that he held Bo Peep. He wants to fix this like he wanted to fix her. I look at his hands. Strong hands.

"Do you remember anything else?" he asks again.

I manage a nod. How can I tell him? Will he even believe me?

Reyes regards me sympathetically. "Maybe we should start with why you went out to the barn."

My mind starts churning over the nightmare. I don't want to remember any of this. None of it. I want things to go back to before, before Tara, before Gus, before Mia . . . "Why? Why did he have to . . . my Gus." A knot swells in my throat. "Why did he have to die?"

Reyes leans closer, lowers his voice. "I'm so sorry, Mona."

Something about the way he says my name, so personal, like a friend. It feels good to have a friend. The voices have quieted, and I take a breath. "I went out to the barn because Gus told me to."

He looks at me patiently, quizzically, and I want more than anything to tell him, to share the misery I've suffered, to have him piece together this broken doll. My words come haltingly at first in staccato words, but slowly form into broken sentences. "But that can't be right. I know now that it's not Gus. Because he's dead." I look up at him, deep into his eyes. "Right? My Gus is dead?" Tears are forming, ready to cascade, as I search his face for . . . what? Understanding? Reassurance that I'm wrong? But it's true. Gus is dead. I know it was true. I've known all along, even before Alice and Tara and Selma told me again yesterday. Why is it so difficult to accept? Why does it have to be true? And now the tears flow and I close my eyes to his body hanging from the rafters and to the bloody scene in the barn.

Reyes's voice is far away now, soft and kind. "Get some rest. We'll talk more later."

CSI Response Form—Request for Forensic Services

Belington Police Department
Criminal Investigation Bureau
Crime Scene Investigation Division

Homicide
Case No. 3167 – 9824
Outside Agency Report No. 38675G
Comments: I arrived on the scene at 0245 hours, the perimeter had been established by responding officers, Schmitz and Cagle. I conducted an initial walk-thru and established scene access. All agency protocols followed.

The body of Tara York was positioned facedown, top of the head facing north wall of the barn. Approximate position: fifteen feet from the north wall, twenty-five feet in from entrance of the barn, eighteen feet from east wall. Tara York's left arm was raised, positioned at approximately a ninety-degree angle, her right arm raised at approximately a seventy-degree angle, face turned slightly toward east wall of barn, fully clothed and wearing blue jeans, red sweater, gray parka, multicolored scarf, dark leather snow boots. Tara York's skull was cracked open, injuries consistent with a bludgeoning. Blood pool surrounding the body contained fragments of bone, hair, and brain matter.

Evidence Search

Evidence markers assigned to the following areas of apparent blood spatter/stains and items of evidence collected:

A. blood pool on floor surrounding victim
B. skull and hair fragments on floor surrounding victim
C. blood spatter on vertical wood support beam
D. blood spatter on black tractor tire
E. dark matter on black tractor tire
F. damaged black cell phone, clear case, wedged under victim's right hip, found by ME assistant as the body was being moved for transport
H. unidentifiable dark spots located near victim's left foot
I. evident partial shoeprint in blood stain to the right of victim's body
J. evident second partial shoeprint near victim's right hand

CS Investigator Shelby Hamilton accompanied the second victim, Mona Ellison, to Belington Hospital, where she was treated for moderate hypothermia. The following evidence was collected at the hospital.
1. muddied shoes

2. sweatshirt, blood stains, spatters, and smears evident
3. jeans, blood stains, spatters, and smears evident
4. undernail scrapings collected from both hands
5. buccal sample

Crime Scene Investigator's Signature: Michael Sievert, Shelby Hamilton

TWENTY-SEVEN

The county coroner works out of a squat brick building across the river from the sewage treatment plant and two blocks down from the Jolly Burger joint. Reyes and Meyers pull into the lot and park facing the river, oily smudges staining two Jolly's bags.

Meyers tears his open, bites into his burger, and tips his head toward the sewage plant. "Appetizing view."

Reyes agrees. "Wonder which was here first. The morgue or the sewage plant?"

"Who knows? They'll be here longer than us. I mean, no chance they'll go out of existence, right? Everyone spends their life shitting and then they die." Meyers takes another bite of his burger, swiping his tongue at the runny catsup on the bun's edge.

Reyes removes his scarf before unwrapping his own sandwich.

Meyers eyes the scarf. "How's the kid doing?"

"Stella's fine. She's at her Aunt Camilla's for the weekend. They're doing a girls' spa night, or something. Having more fun with her than she would hanging out with me, that's for sure."

"No doubt." Meyers held out his hands and moved them up and down like a scale. "Let's see. Spa time or viewing a dead body. Spa. Dead body. Hmm."

"True." Reyes unwraps his chicken sandwich, takes one

bite, and tosses it back into the bag. He knows better than to wait to eat after a morgue visit. But today even eating before doesn't settle with Reyes. Shitting and dying. Meyers's cynicism hits a little too close to home and leaves little room for appetite.

Meyers talks with his mouth full. "What's up?" They haven't been partners long, Meyers transferring in, but Meyers picks up quickly on clues both in cases, which Reyes appreciates, and in Reyes's moods, not as much.

"Nothing. I just wonder how Stella's really doing, you know? This job. The schedule. And I can't give her what Teresa would give her—a woman's touch."

Meyers sets his burger aside. "No. You can't give her that, but I've seen you two together. She adores you, buddy. And you've got Camilla to help out with all the girl-type stuff."

Reyes picks at a few fries. "What's your take on Ben Ellison?"

"Jackass."

"Besides that."

"He was probably doing the York woman. Which gives the wife motive for bashing in her head. She's half out of her mind already, wouldn't take too much to push her over the edge."

Reyes thinks of Mona with her dolls, the way she tenderly cares for them, down to every detail. Her vulnerability. The sadness that radiates from her. Her tears at losing her son. "I have a hard time seeing her bashing in someone's skull."

"She had blood on her. Spatters, consistent with being in close proximity to the victim."

"So did her husband, only he washed it away."

Meyers crumples his empty burger wrapper and tosses it into the bag. "Him? Her? Maybe they were in on it together. Who knows? Maybe Tara will have some answers for us. You ready to have another chat with her?" Meyers chuckles.

He's joking, but Reyes knows that it's too late for Tara to

tell him anything. Just like most evidence at the scene, finger-prints, shoe prints, trace evidence, the victim is at their most informative only while the crime is still fresh.

Reyes and Meyers ride the elevator down to the ground floor of the coroner's building with a youngish woman in green scrubs, short-cropped hair, and no jewelry. No one talks. All three study the numbers flashing above the door like they're the next million-dollar lotto pick.

The elevator opens to a long gray hallway. Reyes and Meyers step aside to let the woman exit first and then head in the same direction, stopping off at the clerk's desk to sign in and get directions to the correct examination room. Then, another door and a short hallway to a prep room, where they wiggle into biohazard protection: masks, gloves, shields, and hair coverings that remind Reyes of his short high school stint flipping burgers.

Inside the lab, the smell of formalin and death settles in Reyes's nostrils. This isn't his first morgue rodeo, but the smell still catches him off guard. He coughs, gags, clears his throat, and then shivers. The external temp is mandatory low sixties, but his shiver has less to do with coldness as it does the sight of Tara York's body on the gurney.

Meyers hesitates, cursing under his breath. "I'll never get used to this."

Doctor Mendez looks up from the body. "Come on in, gentlemen."

They join her around the gurney. This is Meyers first time meeting Dr. Mendez. "Meyers, this is Doctor Gabriella Mendez. She's worked on a few of my people in the past."

"Once they're in here, they become *my* people, Detective."

"Understood."

She gives Meyers a slight nod and then waves her hand toward a tech standing by another table, weighing something gelatinous and glossy in a bag. She introduces him as Martin and then gets right down to business. "Okay. I know you're mostly interested in her head." She starts toward a table, and they follow.

Reyes rolls his neck, his muscles popping. Just a few days ago, Tara York was a vibrant, beautiful woman, and now her soulless body is naked on a cold metal, every inch of her flesh being poked and prodded, and stared at by strangers. It rankles him any time he meets a person in real life and then sees them exposed like this in death. Like he'd violated some unspoken trust shared in those living moments.

Reyes tries to keep his focus on Tara's head, her injuries there, but his eyes wander to the massive Y-incision that runs between her breasts, the breasts of a fifty-something woman, wide and jelly-like, flattened due to her supine position, darkened nipples stretched with age, a soft belly, plushy hips, a dark tangle of hair between full thighs, and he remembers his wife's legs, both soft and strong as they wrapped around his waist, pressing closer and pulling deeper and . . . he catches himself and shifts uncomfortably—thoughts of Teresa and now he's aroused. How long has it been since that happened? Grief and loneliness wash over him. Why are his emotions catching up to him now? Here? He knows better. This is Tara York's last medical exam, a chance to get any sort of justice. He'd promised her as much at the crime scene.

He blinks, looks away, and notices that Meyers's hairline is soaked with sweat. He looks ill.

Dr. Mendez clears her throat and Reyes's attention is drawn back to the table as she swings the overhead fluorescent light lower.

She asks the tech to flip on a large screen that's mounted to the wall behind them and traces a gloved finger along Tara's fractured skull. "Okay. What we have here, according to my gross examination and CT imaging, are focal contact injuries, three of them, caused by blunt force contact to the head and including scalp contusion and laceration, skull fracture, brain contusion, epidural hemorrhaging, and focal subdural hemorrhaging."

Meyers speaks up. "So basically, her skull was beaten to a pulp."

Dr. Mendez's features tighten. "Basically, yes. Anything I'm telling you today is preliminary. All official diagnoses are reserved for my final report. You won't see that for a while."

"What was used on her?" Reyes asks.

"The cranial lesions are geometrical, as you can see here and here. Square shaped. The edges of the wounds are sharp and regular, with the inner table of the skull showing some beveling, consistent with skull fractures of this nature." She reaches for a nearby cart with a small laptop and hits a couple keys. Several pictures of skull wounds appear on the wall-mounted monitor. "I called these up earlier, so you can make your own comparison. These are wounds known to be made by hammers. Basic claw hammers like you would find in most people's garage. They all vary a little, depending on the tool and the person who used it."

Reyes studies the photos and looks back at the wounds. He'd expected as much, but now it's official. "A claw hammer. You're sure?"

"I'd say so."

Meyers turns toward the door, as if satisfied but likely just anxious to leave. "I'll call the guys at the scene. Let them know what we're looking for."

He steps out and Dr. Mendez turns back to Reyes, lifts an eyebrow, and offers, "Want a minute with her?"

Like Meyers, she's known him to converse with the dead, but this time he senses the slightest hint of accusation in her tone. Or maybe he imagines it. Either way, she's either noticed his earlier display of emotion, or worse yet, his arousal. What does she think? That he was reacting to a stone-cold dead corpse when he was simply missing his wife?

He lowers his voice and stammers, "Ah, no, thanks."

And, like Meyers, he quickly turns and leaves.

TWENTY-EIGHT

Monday, November 2

The room is as dark as my mood as I stand at the window, watching for Ben to come home. The neighborhood is still abuzz with activity, people searching the fields, police going in and out of Tara's house, news vehicles perusing through, sometimes stopping to take pictures or film a brief interview, neighbors out and about, huddling in groups with their heads bent together, discussing Tara's death, no doubt. And Reyes and Meyers canvasing the neighborhood, door to door like trick-or-treaters, *ding dong, your neighbor is dead.*

I watch as they knock on Alice's door, Reyes wearing the same colorful scarf I'd seen him wearing before. From his daughter, I'd supposed. I wonder if she likes dolls. Alice answers and steps onto the porch, wrapped in a long sweater, and immediately they lock into an animated conversation. Meyers scribbles in that notebook of his while Alice talks and talks, and glances toward my house, looking up at my bedroom window as if she can see me standing here behind the gauzy inner window covering. Doubtful, but maybe she senses me watching. Perhaps she's worried that I know what she's saying, can read her lips from across the street, or know that she's telling the police all my long-lost secrets. Things I've confided over wine and girls' night out, where it had always felt like I could let my guard down, be myself, reveal my most inner thoughts. But that's not true, is it? I can never let my guard down. I can trust no one. Maybe myself the least.

Reyes turns and looks up at my window. I jerk back, into the shadows of the outer drapes, and then precipitously decide to step forward, showing myself, letting him know that, yes, indeed I am here, me, Mrs. Ellison, locked in the tower room, all alone except for the company of my dolls. See the broken pieces of me, Detective Reyes? But he's already turned back to Alice, leaning in and focusing intently on her words.

My gut turns sour.

Anxiety probably, or a side effect of one of the meds they gave me at the hospital. They kept me just under forty-eight hours, discharging me this morning with an appointment to see a new psychologist. Like I need another mental health professional in my life besides a husband who overdoses me and a counselor best friend who slept with my husband. Not that she'll ever be in my life again. Sadness pricks along the edges of my subconscious along with a strange, fleeting sense of relief, which I quickly push away.

I'd called Alice to pick me up at the hospital earlier, not Ben. And thankfully, Ben wasn't home when I got here. I can't face him yet. So, I locked myself in the house, closed all the drapes, and then came straight to my doll room, where I plan to stay until I can get things straightened out in my mind.

What happened in the barn? Bits and pieces have come back to me, but the whole picture is still beyond my grasp.

I'd refused to let Ben visit me at the hospital, but the nurses told me that he'd stayed in the waiting room, hoping that I'd change my mind. I didn't. Ben likes to play the part of a devoted husband, but I know the truth. There is nothing devoted about him.

I double-check the lock on the door.

And breathe easier. I'm safe and plan to stay ensconced in my happy place.

I go to the settee, surprised to see Bo Peep, Blythe, and Mia sitting there, pretty as can be. "I didn't expect to find you all here," I say and sit next to them, putting my feet up on a small, pin-tucked ottoman. I settle in, wishing I had some tea, or a snack, but I don't. My stomach rumbles. "At least I have you three."

"Always," I hear Blythe say. Her blue eyes twinkle, both now open after a bit of my earlier tending.

"It was horrible what happened in the barn. The worst nightmare ever." My voice cracks. Just thinking about it makes it seem all too real again, even though the details evade me.

Mia nods encouragingly—*let it all out*—and I think to myself, I'm safe with them. I probably told that Detective Reyes too much already. I can't recall exactly what happened or was said at first. But I know I didn't tell the nurses, not even the psychiatrist that talked to me in the hospital later. But I can tell my dolls—they're my true friends.

"I don't know if it's real," I start. Bo Peep leans in. She's always been the most attentive. "But it still haunts me, the way it happened. I was only there for answers about Gus, you understand?" The three listen silently. They understand. "But it wasn't Gus, it was . . ." And I close my eyes, unwilling to accept what I've seen. Tara . . . Ben . . . the hammer . . . *thwack, thwack, thwack* . . . blood spurting, the sickening crunch of Tara's skull cracked open, white veiny tissue between jagged edges of bloody bone . . . It can't be true. I squeeze my eyes tighter against the sights, but I hear the other voices, the ones that have haunted me so often these last days, rise up in the back of my mind. *It's true, it's true, it's true,* and my dolls join in, all of them chanting, *it's true, it's true* . . .

And then I hear the garage door open. Instantly the voices stop. We listen.

And wait. I know the sequence of sounds by heart. I've heard them a thousand times before, never changing. When I'm downstairs, I hear every motion. Up here I hear it as a memorized metronome to my husband's predictable life: First the door shuts and the click of the lock as he turns it back into place. The jingling of his keys as he tosses them in the basket on the front entry table. The front hall closet door opens, a shuffling of his coat being hung, and the closet door shuts followed by footsteps, even and uniform, as if his weight is perfectly balanced on both feet as he makes his way up the stairs.

"Mona?" His voice echoes down the hall. "Mona? Where are—"

He's in our bedroom now. I imagine his face twisting in disgust as he sees the dirty clothes I peeled off earlier and tossed in a heap on the floor. "Mona!"

Heavy footsteps now and my pulse thumps louder, too. I hear the door to Gus's room fly open. *Wrong again, dear Ben.*

"Mona!"

My heart pounds in my throat.

"Mona, I know you're here. Your car is parked outside."

I try to read his voice. Even and measured, as always, yet with an edge. Irritation? Anger?

More footsteps. Close? Far? I can't tell. I cross the room and press my ear to the door. Nothing. I let out a huge sigh and sink against the wood. He's left.

The doorknob turns.

I jump back.

"Mona?" He sounds eerily calm. "Mona, dear. Open up. We need to talk."

I step back from the door. *Go away, go away . . .*

The knob rattles. His voice turns thick with panic. "Mona. What are you doing? Open this door!"

But I'm frozen in place, indifferent to his pleading while my mind whirls: the barn, Ben, Tara, the hammer . . .

He pounds on the door, *bam, bam* . . . but all I hear is the sound of a hammer against bone, *thwack, thwack, thwack* . . .

I bend over, clasp my hands around my ears, and mutter, "Go away, go away. . ."

Splintering of wood shatters the air. He's breaking in the door!

TWENTY-NINE

Reyes and Meyers catch Alice Parker just as she's heading out to walk her dog. They stand on her porch and talk. "I just can't believe it," she says. Her eyes are red rimmed and puffy. "We've been friends since childhood."

"When did you see Tara last?" Reyes asks.

"That day. Several hours before she died. We'd all gotten together at Selma's house earlier to talk through a few things."

At "things" Reyes sees her glance briefly across the street, toward the upper floor of the Ellison house. "What kinds of things, Ms. Parker?"

"Well"—she swallows—"to talk to Mona. She'd been acting strangely the entire week and we were concerned."

"Strange how?"

"Down. Withdrawn. It started after book club on Tuesday."

"Why?" Meyers wants to know. "Did something happen at book club?"

"We shouldn't even call it book club. We rarely talk about the book. Mostly we drink wine and talk about other things, kids and work, and husbands. Or ex-husband, in my case." She fingers the gold cross that dangles in the hollow of her throat. "That night we talked about Mia Jones."

Meyers takes note. "Did she seem upset about that?"

"We were all upset about it. It's tragic, but it happened so close to here . . . it's scary. We all have kids, except Tara, and to think of something like that happening to one of them . . . That's why I thought the topic might upset Mona. Because of Gus . . . I mean, I just can't imagine." Alice looks over at the Ellisons' house again. "Ever since he died, she's spent most of her time up there with her dolls. When I brought her home from the hospital this morning, that's all she talked about. Her happy place, she calls it. Up there with those ugly things."

Meyers asks questions while he writes. "Her husband didn't bring her home?"

"No. I didn't ask why. She called and needed a ride home, so I went."

Reyes turns and looks up at the tower. It's the focus of the home, red brick accented with white fish scale-like shingles and a top that looks like a witch's hat. Movement flashes in the center window. Is Mona up there now, watching them?

He turns back to Alice and says, "She does enjoy her dolls."

"That's an understatement. I've heard . . . I've heard her talk to them."

"Have you heard them talk back?" Reyes asks without expression.

She flinches. Meyers chuckles.

"No! Of course not," she says, then clears her throat, and continues: "Anyway, like I said, we got together that evening because we were concerned about Mona. She had an episode. You see, Selma had come home from a trip earlier in the day and we were all standing outside visiting in her driveway—"

Meyers looks up from his notebook. "All? You and . . .?"

"Selma, Tara, Mona, and me."

"Okay."

"And Mona saw the tag on Selma's luggage and confronted her about being in Phoenix, accused her of being there with Ben. Which surprised the rest of us because we thought he was in Seattle."

Reyes thumbs toward the ultramodern house two doors down. "That's Selma's place, right?"

"Uh, huh. Later, I went over to talk to Mona. I thought if she and Ben were having trouble, that maybe I could help."

Reyes's brows furrow. "By trouble you mean?"

"Infidelity." Alice looks down the road, her eyes tracing the movement of a black Mercedes SUV. She plasters on a smile and waves. "Here's Ben now."

They watch him pull into his garage and the door close.

Reyes turns back and asks, "Do you know him as well as you do Mona?"

"Mona and I were childhood friends, but I've known Ben for years now. Even before they were married. We were all in college together."

"In your opinion, is he the cheating type?" Reyes asks.

Alice's features turn hard. "In my opinion, most men are cheaters. But that's just me. I'm in a bad place in my life right now." She shakes her head. "To be honest, normally, I wouldn't have thought that about Ben. He's always been devoted to Mona. They seem like the perfect couple."

"Things are rarely what they seem." Reyes bends down and pets Milo with his own ring-bare hand, and then straightens at the sound of someone yelling. He looks at Meyers. "What was that?"

Meyers turns toward the Ellisons' house. More yelling and then a loud scream slices through the air.

Reyes bangs on the Ellisons' front door, but no one responds. The screaming continues. Meyers rings the bell and yells, "Police. Open up."

Footsteps echo inside the house and the front door flies open. Ben Ellison's face is flushed, and his tie skewed. "It's you. Thank God." He opens the door wider. "Mona has locked herself in a room upstairs and I'm worried about her."

Reyes and Meyers push past him and up the stairs. "Which room?" Reyes calls over his shoulder.

Ben catches up to them and gives directions. The detectives rush down the second-floor hallway to the back staircase. The screaming has stopped and it's quiet now, more frightening to Reyes than the screams.

They move past the attic door and ascend the narrow steps to the door at the top of the tower. Reyes knocks gently. "Mrs. Ellison, it's Detective Reyes."

THIRTY

At the sound of Detective Reyes's voice, my muscles loosen, just a little, and the pain in my head recedes, just a little, and I'm able to catch my breath, just a little, and for a second, when I open the door and see Reyes and Meyers, I think that maybe things will be okay. But then I see Ben standing behind them and I know that things will never be right again. Oh, he's acting concerned, like any good husband would, but there's a flicker of anger in his eyes that only I would recognize. I've seen it many times before when things aren't going his way.

He elbows past the detectives and comes to me, his hands outstretched. I shrink back, but he wraps his fingers around my face. I freeze in panic, and he pulls me forward and softly kisses my forehead, his lips a tarantula's touch. "What is going on inside this head of yours, Mona? Why wouldn't you let me in? I was so worried about you."

I shake him off, swipe off his kiss, and step back. I'm trembling and can't stop. I turn to Reyes. "Get him away from me."

"Mona, you're not yourself," Ben says. "Your mind is playing tricks on you." Then to the detectives. "I know what's going on here. I just finished a meeting with one of my colleagues, Doctor Adler. He questioned me about overprescribing medications to my wife. Benzos and SSRIs and other things that I would never prescribe in combination with one another. I believe she's found some sort of illicit source for prescription pills. If she's taking what he described, it could be contributing to her delusions. Or worse."

Anger wells inside me. "Those pills were in the pillbox that *you* filled for me. You kept reminding me to take them."

Ben's skin grows blotchy, and his eyes are a little too wide. "Just the ones I prescribed. I didn't put those extra pills in there, Mona, and you know it." His voice seethes with anger. "Do you want me to get into trouble? Is that what you're trying to do? Make me lose my license?"

"No. Of course not. I . . ." A dull ache swells behind my eyes. I rub at my temples. It always boils down to his image, his career, doesn't it? But . . . then why would he jeopardize it by overdosing me? "I . . . I don't know what to think anymore." I don't remember putting those pills in there. Where would I even get illegal drugs? The image of that drug house I went to flitters through my brain—did I . . . Is my mind that far gone?

Meyers steps forward. "Did you buy prescription medications from someone, Mrs. Ellison?"

"You don't have to answer that, Mona." Ben is near me again, his hand on my shoulder, his voice soothing, the ever-supportive husband.

I look to Reyes. "Am I in trouble for something?"

"It's going to be okay," Ben answers. "I'm going to help you, I promise." He turns to Reyes and Meyers. "Try to understand. She believes that what she's saying is true. Paranoid delusions. It's part of her illness. It's like what I was telling you earlier."

What he told them earlier? "You were talking to the police about me?"

"They questioned me," Ben says. "About Tara's murder."

Tara. The barn.

I shrink from Ben's hand, move to the settee, pick up Mia, and snuggle her close as I sit hunkered in on myself. "I saw Tara out there in the barn."

Ben starts to come my way, but Reyes motions for him to stay put. The room is silent. I can hear my heart thudding in my chest, and the sound of the blood whooshing through my head. It reminds me of when I was eight, standing on the beach with a conch shell to my ear, listening to the ocean waves. But these waves carry only fear and dread.

Reyes is perched next to me now. He's picked up Bo Peep and is studying her. "You did an amazing job with her face. It was in several pieces last time I saw her."

"Thank you. I worked hard on her." My heart soars as I glance at her. "Do you like her dress?"

He raises a brow. "Yes, it's nice."

"It's new. I made it from scrap material. One of Ben's old sweatshirts. It was badly stained, but I was able to salvage enough material for the dress." I glance at Ben and see his eyes glued on Bo Peep's dress, his expression rigid. He's never cared about my dolls' attire before, and I almost find it funny that—

"That's amazing." Reyes interrupts my thought. "You treat your dolls well."

"Thank you." I blush at the compliment. "She'll never be like she was before, but at least she's still alive." What did I just say? "I mean that figuratively, of course."

"Of course," Reyes says and smiles. His fingers lovingly caress Bo Peep's face and his smile fades. "When I look at her, I can't help thinking about Tara and how someone broke her in much the same way."

Thwack, thwack, thwack . . .

I cringe and cling tighter to Mia. "Bo Peep was an accident. Tara was hurt on purpose. It was nothing like Bo Peep."

"Be quiet, Mona," Ben yells from across the room. "Please. You're in no shape to be interviewed. Let me get you an attorney, and then you can talk to the police."

I pull Mia closer and shrink further into the cushion.

Reyes keeps his gaze steady on me. "Your husband has a point, Mrs. Ellison. There has been a homicide. Your friend Tara York has been murdered. You understand that, right?

"Yes."

"And you know who I am and that I'm with the Belington Police Department. And that I'm investigating Tara York's homicide."

I look Reyes straight in the face. "My husband thinks I'm crazy, but I'm not. I know what's going on. I'm not incognizant, Detective."

Ben groans and throws up his hands. "Don't be stupid, Mona."

You stupid girl! What are you thinking? I hear Daddy's voice. I feel my lips tremble but at the same time something inside me hardens. An intention or resolve or maybe I'm just closing a door. Or opening one.

Reyes slides a sideward glance Ben's way, and then turns his full attention back to me. "I've never thought you were incognizant, Mrs. Ellison. And there's nothing stupid about you. Anyone can tell that."

Warmth flushes over me and I decide to ignore Ben. He's the stupid one. Sleeping around, thinking I'd never know.

"But you need to understand that your husband is correct about one thing. You don't need to talk to me. You have the right to talk to an attorney. Is that what you want to do, talk to a lawyer?"

"No." I see Bo Peep still held gently in his hands. "I just want to talk to you."

He reads off a list of rules, my legal rights, and then nods at Meyers, who points Ben to the door. Ben argues, and then reluctantly leaves. Meyers shuts the door behind him and then sits in the Queen Anne across from us, his notebook in hand.

My eyes drift to the window. "Why are all those people outside by the barn still?"

"We're still trying to find the murder weapon." He glances around the room, and I know the police will search this place soon, too. The idea of my dolls being handled by strangers upsets me.

Detective Reyes's focus snaps back to me and he smiles. "I do appreciate your cooperation."

I see Bo Peep is happy in his strong hands, and suddenly my world is safe again. And this room . . . well, it's my happy place again. When my dolls are happy, I'm happy. I take a breath. "I want to help you any way I can."

Our gazes connect and his eyes soften. "I'd like to discuss what happened out there in the barn, if that's okay with you," he says.

Anxiety stabs my stomach. "I really thought we would talk about my dolls."

"Sure." He points to Mia. "She's a pretty little thing."

"She's new. I just . . . uh, found her this past week. She's part of a set of five. I had the others, her four friends, but not her." I pull her to my face and nuzzle her, enjoying the softness of her hair against my cheek. "At first, I thought she was a gift. From Gus."

I watch him closely as I say this, but there's no reaction. He just continues to watch me with those kind brown eyes of his. My own gaze slides to a nearby shelf and my containers of doll eyes, all stored neatly in recycled baby food jars, the old ones, Gus's old ones, actually. I'd stored them for years in the attic, finally putting them to good use. I search the rows, settling my gaze on the browns, maybe a dozen different shades of brown, from barely brown hazel to a deep rich chocolate brown, but none of them come close to Detective Reyes's shade of brown.

"Mrs. Ellison?"

I blink and refocus on our conversation. "Yes?"

171

"I was asking why you don't believe that the doll came from Gus?"

"Because he's gone. My Gus is gone. Dead."

He nods. "I'm very sorry."

"Everyone says that."

"Because there is nothing else to say."

I shrug. "True enough."

We stare at one another. He shifts, and I feel horrible. I'm making him uncomfortable. Everyone feels uncomfortable around me now. "I'm sorry."

"For what?"

"I'm not explaining this very well. It's just that I don't really understand it myself."

"You're okay. Take your time. Maybe start at why you first thought that the doll came from Gus."

"Because of the posts on Instagram. That's why I went to the barn, too."

Reyes straightens. "Please explain."

I tell him about the post of the doll and the barn and a few other things from ICU2, who in my tormented mind, I'd believed to be Gus. "I really did think it was him. That somehow, he'd been able to reach out to me. You can understand that, right? It's not really crazy to want to keep someone you love alive, is it?"

Reyes flinches. "No, not at all. I think that's perfectly normal."

"Perfectly normal." My breath escapes in a small sigh, then another. I start to laugh, and it feels good. Damn good.

Reyes appears puzzled.

I get myself under control. "I'm sorry. It's just that you called me perfectly normal. No one has called me that in a long time. Ben always says I'm . . . I don't know, he uses all sorts of different words, but they all mean the same thing. Crazy."

"I understand how that is. People have said those things about me, too."

"They have? You?" I want to laugh again, but I don't.

"Yes. I have an unusual way of investigating homicides . . . I . . . I think out loud . . . sort of like talking to the victims . . . it helps me sort things out in my mind. Helps me make sense of things."

"I talk to my dolls." My voice is barely a whisper, and as soon as the words are out, I feel vulnerable.

But all he says is, "I completely understand."

My heart melts, as if I could cry from relief in finding someone who really understands. And I briefly wonder if I should tell him that my dolls sometimes talk back. Then I decide against it. He won't get it, because certainly his homicide victims can't talk back. Not like my dolls.

Reyes clears his throat. "I don't understand how a post on Instagram led you to this doll."

"Let me show you." I reach into the pocket of my sweater for my phone and power it on. My screen is full of notifications, Selma and Alice, and Ben. Most of them from Ben. I click past them and open Instagram. I click over to ICU2's account and show Reyes the posts, starting with the ones that showed all the places where Gus had been. "At first, I didn't know who this was, I mean, I wanted to believe it was Gus, but how . . .?" I shook my head.

"What is it, Mrs. Ellison?"

"I'm embarrassed to admit this. I don't know why, but I think it was all the medication Ben had given me, but I really did think I saw our son. That night of the storm, outside in our backyard. It looked like Gus. And I thought maybe he was reaching out to me with these posts."

"What did your son's cell phone look like, do you remember?"

"Of course, I do. I gave it to him—well, we did, Ben and I, for his birthday two years ago. It was the latest model and he—"

"What color was it?"

"Black. Anyway, I thought he led me outside with this post." I scroll down to the post of the backyard and show it to him. "Like maybe he needed me to know something."

Reyes stares down at the picture. "You were outside that night? What time?"

"Around midnight. The storm had blown open the cellar door. Which was strange because I always keep it secure. I realized later maybe you had opened it."

"Me? Why?"

"This happened right after I saw you behind my house that day."

"No," Meyers interjects, and I startle. I forgot that he was there. "We wouldn't go into your cellar," he adds. "Not without a warrant."

Then who? I hear, "Maybe Gus opened it." This from Mia. I give her a little shake. *No, my dear. I know better than that. At least now I do.*

Reyes doesn't notice as he reads through the posts on my phone, pausing here and there. "So, which post led you to your new doll? What's her name?"

I reach over and run my finger along the screen, scrolling. My heart thudding. How much can I trust him? "This one with the wheelbarrow."

We're looking at the post with the wheelbarrow parked by the dumpster in the alley. I think back to the homeless man, John, and how he had poor Mia wrapped in a rag and I feel a strange mixture of indignation and gratitude. Grateful that he'd kept her safe. Irritated that she was so poorly kept.

"This doll was left in *this* alley?"

"That's right. In that wheelbarrow."

He squints closer. "This is by Carmen's, downtown."

"Yes. That's how I found the alley. I matched the partial sign in the photo to that restaurant. I didn't recognize it right away, though. You must know the area better than me."

He and Meyers exchange a look and he resumes scrolling. "This park bench. It looks like it's at Simon Park."

Meyers gets up and moves behind the settee, looking over our shoulders at the screen.

"That's right," I say, pointing to the post of the balloons. "And the next post is at the lake there." I look to Blythe and shudder. These three beauties, all going through such difficult times. Hauled around in a dirty wheelbarrow, drowned in a lake, Bo Peep's head smashed to pieces. "That's where I found Blythe. But I wouldn't have found her if it weren't for the balloons. The strings were tied around her and she was submerged underwater."

Reyes's hand starts to tremble. "Which doll is Blythe again?"

I pick her up and smooth her dress. "This one, of course. Don't you remember? I introduced you to her the other day."

He nods slowly. "I remember now." He points to the only one of the three whose name I haven't mentioned yet. "I don't think you've introduced me to this one."

I hesitate.

"Mrs. Ellison. What's this doll's name?"

Don't be stupid, Mona!

I could lie. I could give him one of the names that are on the tip of my tongue, Rachel, or Tina, or Meg, but Detective Reyes is thorough and smart, and it will only take him a couple clicks on any doll reference site to find her true identity. My stomach clenches. *Stupid, stupid, stupid!* The words echo around me from the voices in my head and I squeeze my eyes shut. The voices are lying. I've listened to Daddy's voice and Ben's voice and the voices that whisper to me in the dark and shout at me in the daylight and they are all lies.

That hard resolve comes back to my gut. I can trust Detective Reyes. I know I can. I take a deep breath, open my eyes, and tell him the truth. "Her name is Mia."

Meyers's cell rings. He steps aside to take the call. When he returns, he looks excited. He motions for Reyes to join him by the door. They exchange a few words, and then Reyes tells me that he'll be back later. Before he leaves, he pauses and says, "I have to go now, but I'm going to need you to give me a full statement about these posts. It's important. Will you do that for me?" I nod and they leave the room.

A part of me thinks I should feel better now, but my happy place seems emptied of whatever short-lived hope had kept my head above the waves of fear. I set Mia down, run a finger over Bo Peep's new dress, and hurry over to lock the door again.

THIRTY-ONE

Supplemental Crime Report (continued)

Case No. 3167 – 9824

Belington Police Department, Homicide Unit

At approximately 1500 hours on November 2, Detective Meyers and I were at the Ellison residence interviewing Mona Ellison, when Officer Cagle called and notified us that he had located a steel claw hammer in the culvert drain located under the crossroads of Midfield Rd. and Blackberry Farm Road, approximately halfway between the crime scene and the residence of Ben and Mona Ellison. The tool was photographed, documented, taken into evidence, and transported to County Forensics Lab for analysis. On November 4 at 1130 hours, I received a phone call from forensics indicating that blood removed from the instrument showed an initial match to the victim's blood type, DNA match pending (see attached form). Forensic specialist also indicated the lifting of several viable prints on the steel handle and cheek portion of the hammer that were a positive match to prints for Ben Ellison, placed into record upon a DUI arrest in 1992. An arrest warrant was issued for Ben Ellison on November 4 at 1215 hours.

Report Signature: Detective Lucas Reyes

WHAT THEY DON'T KNOW

Wednesday, November 4

M ia and I stand at the tower window, watching the murder
tourists cruise through the neighborhood. A dark, grue-
some crime, happening around Halloween . . . just the right
mixture to attract every freak in town.

They drive by the barn first, hopping out of their vehicles for
selfies, and then some of them venture into the neighborhood to
peek at the dead woman's place. A half hour earlier, a dark van
pulled up to the barn with several teens dressed as zombies.
They drank beer and shot videos of themselves before taking
a slow drive-by, gawking and pointing at Tara's house. At one
point, one of them slid the side van door open and dumped a
couple dozen empty beer cans into the street. The wind instantly
scattered them. Ben is in the side yard now, picking cans out of
the boxwoods, one by one, with gloved hands, like a truant on
the side of the highway picking up litter to fulfill his community
service hours. His shoulders are stooped, his hair disheveled,
and his shirt half untucked. I've never seen him look so untidy.

After the police left Monday, I was scared he'd try to break
into the tower room again. Instead, he brought up dinner and
set it by the door and then left. I don't know where he went, but
he must have talked to Alice and Selma at some point because
they stopped by several times while he was gone. I ignored the
bell. Finally, I fell asleep, only to drift in and out of nightmares
and then wake around three in the morning. It took a moment
to register what had disturbed my sleep, but then I heard a long
soulful groan emitting from the bowels of our home and echoing
through the old heating grates. Instantly, I knew what it was.
I'd recognized it from before. The cellar door. Not the outside
bulkhead door, but the one that allows access from the kitchen.
Like a trap door, it swings open in the corner of the kitchen
to reveal a set of rickety wood steps leading into the cellar.

Convenient for the turn-of-the-century wife who might need to run down for stored root vegetables while cooking dinner. I've always thought it was creepy. We'd secured it that night, after we'd discovered that Gus had been using it for clandestine meetings with Mia. Ben had apparently reopened it last night. Why?

I'm wondering about this and scrolling on my phone, googling the name Tara York and reading news reports, when a familiar sedan cruises around the corner, followed by two marked police vehicles.

Reyes and Meyers.

A few minutes later the bell rings. Have they come for me?

The bell rings three more times before I reach the foyer. I've brought Bo Peep with me and clutch her closely as I open the door to Reyes and Meyers and two other officers. My chest muscles constrict with anxiety. I suck in a long, jagged breath and exhale, "Yes?"

Reyes speaks first. "We have a search warrant. It covers your residence, vehicles, and outbuildings. Where is your husband?"

Meyers and the other officers push past me and enter the house, dispersing in different directions. Reyes lingers and gives me a hard look. "Mr. Ellison. Is he home?"

"Yes. Outside. Around the side of the house." I'm surprised he hasn't come around yet.

Reyes steps aside and says something to another officer, and then comes back to me. "Is there anything in the designated premises that we should know about? Anything thing that might be evidence in a crime?"

I nod and whisper a dry, "Yes." My mouth like cotton. "Please, I'm sorry . . . I wanted to tell you before, but I . . . Ben told me I was hallucinating . . . and then when I started to realize . . . he . . . I was afraid of Ben . . . of what he might do to me."

Reyes's features soften.

"Ben accidently killed that girl, Mia Jones." I hold out Bo Peep. "I have proof here. Bo Peep's dress. It's made from the sweatshirt he wore that night when he took Mia Jones's body away in our Range Rover. Ben told me to get rid of it, the sweatshirt, but . . . this is the only way I knew to hide it. It has Mia's blood on it."

The officer returns and interrupts. "Ben Ellison isn't here. He's gone."

THIRTY-TWO

M. ELLISON: I do.

M. ELLISON:

Transcribed Report
Recorded Interview – Part 1

Belington Police Department, Investigative Unit
Case No. 3167 – 9824
Date filed: November 4

DET. REYES: This interview is being recorded. I am
Detective Lucas Reyes and I'll be conducting this interview. Detective Meyers is attending as witness. Also
attending is Trish Lee, attorney for Mona Ellison. We
are conducting this interview in Interview Room 2B,
Belington Police Department, 1400 West Indian Trail
Road, Belington, Illinois. Please state your full name
and address.

M. ELLISON: Monica Anne Ellison. 13 Harvest View
Lane, Belington, Illinois, 60500.

DET. REYES: Thank you. Please state your relationship
to Ben Ellison.

M. ELLISON: He's my husband.

DET. REYES: Thank you. You understand that this is a formal statement and that anything you say here may and will be used in a court of law.

M. ELLISON: I do.

DET. REYES: Do you know the current whereabouts of your husband?

M. ELLISON: I do not.

DET. REYES: Earlier today, during the course of a search conducted at your residence, you presented me with a collector doll as evidence to a crime. Can you explain this for the record?

M. ELLISON: That doll was Bo Peep. And I didn't mean to give her to you. Just the dress. I'd like her back, please.

DET. REYES: Don't worry. I'm taking good care of her. About her dress?

M. ELLISON: I made that from one of Ben's sweatshirts. It was the only thing I knew to do with it, you see, he told me to get rid of it because it had blood on it. Mia Jones's blood.

DET. REYES: Can you explain how the sweatshirt came to have her blood on it?

M. ELLISON: Mia Jones and our son, Gus, were dating, but Ben didn't approve. Gus actually met Mia at Ben's clinic (laughs), isn't that ironic, but anyway, Ben told him to not see her and you know how that goes with kids, he did it anyway. He snuck around behind our backs. Ben was furious. That night that it happened . . . (inaudible articulation) . . . that night Mia died, it was horrible.

DET. REYES: What night was this?

M. ELLISON: (long pause)

DET. REYES: Mrs. Ellison? Do you recall the date that this occurred?

M. ELLISON: I know that it was three days before our son died. (inaudible articulation)

DET. REYES: Please continue, Mrs. Ellison.

M. ELLISON: We were in bed and we heard something, and Ben went down to see what it was. When he didn't come up, I thought maybe I should call the police, but I went down to check first and . . .

DET. REYES: Take your time.

M. ELLISON: I went to the kitchen and the trap door to the cellar was open. I called to Ben, but I was so scared, thought a burglar hurt Ben or something, but it was so much worse. I found him in the cellar. The girl, Mia Jones, I didn't know right then, but later, Ben told me he'd found her coming up the cellar stairs. Apparently, Gus had been meeting her there and she hadn't heard from Gus and was sneaking in to see him. Ben was furious. There was a fight and he, Ben, well, he said it was an accident. She fell down the stairs and . . . she was dead. (long pause)

DET. REYES: Then what did you do?

M. ELLISON: Ben was in a state. I've never seen him so out of control. He begged me to help him. He said he knew the girl from his clinic . . . she didn't have any family, no one would know, but if her death was linked to him, he'd lose his license, his career, everything we'd worked for, or worse. (long pause) He said maybe someone would blame our son and I couldn't let that happen. I . . . I helped him cover her death. But he said it was an accident. An accident.

DET. REYES: Tell me how you helped. What did you do?

M. ELLISON: Ben did most of it. He told me to find something heavy that he could tie to her.

DET. REYES: Did you?

M. ELLISON: I tried. But I was so upset, I couldn't think. I didn't find anything. Ben got angry. He told me to go get the wheelbarrow instead. So I did. By the time I got back with it, he had found something, I don't know what. He told me to drive the Range Rover to the back road behind our property and he used the wheelbarrow to bring her out there. I helped him . . . (inaudible articulation) I can't believe I . . . God forgive me, but I helped him put her body into the back of the Range Rover. He took the wheelbarrow, too. And left.

DET. REYES: You didn't go with him.

M. ELLISON: No. He told me to clean up the blood stain on the cellar floor. Where she hit her head.

DET. REYES: Where was your son at this time?

M. ELLISON: Sleeping upstairs. He had always been such a heavy sleeper. (crying) The next day, Gus came home and was (crying) . . . he kept saying her name over and over . . . (crying) . . . I think he'd been looking for her and thought she'd left town or maybe that Ben had threatened her to make her leave Gus alone or something. He was so upset and wouldn't talk to me, locked himself in his room. Later that night I heard Ben and Gus arguing downstairs and I went to see what was wrong, but Gus just screamed at me "Why?" and ran out of the house . . . (crying) . . . Ben refused to talk to me, too. I've lived in a dark hell since then, not knowing what Ben told him, what Gus believed . . . or why later he . . . (crying)

T. LEE: This is enough. My client needs a break.

DET. REYES: Okay. We'll take a break.

Reyes meets up with Meyers in the hallway after the interview. "Has forensics been able to retrieve anything from the cell phone found under Tara York's body?"
"Haven't heard."

"Can you check with them?"

Meyers nods. "Will do. Not likely, though. It was damaged. Nonoperable. Why?"

"Mrs. Ellison said that Gus had a black phone. I looked at the death report from his suicide. There was no phone recovered from the scene. What kid goes anywhere without their cell phone these days?"

"You got a point there, buddy."

Reyes frowns. "See if they can make it a priority. Any leads on Ellison?"

"Nothing yet. He seems to have simply vanished."

THIRTY-THREE

Thursday, November 5

Hard times change a person mentally, I know this. I measure the emotional effects of my difficulties all the time, but this morning, I notice just how cruel the stress of the past couple weeks has been to my appearance. I barely recognize the woman in the mirror. My jawline is softer, my eyes dulled, my dark hair faded from rich brown to something that looks like a dusty schoolroom chalkboard, fleshy bags puff out from under my eyes, and creases radiate from the edges of my mouth. Stress and grief and anger have aged me almost overnight. I'm living in fear that Ben will show up at any time, angry that I'd told the police about what happened that night when Mia died, and angry that his crazy wife hadn't kept quiet and retained the image of the bereaved mother who knew nothing.

The whole world is looking for him. Reyes suggested that I temporarily relocate somewhere safer, with friends or family. But both my parents are gone, and over the years, the scope of my life has become narrow, constricted to just Ben and Selma, Alice, and . . . it doesn't really matter. The truth is that until Ben is caught and locked up, I'm not going to be safe anywhere, so I might as well be here, in our house, with my dolls. I nod across the vanity to Mia and Blythe, but not Bo Peep, she's still with Detective Reyes, and I offer them a smile. Despite everything, I want to be strong for them, but my hand tremors as I slide on my lipstick and add a coat of mascara. I dab and blot, nod my approval at my reflection, and then squirm into trousers and a sweater, tie my hair back, and add simple earrings. I pick up Mia and Blythe.

Downstairs, I take another quick peek in the foyer mirror. I can't help it. Keeping up appearances is exhausting. The press is everywhere, snapping pictures, shooting video, asking questions. And the murder tourists are worse than paparazzi. They trapped me yesterday on my way home from the police department, out in the front yard, with their phones in my face. I've started showing up in social media. At first, I was mortified when I started seeing public photos of me. *Do I really look that old? That hip-heavy?* But then I noticed the accompanying hashtags: #SupportMona and my favorite: #MomOfGus

To my surprise, I've become the new poster mama for women in misery: scorned women, bereaved mothers, mothers with mental illness . . .

My cell rings. It's my attorney, Trish. My stomach clenches. I usually call her, not the other way around. "Hey, Trish. Is everything okay?"

"I'm outside."

"What?" I move to the front window and part the curtains and scan the group of reporters and gawkers gathered in the street. "I don't see you anywhere."

"Right. Make sure your back door is unlocked, okay?"

I position Mia and Blythe comfortably on the sofa before opening the back door. Trish is picking her way across the yard in wide trouser pants and stilettos, her wickedly angled silver-blonde hair bouncing along her jaw line. She half stumbles across the threshold of my mudroom in a chilly gust of decaying leaves, wood smoke, and Chanel perfume.

I shut the door behind her and flip the bolt lock. "What is it? Did they find Ben?"

"Coffee first." She breezes past me to the kitchen and shimmies out of her black trench, tossing it over the back of a chair. I pour two mugs, add cream to mine, and we settle at the kitchen table in partial darkness. I've pulled every drape and blind in the house for privacy.

She leans back confidently in her chair, mug in hand, and crosses her legs. I notice a clump of sod stuck on the point of her heel, like a shish-kebabbed piece of meat. "We're at a major tipping point here, thanks to Ben," she says.

"What do you mean? Did he turn himself in?"

"No. But don't worry—they will find him soon. He's getting sloppy. He videotaped himself making a statement and put it on YouTube. He sent a link to all the major news outlets. It's got tens of thousands of views already." She slides her mug onto the table and extracts her phone from the outer pocket of her briefcase, taps and scrolls, and turns it my way. Ben's front and center, buttoned up tight, tie straight, hair in place, and speaking in his sage doctor voice.

I want to assure you that these allegations against me are false. I am not responsible for the tragic deaths of Mia Jones or Tara York. I am a victim of my wife's delusional emotional state brought on by the unfortunate death of our son. I beg you to show her mercy during this time of intense bereavement. Mental illness is a disease that wreaks havoc on one's perception of reality. She can't be held responsible for bringing false allegations against—

"Okay, that's enough. I can't listen to this." I sip and swallow. My hand jitters, and coffee slurps over the brim. I give up and set the mug down. That voice, so calm, so right, from the one who has calmed me, soothed me, cared for me for all these years, and now he is saying . . . *my wife's delusional emotional state . . . false allegations . . . I am a victim . . .* "Is that true? Is what he's saying true? Has Gus's death done something to my mind? Am I imagining all this, falsely accusing—"

"Stop, Mona. Stop and listen to yourself. Don't you see what he's done to . . . well, of course you don't. You've been conditioned to this type of treatment for years."

"What do you mean?"

She studies me for a second and then goes back to her phone. "He's manipulating you. Can't you see it? Here, I'm not the only one who thinks it. Listen to some of these comments: *Classic example of narcissism, Doc. I feel for your wife. Play the victim, blame the victim. Gaslighting anyone, Dr. Ellison? Anyone diagnosed you as a sociopath. I hate to think about all the kids you've screwed up, maybe even your . . .*"

Trish's voice trails off, but I can fill in the blank. *Maybe even your own son.*

I pull back and fold into myself.

"Mona? What are you thinking?"

"I'm thinking that I don't know what the truth is anymore."

She looks alarmed. "What do you mean?"

"It's just that I used to think things would be different if Ben had been around more and taken more interest in Gus instead of pouring himself into the new clinic. That he should have concentrated his skills on helping our son instead of helping other people's kids. Now I wonder if Gus would have been better off if Ben had been completely out of the picture. Was Ben some sort of toxin, poisoning our family, destroying it from within?"

"I can't answer that, Mona. I'm sorry. I think you have to focus on your future now." She taps her phone. "You can see how great this is for your case, right?" Trish says.

"No. Not really."

"It's not Tara York's murder that I'm concerned about, Mona. Evidence is mounting against Ben. But don't forget, by your own admission, you helped cover Mia's death. You're still looking at a possible charge, a record, a—"

"But I . . . I explained to the police that Ben told me to . . ."

"I know, Mona. I know. That's why this case is so important to me. You deserve someone who will look out for you and protect your rights. And this . . ." She points to the phone. "This video Ben posted is a gift."

"I still don't understand."

"York's murder has thrust Ben into the spotlight. It's a titillating story, right? A beautiful victim, a love affair, blood and gore, and all the evidence clearly points to Ben, a once well-respected family man, wealthy, successful, and now on the run from the law . . . let's face it, the higher you are the harder you fall. And the public loves to watch the descent."

"That's a depressing thought."

"Not in this case. I can use the whole manipulation thing in your defense. The public buys into it, the state's attorney will, too. There's a good chance you'll come out of this without any charges." She glances over my hair and nails. Examining me, analyzing me. I swear, her brain never shuts off. "You know," she says. "Don't make any changes to your appearance. The way you look says 'mother.' That's what we want. Just don't leave this house with any of those damn dolls, understood?"

I feel my jaw clench, but she doesn't notice. She glances at the watch on her wrist, an oversized, chunky piece, paired with several gold bracelets. "Looks like we've got enough time to practice."

"Practice what?"

"Your talking points. You need to solidify your story: Ben manipulated you, you believed him, he convinced you that you're crazy. Has he ever called you crazy? You could play that up. And be sure to mention the toxic cocktail of meds he was feeding you, and the posts, the posts are important."

She speaks with such confidence and so casually that it makes it sound as if organizing and reducing someone's life into a few hand-picked and well-spun dramatic points is as normal as brushing your teeth. Maybe to her it is.

She continues: "You know, I was impressed with the way you handled that interview the other day with Detective Reyes. When you told him about those posts, I got chills all over. So scary what someone will do to manipulate another person. Anyway, I made a copy of it. I think you should read it over a few times. Then when the time comes, just tell your story the same way you told Reyes in the interview. The girl you told him about, Ru, well, I got word today that they picked her up on a petty drug charge. She'll make a statement in exchange for leniency." She leaned over and patted my hand, a big fat smile plastered on her face. "It was brilliant the way you dropped that little bread crumb at the end of the interview. Damn brilliant."

Brilliant? Trish thinks my testimony was brilliant? Damn brilliant even, and those old voices, Ben's voice—*Stupid girl . . . Don't be stupid, Mona*—start to fade, and I'm left to wonder at the new Mona who began to emerge during this interview just a few days ago:

Transcribed Report
Recorded Interview – Part 2

Belington Police Department, Investigative Unit
Case No. 3167 – 9824

DET. REYES: This is part two of a recorded interview conducted today, November 4. This is Detective Lucas

Reyes, interviewer. Detective Meyers is attending as witness. Also attending is Ms. Trish Lee, attorney. We are in Interview Room 2B, Belington Police Department, 1400 West Indian Trail Road, Belington, Illinois. Please state your full name and address.

M. ELLISON: Monica Anne Ellison. 13 Harvest View Lane, Belington, Illinois, 60500.

DET. REYES: Thank you. I want to move on from the night of Mia Jones's death and discuss the events leading up to the murder of Tara York.

M. ELLISON: (sighs) Okay.

DET. REYES: I just need to cover all our bases. You understand that this is a formal statement and that anything you say here may and will be used in a court of law.

M. ELLISON: Yes. I understand.

DET. REYES: Thank you. You are aware that two cell phones were discovered at Tara York's homicide scene. One belonged to the victim, the other has been identified as belonging to your son, Gus. Can you tell me when you saw that phone last?

M. ELLISON: A few days before Gus's death. We'd been having trouble with him, just the normal teen issues that most parents have—anyway, he was caught dating someone that we didn't approve of him seeing.

DET. REYES: What was the name of the girl he was dating?

M. ELLISON: Mia Jones. You see, Gus was seeing a psychiatrist at Ben's clinic, Dr. Adler, because of his issues . . . well, Mia Jones received services there and they somehow met one another . . . which under normal circumstances would have been okay, it's not like we didn't approve of him dating, it's just that she . . . well, she . . . Ben knew that she had a drug issue, and we were afraid she would be a bad influence on Gus.

DET. REYES: I understand. So, Ben took his phone away to keep them from communicating?

M. ELLISON: Exactly. I asked Ben about it after Gus died, but Ben said it wasn't a good idea for me to look at it. He thought it would make things harder on me, I guess. (long pause) I think that's why Mia came by that night she died. She probably couldn't get ahold of Gus on his phone.

DET. REYES: So as far as you know, your son never got his phone back.

M. ELLISON: (inaudible articulation.)

DET. REYES: Tell me about the Instagram account belonging to ICU2.

M. ELLISON: (sigh) Well, when I saw "I see you too," I thought . . . when you lose someone you love, you never stop searching for signs, for messages, for . . . for hope. And I thought I'd found that . . . (laughing) (crying) on Instagram. That sounds crazy, I know. Now I look back and I wonder where my mind was, but at the time . . . maybe it was the medications I was taking . . .

DET. REYES: Was it the name, ICU2, that made you think it was Gus?

M. ELLISON: Not right away, but the photos on ICU2's profile did. They obviously came from his camera roll. Pictures of his school, places he'd been, things that were . . . were uniquely Gus. But then the new posts started and . . . I was looking at Gus's real Instagram profile at a post about the Range Rover, the one that was totaled, and I saw a new comment from ICU2. That's what led me to the account.

DET. REYES: And that comment was?

M. ELLISON: "I know why." That's it. "I know why." I thought at the time that it was in response to Gus's post. He'd shown a picture of the Range Rover after the wreck and he'd written something like, "My dad did this." And the comment from ICU2 was, "I know why."

DET. REYES: Which you took to mean that ICU2 knew that the Range Rover was wrecked on purpose to cover evidence from Mia Jones's death.

M. ELLISON: Yes.

DET. REYES: (sigh) Okay. I'm going to name some of

the posts on the ICU2 account. You can elaborate on each. Okay?

M. ELLISON: Okay.

DET. REYES: The red park bench.

M. ELLISON: I knew right away that it was from Simon Park. I went there. I thought maybe Gus would be there. Like I said. I wasn't quite right at the time.

DET. REYES: What did you find there?

M. ELLISON: I found the balloons. The balloons that are in the second post. They were on the edge of the lake, tangled in the reeds, at least I thought they were tangled—they were attached to Blythe.

DET. REYES: For the record, who is Blythe?

M. ELLISON: My doll. A childhood doll, my first doll. A gift from my mother. (inaudible articulation) She was in the water. Someone had put her in the water. (inaudible articulation)

DET. ELLISON: What did you think when you found her like that?

M. ELLISON: I . . . I thought Gus put her there. That he was trying to tell me that he knew . . . and that what happened to Mia was the reason he hung himself. (crying)

T. LEE: Maybe we should break.

M. ELLISON: No. I want to finish this. I really did think it was Gus . . . because that's what I *wanted* to believe . . . I didn't want to think that it could be . . . (crying) but no one else could have . . . (crying)

T. LEE: I'm going to insist that we take a break.

DET. REYES: I'll switch topics. Can we talk about the ICU2's post with the wheelbarrow, Mrs. Ellison? Or do you need a break?

M. ELLISON: No . . . let's continue, please. I want to finish so I can go home.

DET. REYES: (sighs) Okay, then. Tell me about the wheelbarrow.

M. ELLISON: It was our wheelbarrow. The one we used that night to get Mia into the car. Ben had taken it with him, now I know he probably needed it to get the body to the lake. But I didn't see it again after that night. It's usually in our shed, but . . . the photo showed it in an alley. I was able to track down the location from the photo and I found the wheelbarrow there. A homeless man had taken it over. He showed me a doll. He said she was left in the wheelbarrow. I convinced him to . . . I traded my watch for the doll.

DET. REYES: Did this homeless man say anything else? Did he see who left the wheelbarrow? Or was there a note left?

M. ELLLISON: No. But I remember that the homeless man's name was John.

DET. REYES: Good. Thank you. Anything else about John?

M. ELLISON: No. But it was the doll that made me realize it wasn't Gus making the posts.

DET. REYES: What do you mean?

M. ELLISON: Gus had no interest in dolls and wouldn't know I'd been looking to buy this particular one. You see, she is a collector's doll and her official collector's name is Mia. And well, the whole thing was too clever. A doll named Mia in a wheelbarrow, our wheelbarrow . . . That's when I knew it had to be Ben. Who else would know all these things? He was trying to drive me crazy. Then I really realized about the meds. What they were doing to me. That's when I stopped taking them.

DET. REYES: Did the location of the alley mean anything to you?

M. ELLISON: No. Why? Should it?

DET. REYES. Tell me about the barn post.

M. ELLISON: When can I get Bo Peep back?

DET. REYES: Soon, I promise.

M. ELLISON: (long pause) I don't . . . do I have to talk about the barn post? (inaudible articulation)

T. LEE: The barn is a trauma trigger for my client. I think it's best that any questioning pertaining to the barn be conducted under the supervision of her psychiatrist.

M. ELLISON: But I should tell you about the house. The drug house.

T. LEE: (inaudible articulation) I advise you to refrain. We haven't discussed this.

M. ELLISON: It's okay. I should tell them. It might be important.

T. LEE: I'd like to break. I need to confer with my client.

M. ELLISON: No. It's fine.

DET. REYES: Please continue, Mrs. Ellison.

M. ELLISON: When I found out that Ben had lied about where he was, I searched through his things to see if I could find answers. I found a large sum of cash taped behind one of his file cabinet drawers.

DET. REYES: Yes, we located that during the search of your residence.

M. ELLISON: There was also an address with the cash. Scribbled on a small piece of scrap paper. In Ben's handwriting. At the time, I thought it was where he was meeting . . . well, he'd lied about where he was and I . . . I assumed it was an affair. Things hadn't been going well between us since Gus's death . . . but when I got there, it wasn't a hotel or anything, just an old boarded-up house. People were going in and out, and I thought . . . (chuckles) . . . that it was a place where prostitutes work and maybe Ben had gotten into that sort of thing, but then I saw this girl out on the walk and I asked her if she knew Gus . . . and she acted like she did, so I went inside and then I knew that Gus had been there because I recognized the place from a post he'd made.

DET. REYES: You mean ICU2's post.

M. ELLISON: No. Gus's post. On his real profile. At Ellison underscore Gus eighteen. He was on a sofa in the post and that sofa was there, in that house.

DET. REYES: What was the girl's name?

M. ELLISON: She called herself Ru. Short for Ruby. She said she knew Gus. And Mia and . . . and she said she knew Ben.

T. LEE: (inaudible articulation)

DET. REYES: How did she know Ben?

M. ELLISON: She didn't say.

DET. REYES: This is very helpful. Thank you, Mrs.

Ellison. I'm going to need to get that address from you and a description of Ru. We may have more questions later, but I think we can be done for now.

THIRTY-FOUR

After Trish leaves, I spend the rest of the day brooding. I feel closed in. The press is relentless. I've got officers watching the place around the clock in case Ben returns. For days now, I've kept myself behind locked doors, cut off from the outside world, every possible intrusion sealed off: the heavy damask drapes in the living room, the wood slat blinds of the family room, the in-pane blinds closed on our updated French doors we added when we built on the back deck a couple years ago. Upstairs, *swish, clap, swish, clap* . . . I've battened down the hatches—yessiree!—a tight ship I keep. I laugh. And then wonder why I'm laughing. Am I hysterical?

No, not hysterical, I decide, cold and in need of wine. It's evening already and what have I done with my day? Unpacked a couple boxes, perused social media for mentions, replied to two true crime podcasters who are interested in my story. So much attention, yet why do I feel so lonely?

"Do you know?" I ask Mia.

She's propped up on the sofa next to Blythe, her gaze focused on something off to my right. I turn and see that she's looking at the framed photo on the coffee table: Ben and me and Gus. Magic Mountain, at Disney, we're in the cart, plummeting to the depths, hands up, hair flying behind us, our expressions full of joy and abandonment. A magic shot, captured by an automated camera, we didn't even know it'd been taken until we exited the ride. Ben thought it was silly to shell out twenty-five bucks for it. But it'd always been my favorite. One of the few shots where we didn't all look uptight.

I look back at Blythe. "I know. I miss those days, too."

She doesn't answer. I didn't expect her to. Neither she nor Mia has spoken for a while now. No one has. It's been completely quiet, not even my usual voices.

I pop the cork on a bottle of merlot, stack wood, and roll the newspaper and stuff it into the cracks between the logs. Once the fire is burning, I sit back, wrapped in a blanket with a book I'd retrieved earlier from a box in Ben's office. *The Handbook of Narcissistic Disorders*. I'd remembered packing it away the other day. After my discussion with Trish about narcissism, I thought I'd better arm myself with knowledge.

I consider the irony. This is how it all started, right here, in front of this very fireplace with my friends, a book, wine . . . now it was just me, and a couple of synthetic-haired, glass-eyed, silent toys. I tip my glass their way. "Bottoms up, ladies."

Ben's done this to me. Turned me into the type of woman who sits home in the evening drinking wine alone and talking to dolls, who no longer bother to talk back.

My glass is empty.

I reach for the bottle on the coffee table just as a shadow shifts in the crack of the drapes. My hand freezes midair. Did I just imagine that or is someone out there, peeping through my window? Ben?

I scurry down the hall, away from the window, cell phone in hand, but before I dial 911, the doorbell rings and I hear a familiar voice call out, "Mrs. Ellison. Are you home?"

Reyes. The tension drains from my muscles. I unbolt the door and blurt, "There's someone standing outside my window, in the back of the house. I think it's Ben."

He enters and secures the door behind him. His eyes scan

the place as he tosses his briefcase onto my foyer table and guides me into the powder room. He stands protectively in the doorframe, issuing orders over his phone. "She's safe," he says. A few more words are exchanged, then, "Back window. Check the backyard. Secure the entire perimeter."

Silence stretches on, and it seems like forever before we're given the all-clear and Reyes lets me out of the bathroom. "There was no sign of anyone being out there," he says, and we make our way to the family room, where I show him the window. His gaze sweeps over the room, settling on the half-empty bottle of wine. I see a flash of judgement in his eyes: *so drunk that she's seeing things.*

He checks the window's locks and calls in a couple more things while I pour another glass of wine. I lift it toward him with a questioning look, but he shakes his head. I pull the glass close to my chest. "Ben posted a video today. My attorney showed it to me. The way he talked about me . . . the way he sounded . . . it has me on edge. I keep wondering when he's going to show up."

"We're analyzing the video now. There's not much there, no visuals, no ambient audio clues, but we will find him. Trust me."

"My attorney also told me that you picked up Ru, the girl I told you about in the interview?"

"An investigator from the D.A.'s office tracked her down earlier today."

"Did she say anything about how she knew Ben? Anything about Gus?"

"I wish I could tell you more. I can't discuss it. But know that we're doing everything we can."

"I know you are—thank you." I tip my glass his way. "Are you sure you don't want some wine?"

"No . . . I shouldn't. I was just on my way home and thought

I'd stop by, save you a trip down to the department. I can't stay long. I've barely spent any time with my daughter lately. I just popped by to . . . uh . . . here, it's in my briefcase."

I set down my wine and follow him back down the hall, where he lifts Bo Peep out of his briefcase. She's dressed in her frilly undies.

"Bo Peep!" I'm flooded with gratitude. And in that fuzzy wine moment, I throw my arms around him and then instantly back up. "I'm sorry. It's just that I didn't think I'd see her for a while." I reach out to take her, and our fingers brush together. I'm hit with a zap of nerves.

He retracts his hand and stammers, "I never entered her into evidence, only her dress. Sorry it took so long to get her back to you. I . . . I couldn't figure out the right time."

"Your timing is perfect. I've been feeling low, and she is just what I needed to cheer me up." The hug still lingers and strange notions flow through my wine-infused brain: Reyes rescuing me from Ben, from my life, from my hurt . . . and his warm hands holding my Bo Peep tenderly, bringing her safely home. "Are you sure you can't stay for a while? To celebrate Bo Peep's return."

"No, I really can't. I shouldn't have . . . I need to get home to Stella."

He turns and leaves, shutting the door softly behind him. For a second, I'm left with a strange feeling of emptiness, but I look down at Bo Peep and that lonely feeling dissipates.

"You're home," I say to her, and then promptly take her to the family room. As soon as we enter, a collective gasp fills the air: Mia and Blythe are overwhelmed with joy. And talking again.

Witness Statement

State's Attorney's Office
Belington County, Illinois

1402 West Indian Trail Road
Belington, Illinois

Case No. 3167 – 9824
Name of Witness: Ruby Benson   Date: November 5
Address: Mercy Teen Home, 658 N. River Road,
          Belington, Illinois

I am making this statement voluntarily, without reward, promise of reward, threat or force to: Belington County District Attorney's Office

Please describe the incident in your own words, including dates, times, complete names and locations:

On July 23, my boyfriend Jax Jackson and me gave my friend Mia Jones a ride to Gus Ellison's house out in Belington. She told us to drive onto a gravel road behind the house and let her out. It was about 11:00 p.m. when we dropped her off there. She did not come home to the shelter that night and she never picked up her stuff at the shelter. I never saw her again after that. Two days after we dropped her off at Gus Ellison's house, Dr. Ellison was waiting for me in a car outside the shelter where I stay. He asked me to get in the car with him and I did because I knew him from the clinic downtown. Inside the car, he told me that Mia had told him that I brought her to his house that night to meet Gus. He offered me one thousand dollars to keep quiet about it. I took the money and didn't think more about it until I heard that they had found Mia dead. When I told Jax, he talked me into asking for more. I went to the clinic the next day and told Dr. Ellison that I wanted ten thousand dollars or Jax and me would go to the cops. He told me that he had to leave town for a few days but would bring it when he got home. But he never showed up and I didn't get the money from him.

Under penalty of Unsworn Falsification (735 ILCS 5/1-109), I swear that I have read the foregoing statement and that the facts stated in it are true.

Signature of witness: Ruby Benson
DAO: Peter Lynch

THIRTY-FIVE

B o Peep looks cold, poor thing, sitting here in nothing but
her underwear.

"Let's get you dressed," I say and scoop all three dolls into
my arms, along with the almost empty wine bottle, and drift
upstairs to the second floor, shifting my load when my cell rings.

"Are you okay?" Alice asks. "I thought I saw that detective
at your place. Did they find Ben?"

"No. He's still missing. I haven't heard from him."

There's a long pause, I reach the second floor, and she says,
"I miss her."

"Me too." The end of the hall looms dark.

"And Ben . . . I never would have thought that he . . ."

"There was a lot going on that he kept hidden. Even from
me. You couldn't possibly have known. Don't feel like any of
this is your fault." I pause, and then say, "I haven't heard from
Selma."

"She's taking Tara's death hard. Just like all of us. But those
two were so close and . . . and anyway, she's staying with her
boyfriend for a couple of days." I hear something rattling on the
other end and I recognize the sound right away. Pills. I'm not
the only one needing a little help these days. A while back, I'd
peeked in Alice's medicine cabinet and saw a prescription for
one of the same meds Ben prescribed for me. Prescribed for her
nerves after the divorce probably. I get it. No judgement here.

"Did you see Ben's video online?" she asks. "He says he's innocent, he seemed so sincere on the video, but you . . ."

"I did see it, but I don't want talk about it. Not now." For the past couple days, Alice has been asking about Tara's death, wanting to talk through it all, which is understandable, but Trish advised me not to tell anyone the details of the case.

"Sure, I understand."

She grows quiet; I'm not sure what to say, and the conversation stalls. I reach the end of the hall and manage the light switch with my elbow, illuminating the steps to the tower room. Bo Peep lets out a little squeal of excitement.

"What was that?" Alice asks.

"I didn't say anything."

"Oh. Probably something outside. No wonder. All the traffic in the neighborhood. Those strange kids are out at the barn again tonight."

"Strange kids?" I mount the stairs, parched wood creaking underfoot. The girls squirm with excitement in my arms. I almost drop the phone.

"You didn't hear all that noise last night?" Alice is saying. "I called the police, but they didn't do much. It was some sort of party. Must've been about thirty or more of them out there. That music and the way they look, black hair and black clothing, they look like . . . like demons. If they start in again tonight, I'm going to call the cops right away."

Now I'm in the tower room. I put the bottle on my sewing table with a *clunk* and position the girls on the settee—they're so happy—and cross over to the back tower window, the one that overlooks the field.

Twilight is fading into black as several cars turn onto the road and come to a stop, their headlight beams crisscrossing over the field. Shadowy figures emerge and lurk toward the barn, carrying coolers and cell phones, some coupled up, hands and arms intertwined. Already there is a group closer to the barn, drinking and dancing, smashing against one another, arms flailing. "I see them," I tell Alice. And I wonder if it wasn't one of them at my window earlier, one of these dark, demon-like creatures. I cross to the door, turn the lock, and glance at the sofa. Three worried expressions stare back at me. "Don't worry, we're safe," I assure the girls. Alice thinks I'm talking to her and answers in a tiny voice, "Are you sure?"

THIRTY-SIX

Reyes's daughter is at the kitchen table, head in her hands, staring down at an open book, her long locks done up in a tight bun that resembles a bagel perched on top of her head. Her hair is light brown, like her mother's. She even furrows her brows the same as Teresa did when she concentrated. Her eyes, though, are as deep brown as his, and lately, they reflect the same sadness.

He turns back to the stove, gives the pancake batter another stir, and sneaks a peek at his email while he waits for the griddle to get hot. He spots the message he's been waiting for.

Subject: Electronic Forensic Findings #3167-9824
Electronic Forensics Team <admin@eforensicscrime-unit.bpd.org>
To: lreyes@bpd.org

Preliminary Findings Re: Phone IME:
000101234567120/100/110
Model: Apple iPhone
Color: black
Case: Clear
Issued to: Ben Ellison Family Plan

*Destruction to main circuit board and chip unrecover-
able due to extensive damage. To date, no data recovered.*
Full report to follow.

"Aunt Camilla says you're a workaholic."

He startles, slides the phone onto the counter, and begins
ladling batter onto the griddle. "I'm done now and I'm all
yours."

She shrugs and goes back to her book.

"What are you reading, Bug?" Teresa's nickname for her.
He's tried to keep it going. He's tried to keep a lot of things
going.

"A book."

"I know that. What book?"

"It's called *Little Women*."

"Really? That's a big book for fourth grade."

"You've read it?"

"No, no I—"

"It's not for school. Aunt Camilla gave it to me. We're
reading it first and then watching the movie. We're going to do
a different book every couple of months. She picked this one.
I'm picking the next. We're calling ourselves The Smart Girls
Book Club."

"A book club? That's a great idea." Didn't Alice tell him
something about Mona's downfall starting with a discussion
at book club about Mia Jones . . . he shakes his head . . . . *Stay
present.* "How was school today?"

Another shrug.

"How'd your math test go?"

"Can we talk about something else? You always want to
talk about school. It's irritating."

"Okay, then. How many flapjacks do you want?"

"Three for me, two for Flora."

"Two, huh?" He turns and glances at Flora, Stella's constant shadow these days. Teresa had given her the small rag doll for her fifth birthday. Stella never played with it at the time, but recently she's taken it everywhere. Even sneaking it to school in her backpack.

He looks back at his daughter, his mind clicking away.

"Two pancakes," he repeats. "Flora must be hungry tonight." He flips the pancakes and takes an extra plate out of the cabinet.

"What do you mean? Isn't it okay for her to have two?"

"Of course. I just mean, she must've worked up an appetite at school today, or maybe she's extra hungry because she didn't eat lunch or maybe she was upset because of a grade, or—"

"What are you talking about? Flora isn't real, Dad, she's a doll." The eye rolling is new, but she's become a pro at it already.

"I know that. It's just that we always play this pancake thing and . . ." And what? She wouldn't talk directly to him and he hoped maybe through Flora he could—

"*We* never did the 'pancake thing.' It was Mom's thing, okay? Not yours. I mean it was fun back when I was a kid, and she'd make tiny pancakes for Flora, and I'd gobble them up when she wasn't looking, and we'd laugh about it. But it was just a game. I don't actually believe Flora is real. Never did. You don't really think that, do you?"

"No, no, that's not it. It's just that you've been taking her to school, and I thought—"

"So what? I'm not crazy. I just miss Mom, okay?" She slaps the book shut and storms out of the kitchen. A second later he hears her bedroom door shut.

His fault. All his fault. He *is* a workaholic. And this damn York homicide has wormed its way into his head, making him think everyone talks to dolls.

Another ruined evening with Stella. He flips off the griddle and flings open the fridge door. He grabs two beers, turns, and sees the rag doll staring at him from her chair. *You're a lousy father*, she seems to say. He snatches her by the waist, leaving the pancakes to go cold, and heads to the family room, where Tara York's homicide churns in the evening news.

> *Dr. Ben Ellison, local psychiatrist is still missing after police searched his home on Wednesday in connection with the murder of his neighbor, Tara York. Tara York's body was found early Saturday morning, in a barn near their homes, bludgeoned to death. Reports indicate that the police have found the weapon, but no statement has been released as to the identity of that weapon, or any other details surrounding the arrest warrant issued for Dr. Ben Ellison. Police are asking that if you have any information regarding his whereabouts, to please contact them immediately. Earlier this week, Dr. Ellison released a short video regarding the accusations against him.*

Reyes has watched this post that Ellison made from a nontraceable burner phone a couple dozen times, and still every single time he listens to Ellison spew off about Mona, he gets pissed again. The whole YouTube thing is too slick for his taste. It reeks of manipulation.

He twists the cap off his beer and takes a long swig, and envisions himself collaring the guy, pushing him around a little, and slapping the cuffs on his wrists, and how grateful Mona would be.

The beer goes down smooth, and Reyes reaches for another one just as Gus's high school photo flashes onto the screen. He leans forward. There's a quick report on his death and then the unexpected: someone has leaked to the press that Tara was Ben's counselor. Not much more about it on the official news, but a quick check of his phone and Reyes sees that accusations are already burning their way into the public's narrative on social media: *Ben Ellison: Cheats with Neighbor! Ben Ellison Kills His Counselor. Ben Ellison Is a Cheating Killer.* Direct indictments based on little more than a desire to "go viral." Ben's YouTube plea is going up in smoke against news of his relationship with Tara, even though—so far—their relationship has proven only to be a professional one. But combined with backlash against Ben's earlier YouTube statement, social media will expand to the peripheral as well: *Gus was dating Mia Jones. Gus killed himself after Mia's death. Mia's body, like Tara's, was also found not far from the Ellison's residence.* All facts. And all of them are things that Ben might have confided to his counselor, Tara. Things that would have ruined his career. Ben Ellison had a strong motive for wanting to keep Tara quiet for good.

Reyes takes another long sip and tips his beer bottle to the left, where Flora the rag doll sits slumped against the sofa cushion. "Ben Ellison is as guilty as hell," he says.

And Flora agrees.

215

THIRTY-SEVEN

The moon hangs large on the horizon as the demon creatures continue their frenzied dance. The scene is surreal, something out of a zombie movie, like the ones Gus used to binge watch on the weekends.

I'm entranced and continue to watch for a few minutes, before moving to the other window, careful to remain hidden behind the gauzy curtain. I look over the street. The neighborhood is empty; the press seems to have had their fill for the day. Across the way, I see Alice in her family room, pacing, her phone to her ear. Occasionally, she stops and peers through her front window, and then goes back to pacing again. Probably still upset about the party by the barn.

I back up and scroll through social media, searching #MomOfGus. I'm checking constantly now, eager to see if there are any new mentions of me. It's heady to be in the limelight, and a little daunting. I'm constantly on the edge, my nerves a frazzled jumble as I wait for the rest of the story to unfold. It won't be long before other facts come to the surface: Gus dating Mia Jones, Mia Jones a patient at Ben's clinic, Mia Jones's body found in a park just down the road from our house. Mia and then Tara, not one crime but two, both with connections to our family. The press will crucify us and then pick at the carnage like starving vultures.

Every challenge is an opportunity to grow. Hope you meant it, my dear Ben.

Oh! New photos of me have popped up. I haven't left the house for days, yet they still manage to get pictures: Me at the mailbox. (I look good in that one!) Me opening my door to grab the paper. Me peering through the front curtains.

And the rants against Ben (I secretly enjoy them) are getting crueler. I can't help but grin a little at a few of the comments on a post put out by our local news station: a photo of our family that Ben had used on his professional website: Ben, Gus, and me, sitting on the front porch of our home, dressed in dark jeans and white T-shirts—the casual, monotone look that says we're all in this together. Except our smiles are a little too tight, Ben's forehead vein is popping like a squiggly, throbbing worm descending from his hairline, and Gus, poor Gus, he seems to shrink into nothing next to his father. I hate this photo.

And the caption: Local doctor Ben Ellison is still missing following a warrant issued for his arrest in connection to the murder of Tara York. Police ask that if you have any information regarding Ben Ellison's whereabouts or the murder of Tara York to please call Crime Stoppers at the number listed below. For a full timeline and in-depth reporting, head over to abc4. com.

#BelingtonNews #TaraYorkMurderUpdate #BenEllisonMissing **#MomOfGus**
3 hours ago
1,245 likes
View all 138 comments
duke_perlmutter I'd like to be the one to find him.
   2h 38 likes Reply
   2h **babsplustwo** he can't hide forever
   2h **beamer.lopez** check the dump with all the other toxic crap
maygirl Feel for #MomOfGus, but truly is a comfort to know

217

that I'm not the only one to fall for a narcissistic man. Wish mine would disappear too.

1h 12 likes Reply

1h **timetorecover_1** hope one day you can heal and break away

1h **nicolamatthis** I hear ya!

1h **usedandabused** Mine is out of my life. And the only peace I get is knowing that he'll never be happy.

I pull my shoulders back and take a deep breath. Wow. A lot of women relate to me. They're looking at me and my story to improve their own lives, empower themselves. It feels good to help people. For once, I'm not the defenseless woman in need of a savior.

I read more comments and then move on to a post from a true crime podcast: a photo of me as I step out onto the porch for my grocery delivery, baggy sweatshirt, hair thrown up in a pony. I remember Trish's words: "You look like a mom."

The caption reads: Mona Ellison has remained in seclusion since the murder of Tara York, and the emergence of her husband, Ben Ellison, as the primary suspect. Ben Ellison is at large and wanted by the authorities. This has all occurred only a few months after the death of the Ellisons' only son, Gus. Opinions on social media paint a picture of Ben as a verbally abusive husband cheating on his bereaved wife with the murder victim, who also happened to be his wife's best friend. Here's what we know.

- Tara York – longtime friend and neighbor of the Ellisons, counselor, single, no children.
- Tara York was found bludgeoned to death in a barn near the Ellisons' home.
- Ben Ellison made the 911 call.

- Ben Ellison had been seeing Tara York for counseling.
- The Ellisons' only son was found dead by suicide in the same barn three months prior.
- Police had enough evidence to issue a warrant for Ben Ellison's arrest.
- Ben Ellison is on the run from the law.

Comments? Speculation on motive? Link in bio for more of the heartbreaking story and additional photos. We will be covering this case over the next few segments, so tune in for a deeper dive. At this point, we have more questions than answers.

#truecrime #news #TaraYorkMurder #murder #MomOfGus
#BenEllison #truecrimecommunity #murdermystery #suspicious
1 hour ago
134 likes
View all 18 comments

annabanana Her husband did it for sure. #cheater
17m 1 like Reply
meowmurder News says body found bludgeoned. Did police report the weapon used?
15m 7 likes Reply
8m **TrueCrimeCast @meowmurder** No official report.
Kate_White Tragic
5m 1 like Reply
iam_meangirl so many bad people, so little time #FindBenEllison We love #MomOfGus. Can u get her on your cast?
5m 4 likes Reply
3m **TrueCrimeCast @iam_meangirl** We're working on it!

A true crime podcast! The prospect of being invited as a guest speaker thrills me. I click over and check my email, wondering if they've already reached out. Nothing. What would Trish have to say about me discussing Tara's murder in public? I can almost hear her raspy voice now: "Not a word. Not a single damn word!"

I sigh and glance at Tara's place. Empty, and quiet. Darkness has settled over her home like a pall over a casket. And it's strange to know that she's not there, never will be again. Briefly, I wonder who might move in next. Will Selma list her place? It'll be a hard sell. Selma has said before that houses with a known dark history aren't desirable except to out-of-towners unaware of the background. Our own house contract has fallen through, the buyers pulling out after Tara's death. I'm relieved, actually. Our home will remain a home, while Tara's house already has that abandoned, neglected feel. As do I, in knowing that my best friend betrayed me in the worst possible way. I don't like to think of her dead, but I don't like to think of her alive and sleeping with my husband either. Maybe I simply won't think of her for a while.

Movement draws my gaze two houses down to Selma's place. Her bedroom curtains rustle as if caught in a breeze, and that's what I think is happening, until they suddenly part, wide open, revealing a smudgy figure standing there, looking . . . looking at me? Is that Selma? Did she come home early? I squint, trying to make out . . . and my phone vibrates. A text notification flashes on my screen, but I don't recognize the number. I enter my passcode and open my text app.

8:42 pm
I'm going to turn myself into the police, but we need to talk first. Please. You owe me as much. Ben

My head snaps up, the window is empty, but . . . I scan the front of the house, searching some sign of movement. Nothing. But there was someone there a few seconds ago, wasn't there?

I shoot a quick text to Selma. *Are you home?*

Seconds tick off and then her response: *No. Back next week. Alice should be home if you need something, okay?*

Not Selma. Then who? Ben! I move toward the corner of the room, away from the window, and try to tap in a call Reyes, but blood rushes to my head, and my fingers fail me. I stand paralyzed, my muscles locked in doubts and fear when a sharp screeching noise causes me to startle. The cellar door? My heart thuds wildly as my ears fill with the sound of hundreds of tiny voices in a rhythmic, staccato chorus: *Danger, danger, danger . . .*

THIRTY-EIGHT

I sink to the floor, balled up with my hands over my ears and stay that way, shaking and trembling until I remember to breathe, in deep and out slowly, over and over. Soon my heart rate slows, my muscles loosen, the voices soften and fade, and the house is quiet now. No screeching noises. No footsteps. Nothing.

Was it Ben that I saw? Is that even possible? But I know it is. I force myself to step back to the window and look at Selma's house again. No shadows, no rustling of curtains, and I let out a long sigh. I go back to my phone, my fingers steady now, but I hesitate. What if what I saw was nothing but a reflection on the windowpane, or maybe headlights from a passing car, and my unhealed mind filled in the blanks? Truth is, Ben could have sent that text from anywhere.

My thumb slides over my phone and I reread the text. *We need to talk. You owe me as much. You owe me . . .* The words loop through my mind. All these years together, the life we've made, the sacrifices, the joys, the sorrows . . . and really, all he's asking is a little of my time. Maybe he's right. Maybe I do owe him.

I shake my head. *Stop, Mona. Don't fall for it.* This is Ben's typical mode of operation, a narcissistic man manipulating me, making me believe something is my fault, that I'm the one who needs help: *you're imagining things, Mona . . . overreacting, not thinking clearly, hallucinating, insecure . . . crazy!* The old me would have fallen for this. But I'm stronger now. The new me, #MomOfGus, isn't a woman who can be manipulated.

I look around the room, at all my friends. "He's wrong. I am not crazy," I say to them. My mind may have been muddled with meds before, but I'm better now. *Aren't I?* I look to my friends for affirmation and breathe easier because not a one of them disagrees with me.

My thumb slides over my screen once again, this time to call the police and report this text, but suddenly the room lights up red and blue, circling strobes pouring through the back window.

I cross the room and peer out, seeing four or five police cruisers crawling down the road behind our place toward the barn and the demon-like frenzied dancing comes to a halt, limbs of the partiers suspended in midair, like a kids' game of freeze tag. *One beat, two beats, three . . .* and then, all hell breaks loose. Cops rush the scene, kids scramble, the shrill blast of sirens fills the air, screaming and yelling, engines revving, and . . . *bam!*

I jerk around. *Bam!* The attic door quivers. *Bam! Bam . . .* Ben? A demon person? My muscles seize and my pores instantly ooze fear, the sour musky scent stings my nostrils. *Dial 911, dial 911 . . .* but my palms are slick, I fumble the phone, and it slides from my hand. *Clunk.* I fall to all fours, my hands scrabbling over the floor.

Bam! I flinch and hiss out fear like a startled cat.

The door smashes open. Ben stands in the frame, face twisted with anger, eyes scanning the room for me. I cower at the hem of the drapes. *Don't see me! Don't see me!* But his gaze latches onto me and he launches forward. I swipe my hands wildly across the floor for my phone, finally my fingertips brush against it, I snap it up . . . but it's ripped from my hand. I'm jerked to my feet, face to face with Ben, his eyes ablaze, the white showing around the entire iris, his forehead vein throbbing at the same tempo as my own heart. He spews his hot, sour words at my face: "You imbecile! What have you done? You've ruined me. Ruined everything."

"I . . . I didn't do . . . I only told them what happened . . . they . . . I'm sorry." His nails dig into the soft flesh of my arm. Snot runs from my nose. I taste it as I plead, "I'm so sorry. Please, please don't—"

A shout outside and he whips his head toward the window, studying the chaos at the barn for a second before turning back to me. Beads of sweat dot his forehead, as a thick bile coats my tongue. He jerks my arm again. "Come on. We're going for a drive." He drags me toward the door.

"A drive? No, no . . ." Once you're in the car, you're dead. That's what the experts say. Has Ben ever said that?

I dig in, try to pull away, thrash my arms. My fingernails connect with his cheek and tear his skin. He shrieks, pulls back, and then lurches forward, retaliating with the back of his hand across my face.

My neck twists, and pain radiates from my jaw, down my neck, my shoulder. My vision blurs as my eyes roll back in my skull, and I feel my legs start to buckle. His grip tightens around my arm. "No, you don't, Mona."

Then both his hands are on me, and I'm moving again, half walking, half being dragged down the steps.

THIRTY-NINE

Reyes knocks back another beer before deciding to call it a night. He trudges up the stairs, Flora in hand, and makes his way into Stella's room. She's asleep, book tented on her chest, light from her bedside lamp casting a soft glow over her face. She looks peaceful and younger, like the child he once knew and understood. He draws in his breath, picks up her book, and tucks Flora next to her as the hard edge of their earlier argument fades away.

"Goodnight, bug," he says, and hesitates before flipping off her light. Cocooned in the covers with her eyes closed, she does look like a bug. The most breathtakingly beautiful, miraculous, courageous bug in the entire universe, and at that moment Reyes feels as if his heart might burst with love. "We did well, Teresa," he says, reaching down and finally flipping off the light. "I just don't know if I can do this without you."

Back in the hall, he turns toward the stairs. He knows a pile of dishes etched with dried food sits on the drainboard, and the laundry basket spills over with his soiled uniforms and her "only wash on cold, Dad" delicates, but he stops and turns around. He's too tired tonight.

It's all he can do to drag himself into the shower. Halfway through, his cell rings. He steps out and catches the call. It's Meyers.

"We might have a problem," he says. "Patrol just drove by

the Ellisons' and the garage door is open. Their car is gone, and no one is answering the door. She's not answering her phone either. I'm on my way to . . . hold on."

The line goes quiet. Reyes shoots a text to Camilla and starts dressing. *Damn, damn, damn.* This shouldn't be happening. Mona wouldn't leave her place, certainly not at night—it has to be Ben.

"Okay. You there?" Meyers is back.

"Yeah. What's going on?"

"That was dispatch with more information. Looks like someone broke into the house through the cellar. Patrol is heading inside."

"Which vehicle is gone?"

"His. Hers is parked on the curb."

"Okay. Get the make and license number to patrol. Let me know what they find in the house. I'll be there as soon as I can."

He hoped to hell they'd find her in the house, asleep, not in a pool of blood like Tara York. How did Ben slip through? If he's hurt Mona—

FORTY

My mind is like a dark cave, endless and full of echoes, and as we drive the same nightmare bounces in its recesses: Gus in the barn, the rope taut, his neck bent, the bulging of his eyes, his tongue lax and dangling between his lips, and then Tara . . . poor Tara, blood splattered everywhere. . .

The visions flash like strobes behind my eyelids until I'm shook awake. "Listen to me," Ben says. "I said, listen to me!"

My cheek still burns and my neck hurts, but I manage to roll my head his way. He's moved his hands back to the wheel, precisely at ten and two, and his eyes, illuminated by the light reflecting off the rearview mirror, look like wet glass. Sweat streaks his cheeks.

The whole car stinks like fear. "Take me back," I manage. "To the house—"

"You're not going back until we talk." He turns and levels his half-crazed eyes my way. "You're sick, Mona. You need help. I can get you help."

"I don't need your type of help anymore."

"What do you mean by that? I've done nothing but—" The car jerks to the right. His head snaps back to the road, he overcorrects, and light from oncoming headlights fills the windshield. We swerve again, back over the line, nearly missing an oncoming car.

"Take me home!"

"Tell me what you told the police."

"Nothing. I swear. They found your prints on the hammer that killed Tara."

"My prints were on it because I'd just used it a couple weeks ago. You know that. I used it to fix that damn floorboard. You'd insisted that it was loose." His voice is thin, high, tight. He takes a deep breath, and then quietly says, "Tara was . . . she was already dead when I got to the barn." He swipes his cheeks.

Jealously stabs me in the gut. "You loved her, didn't you?"

He turns my way, his tear-filled eyes going wide. "What? We were friends. We all were. Don't you feel—?" The car shimmies, tires stuttering on pavement.

"Please, pull over. Please." My child voice, tiny and scared. And I'm eight, riding in our old Bonneville, it's summer, and the skin of my legs are stuck to the ripped vinyl, a bottle of Jack clinks on the floorboards, trees whizz by the window, and my tiny hands grip the dash. *Please stop, Daddy. You're going too fast. I'm scared . . .*

Ben's voice goes shrill. "Your mind is making up things, don't you see that? That's what this is. You're sick. Where'd you get the medication? Huh? You told Dr. Adler . . . he's my associate, Mona. My colleague! Do you know how that made me look? Why did you tell him that I gave you all those pills?"

"You . . . you put them in my box."

"No. I did not. You know better than that, Mona. Did you actually see me do that?"

Had I? The pills were always just there, ready when I needed them.

"No, you didn't, did you? See what I mean? And now I'm paying the price for your crazy mind."

Outside, the headlights catch on the bare branches of the

trees. They look like tangled fingers groping at the black sky. "Where are you going? This looks like the road . . ." We're heading down the same road where Ben wrecked the Range Rover. Is that his plan? "You're going to kill—"

"I didn't kill anyone. Why do you keep saying that?"

"I didn't say that, Ben, I swear."

He bangs the steering wheel, and spit spews from his lips. "The sweatshirt. That damn sweatshirt! Why didn't you throw it away like I told you?"

I open my mouth, shake my head, and shut it again. Everything I say makes him angrier.

"Answer me, Mona!"

"Bo Peep needed a dress and—"

"You made my bloody sweatshirt into a doll dress and gave it to the cops!?" His mouth gaps open, eyes wide, at the ridiculousness, the insanity of it.

The speedometer is climbing, 85, 87, 89 . . . I grip the seat, squeeze my eyes shut.

"No . . . I . . . they had a search warrant. They already had a case built against you. I didn't have a choice."

The engine winds up higher, whines and whirs like a giant fan. "Ben, the curve!"

He brakes, but it's too late. The car shimmies and shudders, and my body slams into the car door. Ben curses and his face contorts with fear. He fights the steering wheel, but he's lost control. Tires squeal and the car spins like a tilt-a-whirl. My fingers grip the upholstery. I'm going to die. I'm going to die! Will I see Gus again? I embrace the idea as my body is whipped from side to side like a limp rag doll. My dolls . . . who will care for my dolls? And I see car lights heading our way, and my foot reflexively slams the floorboard. "Bennnn . . .!" A thundering boom, metal crashing, glass shattering, the whoosh of my airbag, a sharp chemical smell, hot searing pain radiates through my neck, my back, blood fills my mouth, I feel the car shooting forward, sliding, squealing on asphalt . . . I'm going to die! And I hear one last voice, my own, screaming, *Gus . . . Gus!*

FORTY-ONE

Twenty minutes later, Reyes arrives at the Ellisons', his nerves like a taut wire about to snap. Several police cruisers are parked out front. The house is lit up like a corner convenience store. Halfway up the walk, he's met by Meyers.

"I was just getting ready to call," Meyers says. "They—"

"Mrs. Ellison? Is she okay?"

"She's gone."

"Gone?"

"We don't know where she is, but it looks like she didn't go willingly. The door to her doll room has been kicked in."

Reyes pushes past him and heads upstairs to the doll room. "Ben did this. He got to her," he says, examining the door. Several heel marks marred the outside, the bolt lock hung from one screw, and the wood along the jamb was broken and splintered. Mona must have been terrified.

"Her phone was found on the floor by the window," Meyers says, pointing across the room. "I already documented it and sent it in. It's being looked at now."

"How'd he get in?"

"Cellar trap door in the kitchen is wide open. Not forced. If it was locked, a key was used."

Reyes scans the room. "Anything else?"

"No. Nothing."

Reyes crosses to the settee and stares down at the dolls

propped against the cushions. Bo Peep, he recognizes, and Mia, who was found in the alley next to Mia's childhood apartment, a detail Mona didn't seem to know when he questioned her. But Ben might have known Mia Jones's former address from her medical records.

He picks up the third doll, the dark-haired one, the one Mona told him was her childhood doll, and the one that she dug out of the pond at— "Check Instagram for @ICU2 and @momofone and @ellison_gus18. Any new posts on those profiles?"

Meyers looks on his phone. "No. Nothing new."

Reyes puts the doll back and runs his hands through his hair. "Time's ticking. It might already be too late. Ben's back is against the wall and he's unraveling. He's going to go down for murder, maybe two, so he's got nothing to lose at this point."

Meyers lays it out. "We're doing everything we can. We've got a BOLO on his vehicle, extra patrol in the area, and we're getting ready to put something out with the press. Once they're on it, something should—"

"We had five units responding to a call in that barn out back, and he still plucked his wife right out from under our noses." Reyes begins pacing back and forth, trying to get a handle on things and think through his next move, but a horrible vision disturbs his thoughts: Mona's body on a steel gurney in the morgue. It was one talk with the dead he couldn't stomach.

"Excuse me, Detective," a voice says from behind. Reyes turns to see a female officer in the doorway. "We got an accident on Route 31, approximately four miles north of here. A black Mercedes. Same make as Ben Ellison's car. Responders are on the way."

"Fatal?" Reyes is surprised at the tenseness in his voice.

"I don't have any details," she says. "But it sounds like a bad one."

FORTY-TWO

The sounds come to me first: an eerie keening mixed with guttural moans, then sirens, car doors slamming, and muffled voices. They penetrate the darkness and lure me to the surface. I claw my way to the top, out of the abyss, back to the land of the living, and just as I break through to full consciousness, I'm smacked with searing hot pain, so excruciatingly sharp that it makes me want to sink back into the murkiness and stay there forever.

Then smells come to me. Foulness permeates the car and reminds me of burned popcorn, wet pennies, and Alice's little blue bags of dog poo . . . I gag, swallow the back of my tongue, and hack out a string of raspy coughs.

And then finally, my eyes flutter open. My gaze slides to Ben slumped over the steering wheel, the deflated airbag splayed over the back of his head like a white hood, his blood-soaked hairline sprinkled with glass shards. He's not moving.

A scream rises in my throat but dies on my swollen tongue.

I reach for him and pain shoots through me. My arm won't move . . . it's broken . . . my bone has snapped in two and torn through my skin and it's glowing milky white against my raw flesh. I shut my eyes against the grotesqueness and waves of nausea overtake me, each surge pushing me closer to the edge, closer and closer, until I fall back into the blackness.

A deafening grinding noise startles me awake, with its

whirring and scraping, and metal popping, and a voice calls out, "Hang in there, lady, we're going to get you out." A high-pitched crunch pierces my eardrums and cold air rushes over my skin. My door is gone, and hands are reaching for me, and then someone's behind me, holding my head. "Hang in there," he says. And something slides behind my shoulders, up around my neck, secured under my chin, and I can't move my head. A rope? Like Gus? And panic seizes me, fear and exhaustion, and I start to fade again, my vision blurring, but I don't fight it. Instead, I close my eyes and allow myself to slip back into the darkness . . . to Gus.

And I'm weightless, free floating through the blackness, shadows whizzing by me, indistinguishable at first, then familiar: Gus in the barn, his body hanging helpless and soulless, and my own soul shriveling at the sight, anguish and overwhelming despair, and so much anger . . . and Tara, my best friend, comforting me, at my side, *talk to me*, but I am silent as cold grief freezes my insides. I see Ben's perfectly knotted tie and above it his eyes dulled by grief, and I reach a hand to him or maybe it is his hand beckoning me, but our fingers slip past each other, so close, so distant, both seeking comfort, but where? The fingers morph into pills: one, two, three, four, five . . . and drop in my box like a flicker in the dark recesses of my mind, and I swallow, swallow, and blessedly separate from my sorrow . . . and the Instagram posts drift past my mind, demanding I open my eyes, commanding fear and desperation and . . . finally the betrayal revealed. Then the barn again as I see the lies I'd been blind to . . . and the blood, so much blood . . . and I run from Tara and Ben and myself, I run, run—

"Mrs. Ellison . . . Mrs. Ellison."

My eyes open and Detective Reyes's face hovers over me. My heart soars and I stop the running inside me. I see it now. I know now. He's here to help me. But his expression is tight with worry. *Am I dying?*

"You're going to be okay, Mona," he says. His voice is soft and reassuring, and I want to believe him, but the pain . . . and memories and words tumble through my mind, and I know what I must tell him. "Ben . . ."

"He's alive. I don't know much more than that. They're still trying to get to him."

"We've got to get her to the hospital," another voice says, and he looks up and nods. Reyes's face disappears from my vision and I'm moving, rolling forward.

"Wait," I say, my voice barely a whisper.

Reyes is back. "Mona?"

"Ben did it."

He leans closer. "Did what, Mona?"

"In the barn. I saw . . . I saw him kill Tara with the hammer. He did it."

~ PART IV ~

NO MORE LIES

FORTY-THREE

Friday, November 6

Belington Daily News
Ben Ellison Found!

A two-car accident on Route 31, four miles north of Belington, occurred around ten o'clock yesterday evening, involving local psychiatrist Ben Ellison. Preliminary reports indicate that Mr. Ellison, wanted on suspicion of murder in the case of Tara York's homicide, was driving a Mercedes sedan north on Route 31 with an unidentified passenger, when he crossed the center line and was hit by a pickup driven by Joseph Burke of Naperville. No deaths are reported. Mr. Burke was transported to Belington Hospital and later released. Both Ben Ellison and an unidentified passenger are reported to be in serious condition. Previously, Ben Ellison had evaded authorities and been at large following a warrant issued for his arrest on November 4.

Reyes checks on Mona's status every couple of hours until the doctors tell him that she's cognizant enough to give a witness statement. Her attorney requests that Dr. Adler be present. He'd hoped to see her on his own first, something less formal than a witness interview, just to see if she was okay. But instead, the room was crammed with people. Meyers and the district attorney are hanging back, out of Mona's line of sight, her attorney and psychiatrist on either side of her, and Reyes at the foot of the bed.

Reyes places the recorder on the bedside table and turns it on:

Transcribed Report
Recorded Interview – Part 1

Belington Police Department, Investigative Unit
Case No. 3167–9824

DET. REYES: This interview is being recorded. I am Sergeant Detective Lucas Reyes and I'll be conducting this interview. Detective Meyers is attending as witness as is District Attorney Peter Lynch. Also attending is Trish Lee, attorney, and Dr. Adler, doctor of psychiatry for Mrs. Mona Ellison. We are conducting this interview in Room 2B, 328 of Belington Hospital, 300 Ogden Avenue, Belington, Illinois. Please state your full name and address.

M. ELLISON: Monica Anne Ellison. 13 Harvest View Lane, Belington, Illinois, 60500.

DET. REYES: Thank you. The purpose of this interview is to question you about the events that occurred in the barn near your home on the night of October 31. Do you fully understand the purpose of this interview, that it is a formal statement that it may be used in a court of law?

M. ELLISON: Yes, I do.

DET. REYES: Mrs. Ellison, you've disclosed the fact that you saw your husband, Ben Ellison, murder Tara York. Is this true?

M. ELLISON: Yes, I did.

DET. REYES: Please start with the facts as you remember them.

M. ELLISON: From the very beginning?

DET. REYES: Please start with why you went to the barn.

M. ELLISON: I . . . it was late, close to midnight and I was in my doll room, it's at the top of the corner tower of our home, we have a Victorian style home, you see, and the room is round, and I can see out in all directions. It's one of the reasons I fell . . . we fell in love with the home, Ben and me, because of the view from up there.

DET. REYES: What did you see that evening?

M. ELLISON: Yes, sorry. I'm babbling, aren't I? I'm nervous.

DR. ADLER: That's understandable, Mrs. Ellison. Relax. There's no hurry here.

M. ELLISON: Um, yes . . . I was looking at my phone

at Instagram, at ICU2's profile, and a post popped up of the barn behind our house. It's like I told Detective Reyes, I wasn't in my right mind at the time, and I thought it might be Gus reaching out to me and telling me to go to the barn. And I saw a light in the barn, too. A small light, like a flashlight, so I went there to see if it was Gus.

DET. REYES: Our records show a text sent from your phone to your husband, Ben Ellison's phone, a little after midnight. It says, quote: *Is that you in the barn?*

M. ELLISON: Yes. I knew Ben was coming home that evening. Tara had told me. She'd talked to him and he said he was catching an early flight home and a part of me, I guess, knew that it couldn't be Gus. (inaudible articulation) I . . . I didn't want to think that Ben was behind all the messages I was receiving, but now I know he was. When I sent that text, I think it was a moment of clarity. Maybe my subconscious warning me, I don't know. That sounds silly, I guess. But on the way to the barn when I sent that text, I didn't know that he was there with Tara . . . (inaudible articulation)

DR. ADLER: Take your time, Mona.

M. ELLISON: (deep sigh) As I got close to the barn, I heard arguing. I knew the voices. Ben and Tara. I couldn't make out the words, but enough to know that she said something about Mia . . . and she must have threatened to go to the police . . . that's it, that's what she did . . . by the time I got inside, something had gone wrong. I heard this horrible noise, horrible . . . (inau-

dible articulation) and I saw Ben . . . he (inaudible articulation) . . . he had a hammer in his hand (crying) . . .
and he had . . . there was blood . . . (crying) Tara was on
the ground and she was all bloody . . . her face . . . and
. . . (crying) . . . (crying) . . . he's going to kill me . . . no,
please no . . . don't hurt me . . . don't hurt me, Daddy . . .

DET. REYES: Excuse me? Mrs. Ellison?

DR. ADLER: Mona, are you—

M. ELLISON: He's coming for me, he wants to kill me,
don't hurt me . . . (crying) . . . please, don't (inaudible
articulation)—

DET. REYES: Who was coming for you, Mrs. Ellison?
Who wanted to kill you? You need to clarify.

M. ELLISON: (crying) I don't know where to go . . .
Ben's going to kill me . . . he's going to . . . (screaming)
No! Please don't hurt—

T. LEE: Dr. Adler!

DR. ADLER: My patient has had enough for now. This
interview is over.

Reyes quickly wraps up the interview. They have everything
they need, enough to shore up the district attorney's case against
Ben Ellison. The only thing left to do is wait for a trial date. A
twinge of sadness hits him.

He should feel a sense of relief at this point in the case.
He's done his job, taken a killer off the street, and gathered all

the facts needed to prosecute the perp and bring justice to the victim and closure to the family. But ever since Teresa's death, he's looked at loss differently. He now knows that some wounds run too deep for healing, and that closure is never definitive but instead grief ebbs and flows like waves. Sometimes those waves are soft and slow, and other times, they come in crashing blows, powerful and devastating. The only sure thing is that they never end. Mona has endured multiple losses: her son, her best friend, and her marriage. Considering her final words, it seems she'd suffered before at the hands of yet another man who should have also been a protector—her own father. Hearing the pain in her voice today only reaffirms that nothing he's done will bring closure to her suffering.

Meyers, the attorney, and the D.A. file out of the room, avoiding eye contact. Reyes stays behind to pack up his recorder. Mona quietly watches as he winds the power cord. He struggles to think of something to say but comes up blank. His hands work in slow motion, his movements are awkward. He drops the cord, curses, and starts over again.

"Has anyone spoken to Ben?" Mona voice cuts through the silence, small and filled with anguish.

"Not yet. He's still under sedation. But the doctors say that he'll be okay." Something flashes in her features. Relief? Fear? Reyes can't tell.

He leans forward and lowers his voice. "Don't worry. We've got a good case against Ben. He'll go to prison for the rest of his life. Thanks in part to your testimony today. I can imagine that it took a lot to do this, thank you. You're very brave."

She smiles a little, and Reyes feels like he's just won a prize, but something shifts, and her smile fades, and fear fills her eyes again. "He's not here, is he? In this hospital?" she asks.

"No. He was taken somewhere else."

"Good." She relaxes and sinks further into the sheets, her eyelids heavy.

She must be exhausted. Reyes steps back, finishes packing his recorder, and places the whole thing inside his briefcase. Before he leaves, he glances back to say good-bye, but she's already asleep.

FOURTY-FOUR

One Year Later

The entire trial has been televised, stretched out over several weeks, every detail rehashed by the press, and today, at 10:00 a.m., the verdict will be read. The world seems to be waiting in suspense.

Alice is with me. She's folded into my family room chair, eyes riveted to the screen and Milo swirled on her lap like a cinnamon roll, his tail tucked, and his muzzle twitching as he sleeps. I watch as she strokes his body slowly, back and forth, in a soothing, steady motion. My own fingers twitch for one of my dolls, something to sooth my frazzled nerves, and I peek at Mia parked at the other end of the sofa, gaze glued to the television. I hate to disturb her, so instead, I pick up my phone and alternate between social media and the newscast on television, where the news anchor kills time waiting for the verdict to be read: *Let's turn now to 4News legal contributor and former federal prosecutor Harvey Lannon for his breakdown of the trial and what we might expect for today's verdict . . .*

"Thanks for being here," I tell Alice. "Not just today, but this whole time." It'd been a long year, starting with the charges that were brought against me for my part in the cover-up of Mia Jones's death. Luckily, Trish got the case dismissed before the arraignment. She and the prosecutor came to a mutually agreeable outcome: my complete cooperation in Tara York's murder investigation in exchange for dismissal and diversion. In the end, no permanent charges were filed. I'd caught a break. That was a big step for me, and today is another: the conclusion of Ben's trial.

"It's all finally starting to sink in," she says. "Everything. It's just really hit me, you know? And Ben . . ." She nods toward the television. "Back in college, when we . . . we used to be so close, all of us—"

"Have you heard from Selma?" I cut her off before she goes too far down memory lane. It gets to me when she talks about how things used to be. Especially the "good old college days" theme. Something that wasn't so perfect for me, and something Gus never even had a chance to experience. My life isn't anything like the younger me thought it would be. I don't need to reminisce about the good ole days.

"Selma? No. I can't reach her. She . . . uh . . . well, you know it would be Tara's birthday this week and . . . well, you know that Selma hasn't dealt well with the trauma of her death."

It wasn't just the trauma—it was also the motive slapped on Ben, which he persisted in denying, that she couldn't handle. Selma told me that there was no way Tara and Ben had an affair, that it would have been obvious. Right. Obvious like her own Victoria getting expelled a few months ago. I threw her own words back at her about that and how she had preferred to live in denial of the obvious choices her Victoria had been making in the crowd she ran in. It's hard to hear the truth sometimes. Much easier to stay in denial.

She hasn't talked to me since.

"Did you see her post yesterday?" Alice asks. Selma copes by spending all her time with her boyfriend, jetting around the world on wild and romantic adventures.

"No. I'll look." I find the post on Instagram: Selma and her new man, Jake, or Jack, I can't remember. This week it's Paris. They're toasting the camera, the Eiffel Tower behind them, champagne flutes in hand. The caption: "Happy birthday, Tara. Here's to a friendship that will always last the test of time and distance."

"She's hurting," Alice offers in explanation.

I shrug and move on to other things.

"What are you looking for?" Alice wants to know.

"News updates." #BenEllisonTrial is trending on Twitter, which gives me a thrill. People from all over the world are commenting on their take on the trial.

Christine Ball @cball8
It's hard to argue with the evidence. Give up defense. He's **#guilty. #BenEllisonTrial**

Ben Ellison Trial Watch @ellisontrial
Jury is out for deliberation. Expected back soon. Verdict pending. **#BenEllisonTrial**

Jim Wallace @skippie1962
Prosecution was strong. **#MomOfGus** not present for verdict. **#BenEllisonTrial**

Nick Banks @nikbanks
He's guilty. No doubt about it. **#BenEllisonTrial**

"Oh wow," Alice says.

My head snaps up to the television screen and a shot of Ben entering the courtroom. His shoulders are rounded and stooped, his eyes sunken, his cheekbones too prominent. His tailored gray suit hangs on his frame. He's a fraction of the man he used to be.

My stomach churns at the sight of him.

"Ben looks horrible," she says.

"He does," I agree. And I'm hit with a wave of sadness. Poor Ben. This has been so hard on him. Then I remember how in my lowest moments, he swore by the scribblings of sage advice he'd plastered to my wall upstairs. Words to help me, he'd said. Words to live by. But those words only avoided the truth, as if a yellow square could erase reality. And I envision the concrete walls of a cell.

He'll be okay, I tell myself. All he needs is a pad of Post-it notes and a blank wall. Assuming a Post-it sticks to concrete . . .

I go back to my phone, click off Twitter and onto Instagram, checking out @TrueCrimeCast. Its newest episode is titled #MomOfGus: Her Own Words. My photo stares back at me and a twinge of excitement squirms in my belly. Their podcast has a huge following. Their last YouTube episode already has over seventy thousand views and counting. Seventy thousand views! And I'm being interviewed this week. The host told me that she expected a record number of viewers. The public is hungry—no, "starving"—for my story, she said.

Alice looks around. "Did you hear that?" Milo unfurls and jumps off her lap.

"What?"

"Hold on." She gets up and heads down the hall toward the front of the house.

I continue reading @TrueCrimeCast and the comments under the announcement of my upcoming guest appearance:

@realtvmom Waiting for the verdict now.
7h Reply
@twiggie Fascinating case.
4h Reply
@jewelrybyrachel Life Lesson: Don't marry a narcissist. He's #guilty

1h Reply

"Mona," Alice calls from the front of the house.

I sigh. "What?"

"You need to come look at this."

"Can't you just tell me?" I keep reading.

@podcastjunkie Excited for this. A lot to unpack in this case.
1h Reply

Alice pops back into the family room. "You should really come look. You won't believe it. There must be more than a hundred reporters out front."

My hand flies to my hair. It's after ten o'clock and I'm in leggings and one of Ben's baggy T-shirts, no makeup, no shower, I stink, my hair is in a ponytail, no contacts, just my cheap glasses with the tortoise shell frames . . .

"Wait," Alice says. "I think . . . it's on, it's on!"

I sit back, set aside my phone, snatch up Mia, and position myself on the sofa with her nestled on my lap, running my fingers over her sorrel hair as I lean forward and watch the screen. The camera is trained on Ben, his face emotionless.

Next to me, Alice sniffles. "Horrible. I can't believe this. It's horrible."

The camera flashes to the judge. A big man, broad shoulders, square jaw, thin lips. "Please be seated. For the record, this is the case of the State of Illinois vs. Dr. Ben Ellison. The bailiff has informed me that the jury has reached a verdict. Will you give the verdict forms to the bailiff, please?"

The camera pans to Tara's family, Mr. and Mrs. York, and her two sisters, Renee and Annie. They hold hands, Mrs. York in the middle. Her pale skin seems ghostlike, as if she's already got one foot in her own grave, straddling this world and the afterworld, unsure where her heart lies, here with the living, or there with her dead child. I know the feeling.

Back to the judge. He shuffles through a stack of papers, reads, and shuffles some more. I watch and wait. My knee bounces.

Back to Mrs. York. She's crying now. Next to her Mr. York puts on a stoic face, but his eyes are shining wild and furious.

Back to Ben. A close-up shot. He's staring at his hands, fisted together on the table, and his lower lip trembles.

And back to the judge, who finally speaks. "The jury has done as instructed. The verdict form in the case of Ben Ellison has been signed by all twelve jurors and the jury foreman. In the case of the State of Illinois vs. Dr. Ben Ellison, as to count one of the indictment, we the jury, duly empaneled, find beyond reasonable doubt, the defendant Dr. Ben Ellison, on the first count of aggravated murder . . . guilty."

Cheers ring out from my front yard. The reporters celebrating the verdict.

The judge continues to tick off the counts, one by one, until all five counts are read with guilty verdicts.

"I can't believe this," Alice says. "I don't even know how to feel. I can't be happy about any of this."

My phone buzzes. It's Trish. I pick up and hear part voice, part squeal. "You saw?"

"Yes." My own voice is neutral. I'm neutral. Numb.

"Big day for us," Trish says. "It's over. Really over, Mona. We should celebrate. Dinner out on me. I'll pick you up out back so we can avoid the vultures. Don't talk to any of them, by the way. Not a word. Let them stew on it. We'll prepare a statement tonight."

As I hold the phone, unsure how to respond to Trish, a text comes in: *Are you okay?*

The number seems familiar, but I can't place it. I ignore

it—probably a nosy neighbor, or even a reporter. They've been calling for days. "I'm sorry, Trish. I really can't tonight. Some other time?"

"I get it. It's been a lot. You're probably exhausted." The flick of a lighter and a long sigh comes over the line. A smoke to celebrate. I imagine her sitting by herself at her kitchen table, a couple case files stacked near her elbow along with a bottle of bourbon and a pack of cigarettes. "Rest easy, Mona, the murdering scum's going to prison."

"Yes. Ben's going to prison." I hang up and clench Mia tighter, trying to imagine what prison will be like for Ben. All I can see are big burly men in orange jumpsuits pinning him against the cell bars . . .

"Look at him," Alice says. She's on the edge of the chair watching the follow-up news commentary, hands clasped like she's praying. "The rest of his life in prison. What must be going through his mind right now?"

That's an easy answer. He'd told me often enough: *Every challenge is an opportunity to grow.*

FORTY-FIVE

True Crime Podcast
Episode 398
#MomOfGus: Her Own Words
The Tara York Murder Case

"This is Serian Rae of True Crime Podcast. Welcome to Episode 398, and the case of the Tara York murder with guest Mona Ellison, better known as #MomOfGus, and wife of recently convicted killer, Dr. Ben Ellison. Thank you for tuning in tonight, folks. First a couple of housekeeping details: This is a live stream, so for any of you joining us live, you may submit your questions in the comment section below. Your questions are being monitored, and anything inappropriate will be deleted. I apologize ahead of time for any lags in streaming.

"Okay, a lot of you have been looking forward to tonight's episode, "#MomOfGus: Her Own Words; the Tara York Murder Case." This may be one of the most complicated, twisty, and truly wild cases I've seen in a long time. But before we jump into the details, let's meet our guest tonight, Mrs. Mona Ellison. Can I call you Mona, or do you prefer Mrs. Ellison?"

"Mona is fine. And thank you for having me, Serian. I'm thrilled to be here." I reach for a nearby glass of water and take a quick sip to wash down my nervousness.

"I'm sure it's been a whirlwind of a week for you, Mona."

"It has." A row of Madames nods encouragingly, and I'm glad I chose to set up in my doll room, where I can feel the support of all my friends.

"I'm wondering if we can start off by having you tell us about your husband and how you met. I think viewers would like a little history on your relationship as a backdrop."

"Sure. Well, we met in college at Northwestern way back when. He was a couple years ahead of me." I chuckle, but my throat's so dry it sounds like a cough. "I know this sounds cliché, but we met in the library."

Serian laughs. "Let me guess. You looked up from your book and into his dreamy eyes, and it was love at first sight. That sort of thing?"

"Something like that."

"What was he like back then?"

"Oh . . . he was smart and good looking and . . . well, I was young, we both were."

I see Serian's nod on my laptop screen. A black headphone edged in lime green adorns her ears. She tilts her head just a bit, that sad look in her eyes of agreement on the tragedy of youth lost and time passed. Then she takes a brief, calculated breath, and plunges viewers to the present, her tone all business. "We heard you husband's verdict earlier, guilty on all counts. We know you weren't in the courtroom, but were you watching it live?"

"Yes, I was. And it seemed surreal to me. It still does. I think it's going to take time for it all to sink in."

"I can imagine it will . . . hey, viewers want to know, heck, I want to know, will you stand by your man?" Her question is edged with a line of accusation, but with dabs of hope in her eyes.

"I can only tell you that I'm trying to forgive Ben and move forward. I don't know yet what that looks like."

"Well, you're a better woman than me because I would

have a difficult time forgiving some of the things he's done."
She pauses and shuffles a few papers and stares directly into the
screen. "And that's the perfect segue into the details of this case.
I'm going to read off the facts for those of you who may not be
up to date. Mona, if there's anything that I've left out, please let
me know."

"Okay, Serian."

I sit back and take a swig of water. It dribbles down my
chin. I swipe it with the back of my sleeve, glad I'm only on
audio. Serian is a pro at this, confident and poised, and she
has that "Mistress of the Night" appeal that pairs well with
discussing murder: long, straight black hair; black dress, low cut
and showing plenty of cleavage; and carefully painted bloodred
lips that overarticulate each word. "It started with a terrible
accident that occurred at the Ellison house. One of Dr. Ben Ellison's patients, Mia Jones, was sneaking into his home to see his
son, Gus, and fell to her death on his cellar stairs.

"Now, most people would have called an ambulance, or the
authorities, but Dr. Ben Ellison had a reputation to protect. A
dead client at his house would look bad for him. And, he figured,
no one would miss Mia. The girl was homeless, with no real
connections to the community. So, he disposed of her body in
a nearby lake and convinced Mona to keep it all a secret. Now
before you judge Mona for her part in this tragedy, remember
that Ben Ellison is *Dr.* Ben Ellison, a famous child psychiatrist,
lauded for his devotion to helping emotionally traumatized
teens. He's a multipublished author and a sought-after public
speaker, and even appeared on several national talk shows. He
helped found The Caring Place, a clinic for troubled teens, using
as his buy-in a sizable investment from his wife's inheritance.
The point is, Ben Ellison knows psychology and he aptly used
it to manipulate his wife into funding his dream clinic and then
into covering up the accidental death of Mia Jones.

"But that's not the end of the story, folks. After the sudden, tragic death of their only child three days later, Ben Ellison sought counseling from his neighbor and his wife's best friend, Tara York, who has worked in the area for over twenty years as a school counselor." The screen flashes to a picture lifted from Tara's Facebook account. She's dressed for an evening party in a strapless gown and looks stunning, with her dark hair spilling over her bare shoulders.

Serian continues: "Tara and Ben became involved; whether the attraction was always there, or if it was something new brought on by Ben's sudden grief, is unclear."

Yeah, right. There was nothing new about it. Their attraction had simmered under the radar since college. Even under my radar.

Serian adjusts a few papers and keeps talking. "Right around the time Mia's body was found in Simon Park Lake, Ben left town for a 'business' trip to Seattle." She makes air quotes with her fingers. "Isn't that what they always say? But when the police tried to reach him for questioning, it was discovered that there was no such work conference in Seattle. In fact, Ben was nowhere to be found. Isn't that right, Mona?"

"Yes. He'd gone to Arizona instead. He'd kept it a secret because—"

"According to his testimony, he attended a grief clinic in Arizona."

I nod and then remember she can't see me. "Yes. That's right."

The tone of her voice drastically changes. "Now pay close attention, folks, because this is where it gets really twisted." She leans closer to the screen, her cleavage spilling out of her dress and those red lips of hers looming large. "It was at that time that Mona started to receive pictures from an Instagram account that belonged to @ICU2. These posts were taking her all over town to different places that were associated with Mia Jones." She holds up her hand and starts to tick off fingers tipped with crimson nail polish. "The lake at Simon Park, where Mia's body was found. An alley next to the apartment high-rise where she lived briefly with a foster family before she ran away and took to the streets. Also, there was a post from the drug house where Mia partied with Mona's son, Gus. And then lastly, the barn where Mona's son died . . . and we'll come back to that in a second."

I feel a lump in my throat. *Please don't come back to Gus's death . . .*

"But first, tell me, Mona, what did you think when you saw these posts from ICU2? You must have been terrified. Did you think that Ben was making those posts?"

"Not at first. I . . . I thought the posts were coming from Gus. That he was reaching out to me from . . . it seems silly now, I know, but at the time . . . I wasn't in my right mind."

"You were out of your mind with grief."

"Yes."

"And medication."

"Yes."

"Let's talk about that for a second. You were on several different medications at once, all administered by your husband, Dr. Ellison, right?"

"Yes."

Serian checked her papers again. "He denied this in court, but correct me if I'm wrong—wouldn't it be easy for a doctor to get ahold of different prescriptions?"

"Pharmaceutical reps often give out samples," I say.

"Very true," she agrees. "Getting back to the posts. We now know that it was more than likely Tara York making those posts, with the help of Ben, in order to drive you to insanity. These posts in combination with the medications and grief and . . . well . . . I mean, that's a lot for anyone."

"Yes."

"And I know this is difficult for you to talk about, so I'm going to just lay out the facts for those who haven't been following the case. On the night Tara York was murdered, you were waiting for your husband to return home. He was expected in on a late flight. While you waited, ICU2 posted a photo of the barn where your son died. When you looked out the window, you saw lights on in the barn and you thought . . .?"

"I thought . . . I hoped . . . that maybe there was a chance that Gus . . . I don't know. I wasn't thinking straight."

"We understand, Mona. We do. I'm sorry." She takes a deep breath. A sad look of commiseration softens her eyes briefly before she continues. "Anyway, you decided to go to the barn, but before you went inside you heard Ben and Tara arguing. You testified that you believe you heard Tara say that she was going to go to the police. Is that right?"

"Yes."

"Then you heard a scream, Tara's scream, and you ran into the barn and that's when you witnessed her brutal murder."

"Yes. That's right."

"You saw your husband killing your best friend, Tara York."

"Yes."

"And after he'd killed your best friend, he came after you."

I pause, and swallow, my voice small now, mousey. "Yes."

"I can't imagine the terror. I'm so sorry."

I reach for my water bottle again. My hands so shaky I can't connect it to my mouth.

Serian pauses, too, allowing the emotions to soak in for viewers, and then she picks up with, "Just a few additional facts: The phone used to make the posts was Gus's phone, and it was found near Tara York's body at the crime scene. But the phone had been destroyed with the same hammer that was used to kill York. And that hammer had Ben's prints all over it." Another big sigh and then more: "Pieces of one of Ben's sweatshirts were discovered during a search of your home. Which is one of the things that stood out to me during the trial. The sweatshirt Ben had been wearing the night he tossed young Mia's dead body in the lake. He had told you to destroy the sweatshirt, but instead you cut it up and made it into a doll dress?"

I reach over and tap Bo Peep's head. She's wearing a brand-new dress, yellow with lace bloomers. "That's right."

"Aren't you clever, Mona?"

"Thank you."

Up comes the hand again as Serian counts off her remaining points. "So, people, there you have the bare bones of the case. Ben Ellison, in an attempt to cover an accident, and save his reputation, decimated the body of one of his young clients, and then after the death of his son, with the aid of his lover, tried to make his wife crazy enough to push her over the edge to commit suicide, in order to get rid of her so he could have his lover to himself and have full control of his clinic. But when Tara York developed a conscience and wanted to come clean, he became enraged and savagely murdered her. If you ask me, Ben Ellison got what he deserved."

My mouth feels like cotton. I need to pee. I had thought this interview would be fun, but it isn't. I feel brutalized somehow, as if on trial myself. I'd anticipated questions, yes. I had to admit that I'd imagined questions and considered what I'd want to answer. But Serian's red-nailed point-by-point rundown of "the case" brings a shiver that makes me clasp my sweater together at the throat. At least she hadn't pressed about Gus's death.

"Okay then," Serian chirps. "Let's go to the viewers' questions. Wow. There are a lot of them. I'll try to get to as many of you as possible. First up is a question from Alison. She asks, 'When did you first know you husband was cheating on you with your best friend?'"

I clear my throat, my fingers releasing the sweater. This was one of the questions I figured someone might ask. "Good question, Alison. I suspected something for a while; he'd been distracted, working more hours, less attentive. But I thought it was from the same emptiness that I felt at losing our Gus. I never thought it was my best friend filling a different type of void for him. I didn't put it all together until after Tara died, and I found out that he had been seeing her on regular basis, for . . . for counseling, and . . . well, you know."

Serian chuckles. "Yes, we do know. Our next question is from Tom. He asks, 'Can you tell us more about how you escaped from Ben that night?'"

"This is a difficult question for me to answer, but I'll do my best. It was dark, and I was so scared, and I . . . I just ran out of the barn and actually . . . I did something stupid. Instead of heading for the neighborhood where there were people who could have helped me, I ran the opposite way, into an open field. It was dark and I was confused and went the wrong way, I guess. But now I know that my mistake probably saved my life."

Serian interjected, "Why do you say that?"

"I'd run maybe three hundred yards into the field before I fell and struck my head on something. Ben must have assumed I went toward the neighborhood, which would have been logical. He would have been looking in that direction for me. The police found the murder weapon in a culvert near our subdivision. I believe that when he didn't find me, he gave up his search and ditched the hammer in the culvert before going home to clean up and pretend that nothing happened. At that point, he knew I could identify him, but who would believe his deranged wife? He'd convinced everyone that I was in a state of psychosis."

Serian shakes her head. "I'm so glad you went the wrong way, Mona. So scary. Okay, next question."

I make it through three more questions, all easy ones:

What's it like to live with a narcissist? Hell.

Will you ever use social media again? Yes, please follow me on all my new social outlets @MomOfGus.

What will you do next? I'm exploring my options. I may write—

Serian interrupts me "Okay, folks, we're just about out of time, but there is one final question I'd like you to answer, Mona. This one is from Rick. 'Your son's suicide happened just a few days after Mia Jones died. I'm wondering if he was home the night that Mia died at your house? Did he know that she had died? Did he see his father carry her body off?'"

My world spins. It was the question that has plagued me since Gus's death over the past year, but that I'd been able to push out of my mind. Now it screams through my brain with a vengeance and my mind flashes back to all the horrible details of the nights following Mia's death: Gus's voice saying *Mia, Mia, Mia*, his seclusion, the violent argument between him and Ben. What had they said to each other? What had Ben admitted? And how angry Gus was when he left, and then a couple days later, in the barn, the rope . . . I look to Mia, and Blythe, and then to Bo Peep. Their blank stares are no help to me.

I need to know. And only Ben can tell me. My eyes wander, unable to focus on the screen. I look back at my phone and a text I'd received earlier. I've seen the number of the sender. On a business card. Detective Reyes. And I remember how he cared for Bo Peep in her time of need, and . . . I glance back at Bo Peep and she gives me a little nod of encouragement. My heart lightens a little. Maybe, just maybe—

"Mona? Mona, are you there?" Serian voice cuts through my thoughts. "Can you answer Rick's question? What did Gus know about Mia's death?"

FORTY-SIX

Reyes is kicked back on his sofa, laptop on his lap, his coffee table littered with greasy take-out bags and empty beer bottles. He's riveted to his screen, watching the quizzical look on Serian's face as she waits for Mona's answer. "I'm sorry, folks, we may be having a tech glitch. Mona, did I lose you?"

"No, I'm here." Her voice sounds little and weak, like a scared child. Something in Reyes shifts. He'd sent Mona a text earlier, just to check on her, but she didn't answer. That worries him.

Serian puts on a compassionate look for her audience, but something tells Reyes that she knew this question would come up all along. That's why she saved it for last. Ending the segment with a bang. She might even have choreographed the whole thing. Reyes would like to crawl through the screen and rip off those fake lashes of hers.

"Can you answer Rick's question? What did Gus know about Mia's death?"

"I don't know. I wish I did. I'm . . . I'm sorry."

There's more, some sort of garbled sound. Reyes leans forward and listens intently, and he knows that what he's hearing is Mona's muffled sobs.

Serian abruptly ends the conversation with a sweet smile and a promise for more to come. "We're not done by a long shot, folks. Thank you so much for joining us tonight,

Mona, and to my viewers: be sure tune back in tomorrow as we hash out the finer details of tonight's interview with #MomOfGus."

Reyes grits his teeth and thinks back to those questions that haunted him when Teresa was dying. "Could he have done more? Was there a cure out there that would have saved her? Why her and not him?" Questions, so many questions and never the right answers. Teresa didn't want to leave, and God knows he wasn't ready to say good-bye, but at least Teresa left with the peace of knowing that her only child would live a full life, with a father who loved her and would care for her. If Teresa were here now, she'd tell him that if it were either her or Stella, she'd die a hundred times over, the most horrible type of death, to save her child. Maybe that's why he understood Mona so well. Her quirks, the hollow look in her eyes, the voices she hears from her dolls. Most people would chalk that up to plain old craziness, but Reyes knows differently. There's something about loss, a loss that shatters your soul, that opens you to receive what others can't fathom. He'd experienced it himself, the way victims sometimes talk to him now. And there were others that he knew that had the same thing. People who'd suffered horrendous pain, like an older woman he'd met some years ago, after her husband was murdered. He'd worked the case and gotten to know her. One day she confided that she was praying for her dead husband when an angel appeared at the foot of her bed. She swore it was real. And that it brought her so much peace. Reyes believed her.

Since Teresa's death he'd come to believe that there is a thin veil between this world and the next. For those who'd loved fully, and lost fully, that veil became more transparent. Whether the voices Mona heard from her dolls were angels or demons, Mona, like him, was more sensitive and able to hear what the rest of the world couldn't.

She knows what others don't. She knows what he knows. And that's what draws him to her.

He looks back at his phone and sees that she's answered. A single sentence: *I need a favor.*

He types back: *Anything.*

FORTY-SEVEN

Reyes makes good on his word.

A month later, I walk into Stateside Prison, a maximum-security prison about forty-five miles south of Belington. It's my first time in prison, and I had no idea what to wear. I'd lost weight over the past few months, got a new hair color, upped my sex appeal, and I wanted Ben to see the new me, the confident me. If it weren't a prison, I would have worn a skirt, on the short side, heels, and maybe a tight blouse, just to flaunt it a bit. As it is, I chose jeans, a sweater, and tennis shoes. Glad I did; my first stop is security, where a female guard ushers me off to a little room and searches me.

Afterward, I'm led through the gatehouse metal detectors and down a long hall. Doors slide open and shut with a clank and thud, bells ring, the pungent smell of sweat and industrial cleaner stings my nostrils, and finally I reach a room lined with plexiglass and cubical-like compartments, each with a phone attached to a long cord. Several men are already visiting with family. I take my place as directed just as Ben approaches the window.

I am shocked by his appearance. Not thin, or depressed, or anything I expected. Instead, his eyes shine clear and bright, he's clean shaven, and his hair is little longer, and disheveled, not his usual precisely combed hairstyle that's sprayed stiffly in place. He's in a jumper, but it fits like it was tailored for him. He's been working out, I realize. And the extra muscle bulk is attractive, in that bad boy, can-handle-himself kind of way. The man I thought would shuffle in, defeated and half-wasted away, instead strides in with confidence, and suddenly my sweater and jeans feel frumpy. I regret the skirt and heels left in my closet.

We pick up the phones and stare at each other. A few beats tick off until he breaks the silence. "Mona. It's good to see you. You're looking well. You must be taking care of yourself."

"Thank you. So do . . ." I bite back the compliment. "I suppose it's difficult in here." Or so I had thought. Maybe hoped.

"It's not what I expected, that's for sure."

"Are you mistreated?"

"What do you mean?"

"By the other men?"

"No, not at all. Many of them come to me with their problems and . . ." His face lights up. "It's good to be useful, you know. I think I'd lost sight of that on the outside."

Irritation pricks at me. "Okay. Well, that's good. I'm glad you feel useful."

He goes on to tell me how he's started a couple support groups and an open discussion forum for young men, short-termers, who need to learn how to make better decisions and make a plan for after their release. This isn't what I expected to hear, and I feel my breath shorten but I refuse to react outwardly. I listen patiently, until I can't be patient anymore.

"Listen, I came here to ask you something."

He sits back. "Sure. What do you need to know?" His voice is kind, patient.

I feel sick to my stomach. "It's about Gus."

"Oh, Mona. I assumed Dr. Adler was helping you through this."

His pitying look infuriates me, as if I need pity, not the man locked behind bars for murder. I smile, as sweetly as I can.

"Oh, he has. I completely trust Dr. Adler. In fact, I sold my half of the clinic to him. He said he'd wanted to be a part of the project since its conception, but you were never in favor of his participation."

After Ben's conviction, Ben was forced out of the clinic by the board of directors. This will be just one more nail in the coffin. I wait for the blow to hit him, that his precious project has been sold off. But instead of shock or dismay, he says, "That's wonderful. I'm glad to know the clinic will continue. There are so many street kids who benefit from it. And Adler is more than capable of running things there. Good choice."

I take a deep breath and rub at the stiff muscles in my neck. "The reason I came here is because I need to know exactly what was said when you and Gus argued that night. If it contributed to his suicide."

"Believe me, Mona, I've replayed that argument a thousand times, wishing I'd said something different, done something more. I finally just had to let all that go. And so do you. Something like that will make you . . ."

His voice trails off, but I already know what he was going to say. "There is nothing *crazy* about me, Ben."

"That's right. There isn't. I've known that for a while. I knew it through the trial, too. I simply couldn't convince anyone else of it. So . . ." He leans back and stretches out his arms. "Here I am."

"What do you mean?"

"Seriously, Mona. Are you that deep in denial? Certainly, there's a reasonable part of you that knows the truth. Even if you don't want to admit it."

"What . . .?"

"About that night in the cellar."

My hand is moist with sweat. "What about it?"

"That night we heard something downstairs, and we went down to see what the noise was. We suspected Gus was sneaking out. He'd done it so many times in the past, so we figured that was what was going on, but it wasn't. It was Mia sneaking into the house. You recognized who she was right away, and you were furious. You called her all sorts of names. Ugly names. And you told her that you didn't want her around your son. That she was ruining his life. She laughed and said that they were in love, and when she started past you, trying to get to Gus, you . . . you stopped her. One thing led to another, and you shoved her down the steps."

"Me?"

"Yes, you. You pushed her down the stairs. And Gus knew it. I tried to explain to him that it was an accident, but . . ."

"You're lying. Is that what you told Gus?" I shouldn't have come here. Allowing him access to me again. This is what he does best—twist things to make them my fault. I didn't do any of that.

Did I? My eyes flicker, my brain starts to doubt . . . and then I stop myself. Never again will I be manipulated by this narcissistic man. "That doesn't even make sense. If this was true, you would have said something. You wouldn't take the fall for me."

"I did help you cover the crime. I disposed of the body. Wrecked the Range Rover to get rid of evidence. I even bought off a witness. I'm just as guilty. But after you so brilliantly set me up for Tara's murder, the crime against Mia seemed insignificant. I chose to pick my battle."

"Set you . . . what are you talking about?"

"You know perfectly well."

I slam my palm against the counter. An officer looks our way and chooses to let it go. I lower my voice and hiss into the phone, "Are you saying that *I* killed Tara?"

"Only you can answer that."

That "just tell the truth" look he's used on patients hundreds of times crosses his features. It's meant to solicit a confession. Remorse. Fear. Whatever the doctor in his wisdom deems to be the correct response. I can see through him, I can.

"Mona, she was dead when I got to the barn. You were nowhere to be seen. I got too close, got blood on me, and went home to shower and call the police. That's it."

I clamp my mouth tight, but my mind spins with his lies. Why is he doing this? And then it dawns on me that this whole conversation is being recorded. Maybe he's wired, like in the movies. Or the telephone, or the booth is bugged. Or he thinks it is. And he wants to point blame at someone else. At me.

"You lie. You're messing with me. You get some sort of cheap thrill out of tormenting me."

He cocks his head with a sad, pitying look. Then he shrugs. "Think what you want. It doesn't really matter. The evidence was mounted against me. The court was on your side. The public was on your side. Still is. I didn't stand a chance from the beginning."

I hate when he shrugs off an argument as if he is right but I'm too stupid to see it. But he's wrong. Dead wrong. "Those posts."

"What about them?"

"You and Tara made—"

"There was no me and Tara. We weren't lovers and we didn't conspire to drive you crazy. I never slept with Tara. Never wanted to. Believe it or not, you're the one I love."

Love, not loved. His words strike at my core. Did he really mean . . . no, of course not. This is another one of his lies. He's incapable of the truth.

"If you and Tara didn't make the posts, then who did? It could only be someone who knew everything about what happened that night."

"Exactly." A grin tugs at his lips. "Criminal amnesia, maybe. You were taking a nearly lethal combination of medications, which could have led to blackouts, much like alcohol blackouts, but I'm leaning more toward symptoms of dissociation rather than impaired neuropsychological functioning. Your childhood trauma, Gus's death, the pending move . . ."

"Stop analyzing me! I mean it. Stop."

"All I'm saying is that it's likely you made those posts yourself, during those black-out periods. Your guilt and grief couldn't be released until you faced the truth, and part of you wanted you to see those sights, to remember what really happened."

I grit my teeth. "No."

"Think about it. You knew everything about that night, and it was your dolls that were left at each spot, I mean, how would I even know about a doll named Mia? That's not even logical. I don't know anything about dolls. But you do. You care for them in your little doll hospital upstairs. Your dolls' ICU."

"Liar. You're lying. You're trying to manipulate me. I'm leaving."

I push up out of my chair, but his hand flies up. "Wait. You need to know the truth, Mona, so you can move on with your life."

"I'm already moving on, I—"

"So, you can move on emotionally. Find peace. Like me. If you'd truly moved on emotionally, you wouldn't be here. Would you?"

Again, I realize the question that has haunted my days and stirred my sleep has yet to be answered: Did Gus kill himself because he knew we'd covered up Mia's accidental death? I sink down into the chair. "I need to know what Gus knew about the way Mia died. I need to know if that's why he—"

"I'm afraid it is."

I shrink back.

"I tried to convince him it was an accident, that you didn't mean to push her, but our son was already troubled, and I think that was the last straw."

I feel myself collapse inside, as a door closes, a veil descends. My Gus thought I'd . . . and so he . . .

Ben leans forward. "Whatever it is you think about me, I have always loved you. I still do. I swear, Mona, I have always been faithful to you and our vows. But my biggest failing is that I neglected you and our family. All for the sake of that stupid clinic. For other people's families. And what happened? I lost *my* family. I know that now. I was wrong. Gus and everything we went through before and after his death, I wasn't there for you. In a way, most of this is my fault."

"You're damn right it is. You're a killer."

"No. I'm a lousy husband, and a lousy father. But I'm not a killer. Oh, I admit, I helped you cover Mia's death for selfish reasons. I told myself it was to protect you. But it was for that clinic and my reputation. That was wrong. When I think of that, I'm so ashamed. But I've grown since being here. I'm a different man. I've found God."

"God?" My mind snaps to Alice, her televangelist shows, all the times she prayed for me, the way she slips God into every conversation.

"Yes, that's right," he says. "I don't know how to explain it. You probably wouldn't want me to, anyway. But know this. I am okay."

I shake my head. "You'll never convince anyone of all this. The public deplores you."

"I know. And I don't care. I admit, my attorney played the podcast for me, and the things you said, the outright lies, they bothered me. After everything I've done for you . . . they bothered me. But worrying about my reputation is what got us into this whole mess in the first place. And three innocent people lost their lives. Mia was an accident, Gus was a tragedy, but Tara . . . Tara was outright murder."

He looks at me hard when he says this last part. I squirm in my chair.

"Come on, Mona. You can't be that far in denial. You know what happened to Tara. And to think, there was absolutely nothing going on between us. She simply went out to that barn because she saw the post from ICU2 and was worried that you were going to kill yourself, the same way Gus killed himself. You planted that in her mind with the rope that was in the cellar. You set her up because you thought she was sleeping with me. All she was doing was counseling me."

No. No, I won't be taken in. Not again. "You're a master at this, Ben. Turning things around to make it seem like someone else is at fault."

"That's called gaslighting. And believe me, I'm not as skilled at it as you are." He glances at the wall clock. "I think that's all we need to discuss. I've got another visitor soon."

"Another visitor? A woman?"

He smiles. "Same old Mona. Did you bring divorce papers for me to sign, or should I be watching for them to arrive in the mail?"

"How'd you know?"

"Just a lucky guess. Is he perfect, this new guy of yours?"

"Better than you."

He laughs. "Time will tell. I won't give you any trouble about the divorce. I hope you enjoy your new life. Good-bye, Mona."

He hangs up, but instead of getting up or moving, he simply stares at me through the plexiglass and smiles.

Disgusted, I leave. A guard meets me at the door and walks me down the hall back to processing. That's when I see her. All fresh and pretty in a blue dress, new color in her hair, full makeup . . . "Alice," I whisper.

She spies me, smiles, and tosses a little wave. A Bible rests in the crook of her arm. She pulls it close to her chest.

What is she doing here? But I already know. It was never Ashley, or Selma, or even Tara, but Alice.

Outside, dark finger-like clouds grip a gray sky. Snow is in the forecast. I shiver and make my way across the prison parking lot to my car. I sit quietly with my mind silent for the first time in over a year. I know now. Ben's lies to our son killed my boy. Ben lives in his own denial about affairs and murder and his efforts to derail my mind. With Dr. Adler's help, I'm on less medication and my mind is clear. Ben is wrong. I have found peace, my own type of peace. And I did it without him.

FORTY-EIGHT

Two Months Later

I lock the door of my house and stare up at the tower room. The drapes are open, and nothing shows beyond them. I will miss that room, but I know another house and something better await me.

A brand-new red four-door pickup sits in the driveway, white smoke pouring from its exhaust, a six-by-twelve trailer hitched to the back. Inside the trailer, packed nicely in individual boxes lined with tissue, and carefully stacked and secured from floor to ceiling, is every doll I own.

A blast of warm air hits me as I slide into the passenger seat.

"Are you okay?" Reyes asks.

"Better than I've ever been."

He looks relieved, and nothing could please me more. I reach between my feet into a large tote bag and turn toward the back seat, smiling at Stella. "Hey, sweetie. I have something very special for you. This is Blythe. My mother gave her to me when I was a little girl. She's my absolute favorite doll. I thought I'd give her to you now to mark the occasion. The start of our new life together, the three of us."

She hesitates.

"Honey?" Reyes says.

She frowns and rips Blythe from my hands, cramming her into her backpack.

I keep my tone in check. "Blythe doesn't look comfortable like that. Maybe you'd like to rearrange her so she can lie flat, you know, with her legs stretched out."

Stella curls her lip. "She's just a frickin' doll, okay."

Reyes rotates in his seat. "Hey! Watch the way you talk to Mona."

He starts to lecture her, but I slide my hand down his arm until I reach his hand. I give it a quick squeeze and a look that promises him much more later. "It's okay. Really."

His expression softens, and he turns back in his seat and puts the truck in gear. As the truck pulls away, I glance at the houses that have been the familiar anchor throughout my adult life. My house, empty and awaiting the new owners, and which sold quickly even without Selma's expert touch.

Across the street is Selma's house, with colorful plastic toys littering her once pristine yard. Not that she would care about the people living there now—she's skiing in Denmark, or is it Sweden, where she has jetted off for her vacation before starting a new real estate job in Dallas.

Next to it, Tara's sad little place still has a for sale sign in the front yard.

And the last of the four houses—

"Mona?"

"Yes?" I turn to see Reyes's concerned gaze.

"Again, I'm so sorry about your friend Alice. I know she stood by you through everything last year. It's such a shame she—"

"Yes. It is." I sigh, and then smile at him. Because, really, it is a shame she took up with Ben. And such a shame she died so suddenly.

The irony isn't lost on me. Out of all of us girls who grew

up together, I was the poor, little abused girl who everyone in the group pitied. Yet now . . . well . . . as Alice would say, "I'm just so blessed."

As we pull around the corner, I turn back to Stella. "It would make me very happy if you made Blythe more comfortable."

Stella's eyes narrow. "Would it?" She leans forward, our faces just inches apart. She keeps her voice low. "Well, I don't really care about Blythe, or how you feel about anything." She shoots me a nasty look. "I see you for what you really are, *Mona*."

I know where this nasty attitude of hers is coming from: she doesn't want to give up her father to another female. And I don't want to share either.

I look straight into her eyes and softly reply, "I see you, too. And I bet you wouldn't like it if someone folded you up and shoved you into a bag like that, hmm?"

Her eyes go wide.

I turn back around and place my hand on Reyes's thigh. He grips the steering wheel as he turns onto the freeway, a smile on his face. Then to me, "Are you ready for our new life?"

"Yes, I am."

"Arizona, here we come. I've always wanted to live some-place warmer. You know, you and me and Stella . . . and your dolls. I haven't forgotten about your dolls." He smiles. "We're all going to be happy in our new home."

My gaze slides to the back again. Blythe is now on the seat, sitting pretty next to Stella. "Yes. Yes, we will." And that's true, because what they don't know won't hurt them.

ACKNOWLEDGMENTS

My first "thank you" goes to my agent, Jessica Faust, for sticking with me through this project and my many other life events over the years. I appreciate everything you've done.

A high five and much gratitude goes out to Dan Mayer, my editor. I appreciate your patience and guidance on this project. Working with you has been a great experience.

A very special thank you to Sandra Haven, freelance editor, writing mentor, and friend. Eleven books so far. Can't wait to see what the future holds. And thank you, Andrea Robb, for your advice and editing expertise in the development of Mona's story.

To everyone at Seventh Street Books and the Start Publishing team, thanks for your hard work and everything you've done to make this book possible.

My sincere gratitude to the following people who contributed their expertise to this story: Christine Beatty, Professor of Chemistry and Forensic Sciences; B.J. Bourg, Police, SWAT, and Chief D.A. Investigator, retired; Police Lieutenant Bruce Ramseyer, retired; and D.P. Lyle, MD. Doctor Lyle, thank you for checking and double-checking my autopsy facts.

Big hugs to my husband and our children, my parents and siblings, for all your love and support. God has blessed me with an amazing family.

CPSIA information can be obtained
at www.ICGtesting.com
Printed in the USA
BVHW030159100723
666936BV00002B/13